POP MUSIC, MEDIA, AND YOUTH CULTURES

From the Beat Revolution to the Bit Generation

Lello Savonardo

Foreword by
Derrick de Kerckhove

Afterword by
Luciano Ligabue

The volume was published with the contribution of the Department of Social Sciences of the University of Naples Federico II, Italy.

Copyright © 2020 Bocconi University Press EGEA S.p.A.

Translation: Enzo Milano, Rosanna Milano, British Language School, San Giorgio a Cremano (Na), Italy.
Translation Supervisor: Francesca Fariello
Typesetting: DataWorks, India
Cover: Cristina Bernasconi

EGEA S.p.A.
Via Salasco, 5 – 20136 Milano
Tel. 02-58365751 – Fax 02-58365753
egea.edizioni@unibocconi.it – www.egeaeditore.it

All rights reserved, including but not limited to translation, total or partial adaptation, reproduction, and communication to the public by any means on any media (including microfilms, films, photocopies, electronic or digital media), as well as electronic information storage and retrieval systems. For more information or permission to use material from this text, see the website www.egeaeditore.it

Given the characteristics of Internet, the publisher is not responsible for any changes of address and contents of the websites mentioned.

First Edition: October 2020

ISBN Domestic Edition	978-88-99902-73-5
ISBN International Edition	978-88-31322-25-6
ISBN Digital Domestic Edition	978-88-238-1977-1
ISBN Digital International Edition	978-88-31322-26-3

Table of Contents

Preface by *Derrick de Kerckhove* — VII

Introduction — 1

1 Sociology of Music — 5
   1.1 Art, music, and creativity — 5
   1.2 Sociological theories — 9
   1.3 Cultural industry and technical reproducibility
       of the work of art — 13
   1.4 On popular music — 15
   1.5 Urban cultures and art worlds — 20
   1.6 Distinction: A social critique of the judgement of taste — 25

2 Popular Music, Urban Rhythms, and Mass Cultures — 33
   2.1 Pop Music — 33
   2.2 Songwriting and its evolution — 37
   2.3 Pop Culture, mass media, and urban rhythms — 42
   2.4 Sound technologies — 47
   2.5 Social role of the radio and re-tribalisation processes — 49
   2.6 Video clip, walkman, and personalisation of listening — 57

3 Bit culture, Sound, and Digital Technologies — 64
   3.1 Liquid sounds — 64
   3.2 Network, file sharing, and cross-media — 68
   3.3 Telephone and media convergence — 73
   3.4 Software culture and connective thinking — 77
   3.5 Sounds, connections, and innovations — 85
   3.6 Creativity and interactivity — 89

4 Youth Cultures and the Social Role of Pop Stars — 95
   4.1 Young people as a social category — 95
   4.2 Cultural studies and youth subcultures — 98

4.3 Youth, rap, and change 101
4.4 Bit Generation 107
4.5 Symbolic power of the rock star 113

Afterword. The Time of Emotion
by *Luciano Ligabue* **121**

References **127**

Preface

by *Derrick de Kerckhove*[1]

"Rock reflects the world of youth, its rituals, its legends, and it represents an important tool to socialize and get together."

This is indeed the driving theme of this new book, one that is recurrent in Savonardo's academic research on the sociology of music, and in his activities in youth culture and media. This new book destined for an English-speaking readership is both a compendium and an update of explorations conducted in the Sociology of music (2010) and Bit Generation (2013), with an enhanced focus on youth and its intimate relationship to music. Being a performer himself, Lello Savonardo knows what he is talking about. Indeed the author's intellectual and professional itinerary combines three large domains of expertise, the first, of course, the chosen discipline of sociology, to which he has devoted his academic pursuits for over two decades; the second, his professional and personal attention to youth culture at political as well as counselling levels; and the third, as a musician, composer, and performer of popular songs, in all senses of the word.

Besides updating earlier examination of the technologies involved and reviewing current theories, the focus of this particular research is on how popular, pop, jazz, rap, and world music connect with its audiences, with a particular attention to its social effects as well lending its voice to protest and social criticism. Thus, the concluding chapter is focussed on the youth. Of particular interest is the section on youth culture music's tribal impact.

The exploration covers all aspects of music creation, production, and distribution in device, place, market, and economy, theory and technology, and the tribes that adopt the specific genres that youth feel define their identity and taste. See in particular how Savonardo updates Bourdieu's sociological analysis of musical taste even as he revisits his benchmark theories. The intimate relationship between youth, music, and their sense of identity is so close that one could debate whether it is the tribe that selects its preferred genres and performers, or, the other way around, the genres and performers bring the members of the tribes together.

---

[1] Derrick de Kerckhove is a guest professor at the Polytechnic Institute of Milan and scientific director of Media Duemila and Osservatorio Tutti Media. Formerly a professor of French language and literature at the University of Toronto, he directed the McLuhan Program in Culture and Technology from 1983 to 2008, and is the author of a dozen books on culture and technology, translated in several languages.

The interesting thing about music is how it penetrates the body and when. Even if heard once, pleasant to the ear or not, it has a tendency to stay in one's head, repeating melodic and rhythmic beats for a while until it is chased away from the mind by something else happening. The power of advertising jingles depends on that phenomenon. At a concert, where sound volume and clarity are drastically enhanced, the music takes over more than the mind; it invades and structures the body almost forcing it to respond. The effect is well known and reported by people who explain thus why the audience rocks, taps feet, and dances even as mere spectators in a tight crowd, actually continues well past the event, overnight, and ends up establishing a core presence in the person, usually a young one, who is thus possessed. Kids dancing to the same tunes understand each other.

One, among many stimulating literary strategies Lello Savonardo exercises in this book to make it more insightful among strict academic concernsis to surf literature and research to pick at the appropriate moment a great many short quotations, almost aphoristic (could we call them "soundbites"?) from a myriad of authors, many among whom one would not immediately associate with a specific expertise in music, myself included. For that reason, I am very grateful that, in his wide-ranging readings, Savonardo managed to find an observation by McLuhan that I had either forgotten, or actually never read before, but struck me as worth expanding:

"McLuhan points out: stereophonic sound is a sound "all around" or "enveloping." Earlier, sound emanated from a single point, in accordance with the preconception of visual culture in favor of a fixed point of view. Stereophony is sound in depth, as TV is vision in depth."[2]

Indeed, the sensation of "depth" in music appreciation, an experience that I had already brought attention to in the postface to Sociology of Music,[3] even as I stuck my ear directly to the loudspeaker when I was in my early teens to get as close as possible to the origin of the sound of Andres Segovia's guitar, and then later marveling at that very effect enhanced by the Walkman, it is the depth of sound – and its point of origin – that I was seeking already. Stereophony is the first step towards total surround both for the depth and the width of the sensation. While getting at the origin of the sound is an unquestionable benefit of earphones, the drawback is the isolating effect, a feature that turns into another benefit for the many users who prefer to be alone to better concentrate on the sound. But the problem is that it precludes air conduction, because it depends entirely on the bone conduction as the music resonates directly via the cranium's bone structure. And for some people, at least for me, despite the enhanced clarity and the seduction of base sounds, this is a limitation that can often turn the experience into a sort of "sound prison". This is why, while not intending to make an advertisement for Dolby Systems, I wish to report here a novel sound experience, thanks to a delightful, but insufficiently distributed application called "Dolby Atmos". This application, by effectively simulating the total surround

---

[2] McLuhan, 1964.
[3] Savonardo, 2010.

without going through bone conduction allows one to "have one's cake and eat it too" so to speak, that is, to experience even with lower quality sound production values, both the fullness of the sound expansion through air conduction and the sense of its origin. It was from the beginning such a joy that it renewed my attachment to all my favorite pieces classic or pop.

Lello Savonardo, in spite of his name is a born and bred Neapolitan. He has breathed Naples' culture along with its Mediterranean air. He understands its stratified social and historical past and present, and deeply sympathises with its youth in trying times, precariousness and little hope for a decent future, even as the Italian economy sinks deeper in the post-covid era. For centuries, the people of Naples have turned to music to find the strength and the resilience that it gives, and the hope against hope. Music in Naples is not a crutch, but a philosophy of life.

It is likely then that the passion for music as an intense communication medium informs this study through and through. A passion that is beautifully expressed in Luciano Ligabue's postface addressing the creative drive that a musician experiences in the act of composing music or writing words for the song. Ligabue puts forward the authenticity of the feeling that inspires the composer and also highlights the constraints of rules of composition that limits the expression of that feeling to a maximum of 250 to 300 words. Likewise, Lello Savonardo is constrained by the rules of the academic game; but in this book, the authenticity of the feeling sustains both writing and reading it.

What we have here is a rare mix of academic and artistic skills that mutually inform all realms of production in Lello's career, so that every word in this book is somehow informed by a vibrant resonance of the sounds of youth culture. It is in that spirit that it could be read most profitably.

Introduction

Get up, as the popular song is getting up, if there's still something to say, if there's still something to do. Get up, as the popular music is getting up, if there's anything left to say, if there's anything left to say, it will tell us.
«The Popular Song», Ivano Fossati, 1992

In 2016, the Nobel Prize in Literature was awarded to the singer and songwriter Bob Dylan "for having created new poetic expressions within the great American song tradition." The award suggests how important pop music is in the contemporary society, and highlights how blurred the traditional boundaries are across all forms of art. Contaminations between tradition and pop culture are increasingly frequent and meaningful, and the languages of pop music keep influencing other forms of contemporary art and expression.

The book is about views and thoughts about popular music, media, and youth cultures, giving special attention to the relationship between the various languages of music and the technology development. In the literature, there are several (and sometimes opposite) ways to define "popular music." However, it is necessary to investigate them from the perspective of the history of music, to appreciate both fixed and variable elements. Music is constantly changing, and popular culture is the turf where all these transformations occur.

Pop music is strictly connected to the widespread media, mass culture, world of youth, and its languages. New generations deliver a revolutionary thrust, exploding at the end of the '60s. This impetus leads to the rise of the youth culture. Pop/rock music (and its sub-genres) brings up new trends and it is equally influenced by cultural, social, and habits turmoil of our time. It is the soundtrack of entire generation, accompanying not only several forms of entertainment but also the social commitment, need of belonging, desire for recognition and limelight. Rock reflects the world of youth, its rituals and legends, and it represents an important tool to and get together.

Moreover, the evolution of communication media is strongly inter-wired with the main social and cultural metamorphosis of our age. Important changes, plurality and complexities of cultural and artistic forms, along with the variety of social contexts made scholars realise that they need to use new categories of interpretation, to better understand the changes. Nowadays, the difference between "elite art" and "mass art" is shaping up in an unexpected way. Art is going towards a new expression through cultural hybridisation, leading to innovative forms of artistic consumption, and diverse mode of reproduction of social inequality. It is interesting to monitor these dynamics while taking a closer look at pop music, mass cultures, and youth languages.

These days, cultural industry and mass media are becoming increasingly instrumental for the production and the fruition of music, as they influence the way people listen and how people in general access it. However, mass media are moving towards the standardisation of cultural consumption and the flattening of the taste in music. However, they also allow pop music to develop and reach a wider audience, even when offering new trends and jargons.

Starting from these assumptions, this book analyses the main changes that occurred from the advent of electronic media in the digital era. Then, we will discuss the connection between music and technology, to assess how they affected sociocultural relationships and promoted hybridisation across musical languages and new creative modalities. With the introduction of digital technologies and new media, the expressive and creative potential of artistic productions and the way the public access them are set for further changes, and the result might at times be controversial. Mass media shook the traditional time–space dimensions, but they redefined the boundaries between the "public' and the "private." This led to both homologation and differentiation. Furthermore, music's digital technologies offered multiple occasions for aggregation and socialisation, and, at the same time, they conveyed new ways in the context of private consumption, within the domestic walls. These are social effects bursting during the digital era, through interaction and connections, and they affect any type of language and communication. The third millennium's youth communicate, create, socialise, and feed on digital technologies, thus supporting the definition of new artistic and creative languages.

The disruptive technical and social changes occurring in the contemporary society in the last few decades affected also the way music is produced and consumed.

The ultimate purpose of this debate is to highlight how the presence of music (from classical to pop) in our daily life has somehow become more complex.

Starting from the most relevant theories about the sociology of music, we aim to analyse these changes, and how they relate to the youth cultures, pop music, mass media, and digital communication technologies. From the *Beat Revolution* (affecting the cultural movements from the '50s onwards) to the *Bit Generation* (stemming from digital technologies and the *software culture*), the last chapter will go over the symbolic power of rock stars.

The goal of this investigation about the sociological role of sound and music in the contemporary society is to gather and interpret the links among the many factors contributing to the sound imagery, within several social and cultural contexts. However, given all the constant changes within the social dynamics, the boundaries between these topics (and the several branches investigating them) are increasingly ephemeral. Modern sociology of music cannot ignore this complexity, and it cannot fail to investigate the various connections among the several cultural factors, to completely comprehend the dynamics typical of the contemporary music industry and the social consequences, both individual and collective.

We aim to contribute to the studies on musical phenomena, part of the never-ending streaming of late modernity, which is increasingly immersed in turmoil of sounds. By doing so, we will take into consideration emotions, which will be discussed further in the afterword section by the singer and songwriter Luciano Ligabue.

1 Sociology of Music

1.1 Art, music, and creativity

The sociology of music is a relatively new topic, and it investigates the complex relationship between the musical phenomena and society. This chapter focuses on some of the theories expressed by the main sociology authors, who also analyse the link between music and society. However, we also aim to consider the major social, cultural, and technological changes affecting several ways of producing, reproducing, and enjoying music.

Music is a very complex sphere of culture, and it expresses feelings, emotions, desires, individual and collective imagination, representation of natural and social reality, and ideas of the world and life, all at once.[1] In this respect, the sociological debate on music is part of a wider perspective of investigation and analysis, and it involves the connection between art and social reality.

There are no fixed criteria to establish what pure art is and what is not. The same concept of "art" and its definition are truly complex, as intricate as the scientific debate about it. However, according to the main theories of sociology of art, "an expression" is defined as "artistic" according to criteria that change over time and to the historical–cultural context. These criteria mutate in relation to social structures and the characteristics of the dominant cultural system, both in its form and content (aesthetical, moral, and social values; lifestyles; consistency; and diversity).[2]

Within the traditional theoretical studies on the relationship between art and society, there are several visions, sometimes contrasting ones. In the 18th century, art was considered "irrational." This stems from the theory by the philosopher Benedetto Croce, who believes that art is an autonomy activity and not linked to the historical and social context. On the contrary, other scholars (from Marxists to Sorokin) believe that the relationship between art and society is quite automatic, and they say that art is just a reflection of the social context.

This approach risks reducing and underestimating the complexity of the art. However, it is not even accurate to consider art as entirely separated from the social context it

---

[1] Crespi, 2006, p. 123.
[2] *Ibidem* p. 124.

was born within.³ The anthropologist Alan P. Merriam believes that if men cannot live without institutions and the "humanistic" objections to them, then they are the two sides of the same coin and must be investigated as if they were the same thing.⁴ The relationship between art and society is real, dialectical, and alive. It is a relationship of mutual influence, and the result cannot be conceived "a priori." On this matter, Franco Ferrarotti says that "art and society are not opposites: art is part of the society" and consequently "the sociological perspective cannot be a simple reference to art, studies, trends, or the specific historical–cultural matrix it generates from."⁵

The relationship between art and society is not antithetical, but ambivalent and of mutual conditioning. On one hand, art "celebrates" and "enhances" the shared social values, while promoting integration and affirmation of social identity; it represents the highest expression of the collective imagery within several historical contexts. On the other hand, art often tends to reevaluate the traditional aesthetical values, as it is a constant source of creativity, an innovation of expression, and rebellion; it brings new interpretations of reality and individual and collective experiences. In its highest forms, the roles of art are not antithetical, as the representation of aesthetic and social values becomes symbolic, and it is not just legitimation or affirmation of the current framework.⁶

The historical transformations of the relationship between art and society show that the former is a result of complex relationships, where creativity, structural influences, and individual and collective factors coexist. At the same time, art is both a reflection and a symptom of social experience, and it represents one of the main symbolic elements which are part of the social reality.

The dialectic between art (as a creative and innovative phenomenon) and society (with its shared rules) leads back to the relationship between ideas and structures. These, according to Georg Simmel,⁷ show a mutual influence between the two. The German sociologist believes that ideas stem from a creative dimension and are not just a reflection of the social context; this, however, may or may not affect the way ideas settle. Simmel says that cultural changes are a result of the dialectic between "the constant stream" of life and the "productions of forms" where the stream gets stuck into.

Innovation and changes in the cultural forms are usually brought by the symbolic mediations' need to adapt to new external factors, but they could also result from creativity which stems from the culture and leads to other changes. When the innovative dimension of actions seems to prevail in the new symbolic state, we could refer to the concept of *creativity*, strictly connected to art and music.

However, creativity is not easy to define, and various studies have investigated it (sociology, psychoanalysis, cognitive psychology, and social psychology).

---

³ Del Grosso Destreri, 1968.
⁴ Merriam, 1964.
⁵ Ferrarotti, 1966, p. 58.
⁶ Crespi, 2006.
⁷ Simmel, 1990.

Recent studies have focused on two main pieces of research: on one hand, scholars analysed cognitive ways of the brain functions, and they see creativity as effectiveness and efficiency; on the other hand, they highlighted social conditions and relationships supporting creativity.

There are three main levels of investigation about this:

- about subjects as socially creative;
- about relationships or contexts, where experiences can be considered "creative";
- about conversations among the actors involved.[8]

The social organization of the symbolic system, where the institutions dealing with cultural production operate, may or may not foster creativity. It depends on the available resources (both physical and abstract), and on the cultural forms, which might or might not be open to innovation.

According to Alberto Melucci, the several definitions of creativity might be placed at the extremity of a metaphorical axis: on one side, the visions of the creative act as an expression of a rich and animated world, populated by impulses and passions, driven by fantasies and turmoil. Genius and insanity, the troubled artist, the romantic vision of creativity are all theories on this side of the axis. On the other side instead, there would be the invention as problem-solving, as those daily activities we all can carry out, and whose success depends on how skillfully the process has been prepped. Hence, creativity could be learnt and transmitted, could be improved and consequently, it could become a technique.[9]

While traditional studies saw a coincidence between genius and creativity, recently scholars have shifted towards a more practical vision, and say that each of our cognitive, ordinary processes are influenced by the relational and social context.

Either way, creation is the capability to stand out from an order, deal with the turmoil, and generate a new order. In the middle of this process, there is transformation, the invention of a different form, in art, music, science, planning, and also in everyday life. This is when our knowledge is rebuilt, when we go through unexplored paths when we create a new order where both the creator and other individuals can recognise themselves.[10]

However, Crespi says that creativity expresses a positive dimension of the human being, and at the same time it could be perceived as a danger for the social order. If we see creativity as the capability to substitute social representations (as well as values, behavioural patterns, socially codified lifestyles) with other representations (as well as norms, alternative lifestyles), or as the cause of events which could change the way we perceive reality (as well as ourselves and the relationships with others), then we have to appreciate why there are some negative visions about it. Each creative proposition could cast doubt on social and individual identities, and it could be

---

[8] Melucci, 1994, p. 9.
[9] *Ibidem*, p. 18.
[10] *Ibidem*.

perceived as opposed to established interests, which could open up a multitude of unexplored landscapes. It is a dichotomy between reassuring conformism and new necessities that we crave for, but it will take time to establish themselves.[11]

Furthermore, creative processes never express "pure" creativity, as they are always the result of distancing or objection against forms of determination and objectivation brought by the existing social context. It is not possible to create something new from scratch, without looking at the existing actual or cultural productions, through a transformative process brought by the dialectic or the conflict between tradition and innovation. As all the artistic or cultural forms, music can express strong creative energy and also a strong function of preservation. Also, music production represents an amazing tool of memory and remembrance. The content of memory, the way it is arranged, and the length of time it can store memories for really depend on external factors, that is, historical, social, or cultural influences.[12] "Remembering" or "forgetting" are not just individual actions, but they are indeed social constructs. In reality, they are paths of actions happening within preestablished institutional landscapes, within well-defined social practices. As Gianfranco Pecchinenda reminds us, each culture has tools and technologies to communicate, to circulate the most relevant element that grant social cohesions among its members. This mediating force is crucial, so as the technical tools to archive and communicate. Music, as well as art in general, represents a crucial element in the processes of social aggregation and memories' preservation as societies are in the habit to use the mediation of social and artistic institutions to "remember" their past. As such, art is instrumental in the building processes of social reality. Collective imagery we tap into daily to elaborate our identities is highly influenced by forms of symbolic productions of society, and the aesthetic form is one of the main settings.

Music is probably one of the main creations of human beings who are capable of creating a memory which is both communicative (horizontally and across generations) and cultural (vertically and within the generation itself). According to Krzysztof Pomian,[13] music has qualities which are typical of "historical objects", objects that have a double temporal belonging and a double space one.

When a piece of music is performed for the first time in a specific historical and social context, it has its own identity but also traces of the various interpretations that occurred in its history. It represents a bridge between our present and the past of which it is a trace. Music, melodies, rhythms, classical music symphonies, operas, national anthems, popular songs, folk, and pop–rock repertoire have always contributed to build a social imaginary and the identity of each community. They record moods and passions of men and women, protagonists of social, political, and cultural transformations in different time eras and times. They tell a story, or even, many stories. Music expresses preservation but also innovations; it rehearses the individual and collective pasts, but it feeds on the present and, at times, it anticipates the

---

[11] Crespi, 2013, pp. 37–39.
[12] Pecchinenda, 2002.
[13] Pomian, 1999.

future through the personal experience of single artists or music consumers. Through music, they express languages and unprecedented communication codes.

As we know, there is an ongoing interaction between externalised and individual memories: forms of the latter influence and give balance to it. According to sociological studies that investigated the relationship between art and memory, "art is a technology of memory." Museum, monuments, cinema, as well as music and theatre are media. As such, they have the authority to communicate and build the social reality.[14] In this respect, art is sociologically meaningful, not only as a form of entertainment and place of cultural consumption, but also as a "negotiation arena" where social identities were born and structured. Even music cannot only be considered the "mirror of society, but it becomes a social factory, a space and place where societies keep building and reproduce."[15]

The following paragraphs describe some of the main sociology authors who dealt with the relationships between musical phenomena and social reality.

1.2 Sociological theories

Luigi Del Grosso Destreri says that among all the form of arts, music could seem "the most immune to a sociological study: its ineffable and transcendent nature might prevent it from being investigated by sociology."[16] The sociology of music was officially born with Max Weber and his essay *The Rational and Social Foundation of Music*,[17] published posthumously in 1921. It does not have a long and solid tradition, even though there have been many inputs from several sources. Initially of German origin, the sociology of music developed in the USA and then in many other countries but not in places with a heavy Catholic heritage (such as Italy), where it only very recently began to get the attention of scholars.

The scientific debate about it is still very much ongoing, as much as the general debate about the sociology of art. Antonio Serravezza[18] says that the width of the socio-musicological debate raises questions about the epistemology of the subject: "Is it a science, or is it an aspiration to science?." This dilemma, already existing for sociology in general, is even more relevant for sociology of music, as it still seems far from getting a clear objective and definition. The boundaries of its field are a flux, not clear. Its definitions could be simple[19] or complex,[20] but they can barely define its framework and raise questions: what are the relationships between music and society?

---

[14] Tota, 1999, p. 79.

[15] *Ibidem*.

[16] Del Grosso Destreri, 1968, p. 161.

[17] Die Rationalen und soziologischen Grundlagen der Musik.

[18] Serravezza, 1980, p. 2.

[19] "The Sociology of music is the investigation of the relationship between music and society", (Engel, 1960, p. 9).

[20] "The Sociology of music's objective is historical evidence of the social existence, stored inside the history of genres and music styles", (Kneif, 1966, p. 16).

And how can we identify them? Furthermore, if a link between social reality and music phenomena does indeed exist, what is its structure?

The discipline is complex both on an epistemological level and on a thematic one. Music has various sociological features and processes: genres, forms, and styles; authors and specific productions; eras and different cultures; procedures and technical elements of both production and consumption; social conditions of composers, interpreters, and audience; patterns of musical communication and institutions; social and cultural functions of music; role of the media and technologies of communication; power plays, symbolic and cultural legitimation, just to name a few. This conceptual framework presents the "continent" of "sociology of music" as a theoretical bunch of possibilities. However, as a matter of fact, each sociological research should prioritise just one or few objects of study. Speaking of the complexity of the subject, Marco Santoro says that "the abstract, ethereal and pure"[21] nature of music, and its ability to carry a wealth of meaning instead makes it a potential key topic for sociologists.[22] Production, distribution, consumption, reception, classification, the structure of music and its phenomena, as well as its strategic usage on a symbolic, cultural, communicative, economic, and political are all key topics in the sociological debate around music.

Given that there is a constant interaction between music and society, and that (as Weber says) the sociological debate around music should help identify all those elements, if music production that relates to the social structure they come from, we will now try to recap the recurring points in the various definitions of "sociology of music":

- there is a contrasting relationship of interdependence between music and the rest of the sociocultural systems;
- the (musical) "text" cannot be considered as independent from the (sociocultural) "context" where it was produced
- the researcher must ignore judgement about the value or any reference to the artistic quality of the music product. This means that creation and musical ideas stem from a process of "social construction" and they will be judged for their socially recognised value within their social context, not for their aesthetic or artistic value;
- a music phenomenon becomes a topic for the sociologist only when it assumes a certain social relevance, meaning when it starts resonating in nonmusical contexts.

The sociology of music aims to investigate not the actual music product, but individuals and their interactions during the processes of production and consumption, of execution and fruition. On purpose, the interest of this discipline for "socially relevant actions" (and for media and mass culture) was slowly brought to relevant sociological

---

[21] Bordieau, 1979.
[22] Santoro, 2000, p. 63–64.

attention of the study of popular music, and it helped the scholars to get over the typical cultural moralism.[23]

Alan P. Merriam[24] says that the sociology of music deals both with "music in culture" and "music as culture", and it investigates music as social construct.[25] However, given the variety of music languages, the word "music" seems inappropriate or at least less accurate than "musics" (even though in this book we will probably refer more often to "music"). As the ethnomusicologist Curt Sachs says, "music is not a universal language",[26] after all. This means that there are several sound and music languages, referring to a multitude of sociocultural contexts. Besides, Del Grosso Destreri[27] argues that the word "music" against "musics" is based on an ethnocentric evaluation. Speaking of this, the sociologists remind us how African percussions or traditional Japanese flutes or the sounds of rock or rave, are "organised sounds" in the same way as a symphony of Beethoven or a Chopin nocturnal or a religious chant by Bach. Social sciences started to deal with music very late, while the advent of mass media and transports encouraged an acceleration of processes of contamination across the several sound languages. Del Grosso Destreri continues his analysis saying that between the 19th and 20th century, elitist music experimented new paths: [...] the traditional harmonic structure had already been challenged before the infinite Wagnerian modulation, Debussy used a whole tone scale from Asia, Strawinsky experimented with percussions and polyrhythms, [...] black Americans music, with its "blue" notes and its ragtimes gained full cultural dignity.[28]

It is an explosive mixture that produced new music phenomena. Traditional musicology, which was based more on the analysis of the music itself rather than its historical and cultural context, showed its limits to comprehend the new musical languages. The tools of ethnomusicology, which these days are crucial to understanding "different" music phenomena (from the ones of extra-European civilisation to jazz and youth music) were very useful to interpret these phenomena, as it was the contribution of social sciences. Studies on music require extra-musicological approaches, and the most important one is the sociological approach.

The main theories of sociology of music refer to classic sociology authors such as, Georg Simmel, Theodor W. Adorno, Max Weber, and Alfred Schütz. In fact, not only had they made a crucial contribution to traditional sociological theories, but also launched the analysis of dynamics and relationships between music phenomena and social reality by defining the main thesis of the debate.

In particular, in his *Psychological and Ethnological Studies on Music*[29] (a book born from his PhD final dissertation), Simmel investigates the origins of music on

---

[23] Pecchinenda, 1999.
[24] Merriam, 1964.
[25] Berger, Luckmann, 1966.
[26] Sachs, 1962.
[27] Del Grosso Destreri, 2002.
[28] *Ibidem*, p. 12.
[29] *Psychologische und ethnologische Studien über Musik*, 1881.

one hand, but on the other, he explores the music processes, the relationship between artists and consumer, and the connection among the piece of art, individual, and society. This was an initial attempt to connect music to other elements, which are linked both to the most intimate dimension of each person and to the social reality. For these reasons, the studies about music by Simmel cannot be disregarded, given also how important Simmel's theories are for the Sociology in general.

However, as mentioned earlier, the Sociology of Music was actually born with Max Weber's essay *The Rational and Social Foundations of Music*. Weber investigates the relationship between music and society within the process of rationalisation. In fact, the German sociologist highlights the important interdependence between social reality and music production, showing the interconnection among the development of Western music in the modern era and the establishment of rationality in our culture and in the social and economic practice.

Simmel and Weber agree about the identification of three decisive moments in the evolution of music: primitive music, the arrival of polyphony, and modern instrumental music. Furthermore, both agree that music comes from the need to express yourself: it is instinctive and linked to the need for expression and communication of emotions and feelings. Like any other cultural product, music language becomes more objective over time, they become rational and autonomous and change the role of music within the modern society: from an expression of human needs to form of art.

Theodor W. Adorno's theory is more complex. Starting from the critical theory of the School of Frankfurt, Adorno's position on art and music is quite specific: it is all about the fracture between art and society. He believes that the purpose of the sociology of music is investigating the relationships among music phenomena, the consumers (i.e., social individuals), ideology, and social classes. In fact, in the various essays on this matter, Adorno says that in some forms of music reflects the ideology and forms of totalitarian repression that are typical of the capitalistic mass society. However, he contradicts the simplistic Marxist theory of reflection and says that music is not just a product of society, but also a form of criticism to it. Adorno says that by opposing and criticising society, art has a liberator function.

While Adorno shares with Weber the theories about macrosociology (i.e., sociology about historical–social processes, institutions, and mass behaviours), Alfred Schütz talks about reality as social interaction. Key ideas of Alfred Schütz's theory are "intersubjectivity" (i.e., the interaction among the composer, performer, and audience), "communication", and the "meaning" of the piece of music. Based on this approach to phenomenological sociology, the Austrian philosopher analyses both the social and nonsocial nature of music, saying that even though it does have a "meaning", it does not refer to a real object or ideas, as it is an idea itself. This does not, however, prevent its communicative processes within a social context where a composer, performer, and an audience interact.

Starting from the theories of Adorno and Walter Benjamin, the next paragraph analyses the concept of the cultural industry and the technical reproducibility of art. These theories heavily contributed to the debate about the social role of art and music. Adorno's theories (whether accepted or criticised) were the ones that most strongly influenced the further scientific production about popular music.

1.3 Cultural industry and technical reproducibility of the work of art

The expression "cultural industry" was introduced for the first time in 1947 by Horkheimer and Adorno in *The Dialectic of Enlightenment*, to indicate the industrial–technological complex that makes possible production, reproduction, and distribution of the art products through mass media. The authors have already discussed this topic in the essay "Sociology or art and Music", part of *Lessons of Sociology*,[30] where they say that the tools of reproduction of art are "ideological" and, as such, they demean the work of art, distorting its meaning.

This theory clearly expresses how Adorno disagrees with Walter Benjamin,[31] who maintains that the reproducibility of the piece of art through modern technologies could be considered anti-individualistic and democratic. Although both Benjamin and Adorno were influenced by the Marxist ideology, they ended up reaching opposite conclusions: the former believed mass media are positive, as they give many people the opportunity to reach works of art; the latter instead claimed that massification of art is the beginning of its degradation. Benjamin highlights that the work of art is not supposed to be reproduced and "massified", as it gets damaged by these processes. This is due to the "aura" or the essence of making the work of art or the artistic event unique.

In his essay *The Work of Art in the Age of Mechanical Reproduction* Benjamin talks about the relationship between art and technology, discussing the "new media" (as per, new at his time), that is, photography and cinema. The arrival of new and more modern technologies of representation and communication dramatically changed both the production of art and its role in society. The scholar believes that the presence of technical tools allowing to produce and reproduce pieces of art favours overcoming an idealistic concept of art, that is, the concept of art as sacred and the artist as "exceptional" human being. The work of art is a unique and non-repeatable object, and its values lie in it, being *hic et nunc*. All in all, we end up losing what can be defined as "aura", because during the age of technical reproducibility of the piece of art, the aura fails. The process is "symptomatic", and its meaning goes beyond art. The reproduction technique subtracts what has been reproduced from tradition. By multiplying the reproduction, we will get a series of events rather than a unique event; and, by allowing reproduction to meet the needs of its consumer, what has been reproduced becomes "current." Both processes bring a violent upheaval affecting what has been handed down. The transformation of tradition entails the current

---

[30] Horkheimer, Adorno, 1956, trad. it., pp. 117–132.
[31] Benjamin, 1936.

crisis and renovation of humanity. Both processes, again, are strictly connected to the mass movements of our era.[32]

The technical reproducibility of the piece of art might get rid of its "aura" but it does not undermine its aesthetic role. According to Benjamin, the technical reproducibility redefines the aesthetic role of art according to the historic context and the rise of the mass society. In this new social context, the work of art's fruition becomes both a necessity and a collective opportunity. According to Adorno instead, the "real" piece of art (whose intention is to preserve its value) shuns diffusion and mass fruition. Based on Adorno's elitist ideas, true art cannot be for everyone, and if it is, then it is not real art.[33]

Adorno's interpretation assumes that in our bourgeois-capitalistic society, both music and art are a "commodity", whose value is decided by the market.[34] In 1938's essay "On the Fetish-Character in Music and the Regression of Listening" (then published within the collection *Dissonances*), Adorno focuses on music "consumption", expressing pragmatical and visionary ideas. In the essay, which is a critical answer to Benjamin's theories, the German philosopher says thanks to the mass diffusion of cultural products (i.e., concerts, movies, songs, etc.), the relationship between the utilisation value and exchange value gets transformed. What consumers spend for and enjoy is no longer the utilisation value (i.e., the aesthetic enjoyment that is truly accessible only to those who have the tools to decrypt and understand the piece of art), but the exchange value.

In other words, the commodity does not have much to do with its own peculiarities: its true value in use lies in the fact that it allows whoever purchases it to be reflected by it. During this process, they reaffirm their personality through the object of worship (fetish of their personality) and reinforce the enjoyment by belonging to the community of consumers. These consumers are either wealthy people who can afford certain commodities, or not so affluent people who admire them and hope to be able to eventually afford them.[35] Adorno claims that in the modern context, even art suffers the consequences of "the decay of the exchanges between individual product and social consumption, increasingly verging on the monopolistic equalisation, required by the commercial *ratio* of the industry."[36] In this perspective, the artist is no longer a free creator, and they go through a process of alienation when they are "just the perpetrator of their intentions, seen as completely foreign entities."[37]

The ideas of the German philosopher have been criticised on various occasions. For instance, Del Grosso Destreri points out that Adorno's analysis of music is just about alienation, and that, as Herbert Marcuse reminds us, "alienation is not the only feature of art."[38]

---

[32] *Ibidem*, p. 23.
[33] Schönberg, 1950.
[34] Petrucciani, 2007, p. 27–28.
[35] *Ibidem*, pp. 39–40.
[36] Rognoni, 1959, p. XV.
[37] Adorno, 1949, Italian translation, p. 23.
[38] Del Grosso Destreri, 1968, p. 168.

The theories by Franco Crespi about Adorno and Horkheimer[39] might help us to better comprehend the cultural industry and the role of the market in the mechanisms of art's and music's production and consumption. These authors believe that the *cultural industry* (i.e., the organised production of culture on the basis of economic and political control aspirations) is an anonymous force, hiding behind fictitious neutrality, on the basis of an empirical assessment of reality (Hockheimer and Adorno, 1947). The main function of this industry is to train masses on conformism, by censoring any discordant voice. To reach this dependency of the masses, mass media grip onto individuals' emotions and primary desires. The more the cultural products affirm the current order of things, the more the individuals appear to be alienated.[40]

In this respect, successful songs seem to be "built" thanks to mass media, and with no consideration of the consumer's taste. Adorno describes the consequences of this process, saying that passive listening (brought by the standardisation and generic cultural industry's dynamics) is the reason for an unavoidable social stultification. Fostered passivity is part of the generic system of the cultural industry as a system of progressive stultification. Stultification is not an effect of any single tune: but the fan, whose needs of imposed products can escalate up to a dull euphoria, gets trained by the generic system of pop music to a passivity that then affects also their thinking and social behaviour.[41] In a nutshell, Adorno and Horkheimer believe that the mechanisms generated by modern society through the production and consumption of art and music, end up threatening the "real" piece of art, its value, and distinctiveness. Furthermore, industrial and commercial dynamics are mirrored by pop music and jazz.

1.4 On popular music

Theodor W. Adorno mainly focused his attention on "highbrow" music, especially in his essays on Wagner (1937–1938), Mahler (1960), Schönberg and Strawinskij (1949), and Alban Berg (1968). However, many of his theoretical works are based on a music genre that was born in America at the beginning of the 20th century and was due to rapidly spread across the world: jazz. His analysis covers not only the music production of Bach, Beethoven, and the other authors mentioned above, but also Kurt Weill, jazz, and popular music. Moreover, Davide Sparti[42] says that Adorno can be considered the first author who tried to define the field of popular music, which includes all kinds of musical expression meant to be consumed by the masses, that he rigorously analysed. This definition has also been applied from Adorno to define jazz, as it was treated as a genre for mass consumption too.

---

[39] Horkheimer, Adorno, 1956.
[40] Crespi, 2006, p. 155.
[41] Adorno, 1962, translation, p. 37.
[42] Sparti, 2005.

According to the philosopher, jazz is a form of popular and "military" regression of music. Sparti explains that, according to Adorno, jazz's tempo is "rhythm-obedient": in spite of the pseudo-variation of syncopation, it reflects the timing of the march (recalling military discipline) and above all to the mechanical and synchronised timing of Taylorism (typical of the capitalistic production). Jazz appears to be "democratic", as it seems to be longing for freedom and emancipation through instinctive and sexual elements but, according to Adorno, it is not a spontaneous phenomenon at all, as it was planned and divulged by monopolistic powers of the cultural and entertainment industry, and it expresses a false anti-conformism. It only confirms and reinforces conformism and submission.[43] Jazz might "simulate" something new, but it is an expression of an "out-of-time" vogue (Adorno calls it *zeitlos* meaning "without time").[44] On its consumption, Adorno says that jazz is a perfect mirror of the colonisation of culture by the market economy: the value in use of the piece of art comes after its value of exchange as a commodity.

Many scholars criticised his theories on this matter: for example, Sparti says that Adorno did not actually have much experience of jazz, except the one he had gained through his trip to America;[45] moreover, jazz developed through various subgenres which do not seem to be evaluated by Adorno and his theories. Adorno's arguments on jazz only refer to a specific era: the *Swing Era*, the era of the great dance orchestras, when the purpose of the music product was just the entertainment of medium and high elites of the American society, ignoring the aesthetic and semantic value of the music product. Although jazz assumed several forms across the century, Adorno was not once open to review his theories, and instead, he kept on reiterating them.[46] In an autobiographical note about his experience in America, Adorno[47] admits that his first studies about African-American music lacked "in situ" knowledge, and probably the purpose of his trip to America was to learn more about jazz directly.

Adorno's target is not actually jazz or jazz musicians, but its consumeristic usage; in general, he reprimands the jazz industry for allowing a flattening of its criticism. In fact, it is worth remembering that Adorno did not actually analyse pieces of jazz, but he did use them to investigate music products in a very different way.

Adorno identifies three types of work of art: the accomplished work of art, linked to the bourgeoisie; the mechanical one, linked to fascism, and the fragmented one, linked to utopia. According to Adorno, jazz is a mechanical art and that is why its pieces are somewhat like fascist marches. Jazz seems to provide an ideal tool for totalitarian usage. However, history seems to contradict his theories: jazz was banned by Nazi-fascism as it was a "damaging and undesired music." Adorno sees

---

[43] Petrucciani, 2007.
[44] Adorno, 1955, Italian translation, p. 118.
[45] Sparti, 2005.
[46] "Abschied vom Jazz" was published in 1933, "Introduction to the sociology of music" was written between 1961 and 1962, "Über Jazz" reviewed and republished in 1964.
[47] Adorno, 1969.

jazz as "fascist" because, like many other forms of mass consumption, it "aggregates and synchronises a crowd of brainless individuals [...], it puts them in synch with the rhythm of the march, creating a non-political and brainless mob. Standardisation and consumption of jazz are the common ground between jazz and totalitarianism."[48]

Some pieces are considered "standard" when they made the history of jazz and have the same structure both for the harmony and musical periods and phrases. The material that Adorno analysed has a rigid metric scheme of 32 cues, and an invariable harmonic pattern, on the basis of a strict alternation of theme (repeated) – variation theme. In this respect, jazz pieces are deemed as commodities: they look alike, they repeat, and they comply. Hence, jazz reflects "the image of a planned and hibernated society."[49]

Adorno's criticism of jazz can be extended to the whole music production defined as popular music.[50]

In 1941, Adorno wrote an article "On Popular Music" (for the magazine *Studies in Philosophy and Social Sciences*), an important reference for those who intend to study this specific music genre. The article represents a meaningful first step in the analysis of the relationship between pop music and society. Although Adorno believes that classical music is somewhat "superior", his essay is crucial as it anticipates many views about pop music. In particular, he talks about the role of the discographic industry, forcing a high level of standardisation on the music it produces.

This process of standardisation gives the feeling that the music product is "predigested"[51]: the audience has the feeling they had already listened to it, due to the recurrence of simple melodies that require no effort. Adorno believes that the habits of mass' listening are based on a mechanism of "recognition" and do not require any intellectual effort. Besides, the familiarity of melodies tends to reassure the audience, reducing the perception of conflict and capability to criticise. This is one of the reasons why, for example, shopping malls play pop music. In fact, many believe that pop music is capable of relaxing customers and increasing their willingness to purchase. In this respect, music is in the service of those who control the economy. Pop music has the power to combine and simulate widely spread emotions, it distracts and comforts the listener, and it acts as a collaborative and productive element within the economic system. It performs a role of social cohesion: even though it is very individualistic, pop music makes the consumer believe their experience is actually a collective experience, through the mechanism of recognition.[52]

Adorno claims that these characteristics are typical of pop music. They cannot be found in music as proper art "where" every single detail, even the simplest, would be peculiar and irreplaceable. The musical patterns of pop songs are so detached

---

[48] Sparti, 2005, p. 72.
[49] Adorno, 1955, p. 119.
[50] The expression "popular music" is translated into Italian as "musica leggera."
[51] Adorno, 1941, Italian translation p. 76.
[52] Santoro, 2006, pp. 31–32.

from the actual musical progress where everything can be replaced with anything.[53] Although it uses standard forms, classical music's modes are creative and unique, and each piece of music is a non-repeatable declaration about the human condition: each piece provides a different understanding of what human beings are. The German philosopher believes that the contemporary hostility towards classical music stems from the fact that each person is embarrassed by it: if there is a piece of music that can remind the listeners of themselves, of their uncertainties, and that there is still a chance to lift their own existence up, it will embarrass them. Human beings become furious if art reminds them that they are actually deprived of their own potential.[54]

In a music piece of art, each detail gets its meaning by the whole flow, and this "wholeness" stems from the "living" interconnection between the details that stand up against and chase each other. The meaning of a classical piece is given by the way the composer puts his work together. Relationships are "alive" and dynamic, so that constant development and new levels of depth are always possible. The meaning of pop music instead gets "imposed" by its form, from the outside, from the social context. Its form does not change, does not develop, but hides behind "ornaments that cover a constant uniformity like masks."[55] Furthermore, Adorno criticises pop music for its excessive emphasis on the form as opposed to the content: "nothing new can be introduced, except calculated effects that add some flavour to the monotone uniformity without questioning it."[56] Finally, due to the commercial logic, in pop music a song must be truly exciting to be memorable, but also recognisable and consequently, trivial. Pop music must answer two questions: it needs impulses to get the attention of the listener, and it needs material that the listener can identify as "natural music." This means that it needs the sum of all the conventions and music patterns the listener is used to and that he can recognise as the basic language of music itself.[57] However, there is a margin of action where the consumer can get the "illusion" of a potential freedom of choice: "the illusion and, to a certain extent, the individual achievement must be preserved."[58] By doing this, the listener gets back a certain level of pseudo-individuality.

Although Adorno seemed particularly interested in pop music and jazz, it is obvious that he preferred classical music (not all of it) as it is an expression of art leaning towards the truth. According to Adorno, the "true" piece of art must always have an ethical value, and it must express itself through an uncompromising radicalism by refusing concessions and manipulations. These characteristics are not compatible with the mass spread. Western Marxists kind of approved these ideas, as until the 1970's they believed that only avant-garde art was truly free from the dangers of a capitalistic commodification.

---

[53] Adorno, 1962, Italian translation, p. 36.
[54] Adorno, 1941, Italian translation, p. 28.
[55] *Ibidem*, p. 29.
[56] *Ibidem*, p. 26.
[57] *Ibidem*, p. 78.
[58] *Ibidem*, p. 80.

In his *Introduction to the Sociology of Music*, Adorno eventually talks about the relationship between music and social classes. He believes that it is possible to understand how music has an important role in the theory of conflict among social classes. However, he warns his readers about the various challenges that the sociology of music meets by engaging this debate. Hence, Adorno focuses more on music production than on its consumption.

In conclusion, it is interesting to appreciate Adorno's ideas in *Neue Musik*, that is, on the new trends of the 20th century within classic or "cultured" music. Adorno sees Stravinskij and Schönberg as two opposite reactions to the new, alienating trends of music: the former reacts through the conservative restoration of tone element from the past (Stravinskij). The latter, by contrast, responds with a total and progressist revision of the sound material (atonality of Schönberg). Adorno's beliefs are not just aesthetic. He does not look at the work of art, but at the role of the composer towards his sources. Adorno believes that the composer is forward-thinking when they are aware of the rational and evolutionary path where the music material reaches a new configuration and catches this material "at the highest level of its historical dialectic.[59] In this respect, the dodecaphony of Schönberg (a twelve-note technique freeing the twelve semitones of the octave from the tonal dependency) is a witness of the process of rationalisation of music. It was already traceable in some of the last works by Beethoven and it was the object of the sociology of music by Weber.

According to Adorno, Schönberg's dodecaphony loses meaning through the negation of tonality. In fact, tonality (similarly to the way grammar rules work for languages) provides music with criteria, opportunities, and limitations to the expression of meaning. "The lack of meaning is a basic factor of dodecaphony",[60] and that is why Adorno focuses on it, as it fully reflects the difficulties of social and economic reality of his time.

Music, and art in general, is a communicative expression, but it seems to have defied its purpose: the massifying industrial society commodifies any form of communication, by alienating it and turning it into a commodity, in fetish.[61] Hence, new music lives by deep contradictions: it has to lean towards the "non-sense", to preserve its communicative function, to keep being a bearer of "truth" and of a witness of the contemporary man's anguish. "The truth of radical music appears to be boosted, as it denies the meaning of the organised society it refuses. It is not capable to convey a positive meaning."[62]

Schönberg is fully aware of the contradictions of contemporary society and that he distorted the conventional rules of the relationships among sounds. He caught and managed change in a progressive way, choosing dodecaphony as an expression of a new reality. Stravinskij, who lived during the same time as Schönberg, came across the same difficulties brought by the crisis of the music code. However, he reacts

---

[59] Zurletti, 2006, p. 226.
[60] Adorno, 1949, p. 228.
[61] Fubini in Zrurletti, 2006.
[62] Adorno, 1949, p. 25.

oppositely: he turns to the past in an anachronistic and nostalgic way, rather than following the river towards the future and the non-sense. In his works, he revived elements of an obsolete tonality. In between Schönberg and Stravinskij, progress and nostalgia, Adorno sees a third option with Mahler. Like Stravinskij, Mahler digs in the music material of tonality from the past but, according to Adorno, he does it more naively (hence, Adorno does not criticise him as he does with Stravinskij). Mahler keeps using tonality, not because of the nostalgia of the past, or as he is afraid of losing meaning, but because he is not aware of the role of music in the dichotomy between progress and reaction.[63]

Adorno sees the creative solipsism and the critical opposition to mass society as the only way for music to survive in a social reality affected by advanced modern capitalism. Music can preserve its social message, thanks to isolation, even though this might wither it: "even the most solitary message of an artist lives because of the paradox of him talking to others thanks to his solitude, giving up on a lame communication."[64] Adorno reckons that the dialectic and critical role of music can only be seen in a "serious" type of music (in particular, avant-garde music), as it cannot just become a commodity.

Adorno's theories heavily influenced the further debate on the social role of music, with a special reference to the relationship between pop music and dominant culture. These theories are echoed also by authors "far" from Adorno and are a strong reference for studies on art, music languages, and cultural processes. The following text discusses the theories of Howard S. Becker, a scholar from the New School of Chicago, and presents some thoughts about urban cultures and the worlds of art.

1.5 Urban cultures and art worlds

In the last century, the development of communications, technologies, transports, and media broke barriers down, removed borders, and blurred margins and limits. They caused an aggressive acceleration of the hybridisation processes that affected any form of language. Moreover, the evolution of the communication media intertwined with the main cultural and institutional transformations of the modern world. As John B Thompson[65] argues, media created new modes of action and social interaction, no longer related to interpersonal relationships or the sharing of the same environment, transforming at the same time the space–time structure where several symbolic and power forms arise. The important changes that affected contemporary societies contributed to the creation of increasingly complex social, cultural, and economic systems.

The plurality of cultural forms and the variety of social contexts revealed that the sociology of the music and art has the need to use new categories of interpretation, helping us interpret these changes. However, music has a progressively important

---

[63] Adorno, 1960.
[64] Adorno, 1949, p. 26.
[65] Thompson, 1995.

role as it is an active ingredient and a valuable meaning resource in the processes of the symbolic and social construction of reality. It is possible to understand and evaluate the music languages and the various expressive forms only within a broader analysis of the social and cultural dynamics. Music (as well as art in general) is the result of collective processes that are socially constructed, and as such, it finds a way to express its content through the media of communication, culture, power, and economy.

As discussed earlier, the relationship between music and society has been analysed in depth by several sociologists. However, only recently there have been studies about the forms of production, distribution, reproduction, and consumption of music. Becker's *art world approach in sociology*[66], the semiotics of the musical discourse in musicology, the investigation of *music-making* in ethnography and the "micro-sociologic" contributions by Tia DeNora[67] (just to mention a few examples) significantly contributed to the debate about the sociology of art and music. The music and art phenomena are strictly connected to the several dynamics and social relationships affecting the contexts in which they are produced.

The last two paragraphs of this chapter analyse the main theories of contemporary sociologists such as Howard S. Becker, Diane Crane, and Pierre Bourdieu. Even when they do not specifically discuss art or music, they provide interesting considerations and interpretation categories that are essential to understand the relationships between society and forms of music production and consumption. Their theories help us understand the artistic and music phenomena through a more detailed study about how the cultural processes come to life.

Before digging in these theories (which will be further analysed in the second part of the first chapter), it would be interesting to talk about the generic concept of "culture" and, particularly, "urban cultures." There is an extensive debate and a substantial literature about it, but in this occasion, we will only touch on the basics.

As Franco Crespi says, culture finds expression through "a multivalent framework (sometimes varied and uneven) of representations, code, texts, rituals, behaviour patterns, values, that in any given social situation, provide a set of resources, whose function will change depending on the specific moment in time."[68] The sociologist then highlights that culture can be defined as "a set of symbolic forms publicly available, and people use them to instigate and express meaning, or as the tool kit (or a repertoire) containing symbols, narratives, rituals, and views of the world that individuals [...] can use through special configurations, changing over time." Crespi then argues that the word "culture" is not "a coherent set of meanings but a complex combination of tools that social actors can use to define natural and social reality, and the strategic modes and their trends."[69] Furthermore, we can distinguish between "core culture" and "counterculture", "sub-culture" or "minority culture";

---

[66] Becker, 1982.
[67] DeNora, 2000–2003.
[68] Crespi, 2006, p. 20.
[69] *Ibidem*, p. 97.

"elite culture" and "popular culture" or "mass culture"; and yet between "class culture", "movements culture", "media culture", "youth culture", and so on. However, all the contamination processes among the several cultural forms got severely accelerated through the spread of mass media and generated more hybrid cultures in complex societies, where it is hard to set the boundaries of the forms they get shaped up into.

The American sociologist Diane Crane highlights the plurality of cultural modes too, talking about the difference between a "recorded culture" where we can find all the recorded forms of culture (texts, movies, records, products built by men, electronic media, etc.) and an "unrecorded culture" that is, beliefs and shared values, that may or may not be expressed through the recorded culture.[70] Furthermore, Crane discusses the idea of urban cultures, that is, "class cultures" reflecting values, attitude, and resources of the social groups consuming them. They contribute to the definition of political and social boundaries and consolidate the elite's prestige and social status.[71] Big international cities show a shocking variety of urban cultures, from the production of graffiti to the rehearsal of majestic operas. We need to find a way to classify them, to compare the environment where they flourish and their consequences on the urban structures.[72] Starting from the theories of Becker and Crane, the paragraph now focuses on the main arguments about the several "cultural worlds."

Howard S. Becker calls all the urban cultures *"art worlds"* or "cultural worlds", both for serious or popular culture. He identifies various artistic worlds that can be considered a sub-cultural system, each with its own features. From here, the sociologist then identifies various types of artists: "mavericks", "integrated professionals", "naive", "folk artists." This shows how art could be socially integrated (professionals) or criticizes and debates the prevailing culture through innovation (mavericks), coexisting at one time.[73] The art worlds made by the set of individuals whose activity is necessary to produce specific works. In a certain world (and may be in others), these works are called "art." The members of these art worlds coordinate their activity by referring to a set of conventional notions, embedded in the standard practice and object usually used. The very same people may cooperate in more occasions or also regularly in the same way and to produce similar works; hence, the art world might be considered a solid network of cooperation among artists. Although people might change, whoever substitutes them are experts in some conventions, so that they can keep the workflow smooth. Conventions make collective activities simpler and less wasteful with regard to time, energy, and other resources.[74]

Diane Crane analyses the theories of Becker and Samuel Gilmore (1987), and identifies three different cultural worlds according to the social class of the audiences who usually use them and of the prevailing features of the environment where

---

[70] Crane, 1994.
[71] Baltzell, 1979.
[72] *Ibidem*.
[73] Becker, 1982.
[74] *Ibidem*, p. 50.

they get produced: network, small profit-oriented and nonprofit organisations. In other words, the scholar believes that urban cultures produced in each of these contexts gave specific features. Some of them are brought by the context of informal social networks, which are made of "creators and the consumers." *Embedded* cultural organisations provide the tools to produce, distribute, and show their works. According to Crane, these networks attract young people who are likely to have fresh perspectives on culture, and at the same time they tend to provide continuous feedback among creators themselves and between the creators and their audiences. The advent of new cultural styles, as Crane reminds us, "is usually accompanied by the emergence of new social networks, sometimes as subsets of the existing networks. When these networks intersect, they provide contacts with creators of other types of cultures, allowing new ideas and approaches to rapidly divulge from one network to the other."[75]

Speaking of which, we can think about the cultural production of the social centres of the 1990s in Italy, and the diffusion of youth music products through alternative, nonofficial channels, helped by a strong connection of social relationships across urban and extra-urban realities.[76] In this context, the intense production of "neo-melodic music" (typical of the Neapolitan context) has become popular, thanks to the social relationships between producers and consumers. The combination of a social network and small nonprofit cultural enterprises seems to be a great tool to produce the aesthetically innovative or provocative culture. Even on this matter, we can use the example of the "Posse" in Italy that except for self-productions, it is about collaboration between the artists of the community centres and small record labels, contributing both to the promotion and the distribution of the product, not only through niche channels but also through more mainstream ones.

Another type of "cultural world" is one of the small profit-oriented organisations, where the activity of the creators is more important than networks. Their purpose is to create works that people appreciate, rather than surprising or provoking them. Becker says that in this case, creators are like artist–artisans, who prefer to make beautiful and harmonic works rather than unique or "rebellious"[77] ones. In this category, we find creators all organisers from the middle class, who sell products or cultural manifestations.

The third type of cultural world is the non-profit organisation, whose typical goal is the preservation of artistic and ethnic traditions rather than the creation of new ones. The creators are often performers who reinterpret the works of creators, most of whom are dead. We can think, for example, about the activities of the most prestigious theatres (San Carlo in Napoli, la Scala in Milano, etc.), of the music colleges, the foundations and institution of preservation of artistic, historical, and cultural goods. According to Crane, if we consider culture as a source of power and a signal of status, urban culture is a prerogative of the middle and high classes that are

---

[75] Crane, 1992.
[76] Savonardo, 1999.
[77] Becker, 1982.

usually more visible than the lower ones and receive more support from institutions or sponsors. There is a broad tendency to ignore that the low-middle classes and the working ones have their form of urban culture that reinforces their status and identity, usually as members of specific ethnic groups or minorities. So, urban cultures have similar functions across different social classes, and they tend to express the differences between social classes and (within these social classes) among the several statuses and ethnic backgrounds. On the basis of Crane's analysis (referring to large American cities), each of the three sectors of urban culture has a specific purpose: the creation, sale, and preservation of of original culture. Most tools get allocated to sell and preserve, rather than create, but of course, it is the creation that brings new ideas, images, and sounds that spread across regional and national environments, especially through the reproduction in other urban settings and only rarely through different entertainment modes.

Going back to Becker's theories, he highlights how the production of the works of art comes from a cooperative process using that relational source called "social capital"[78] by Bourdieu. According to Becker, artists and musicians are not "geniuses" working in isolation, but they depend on the many individuals who assist them in the production and distribution of their works. Hence, Becker believes that art and music are a collective process when "supporting personnel" is as important as artists' personality. These are art critics, patrons, collectors, and institutions (art schools, museums, audience, and art galleries). All the interactions among these social actors define the artistic environment, which is different from other production forms.

> I considered art as an activity carried out by some people, and I mainly looked at models of cooperation among these people rather than the actual works or their creators. [...] My approach seems to be diametrically opposite to the core tradition of the sociology of art, as it defines art as an independent act, where creativity arises, and the peculiarities of a society express themselves (especially in the work of a genius). The core tradition sees the artist and their work (and not the network of cooperation) as the focal point of their analysis, of art as social experience. Based on this difference, we could say that my analysis does not belong to the sociology of art, but the sociology of work, applied to artistic activity. [...] A concert of symphonic music for example is based on the creation, the building and the maintenance of musical instruments, as well as the invention of a musical notation system used to compose music itself. Many people must have learnt to play those notes on those instruments; it's also necessary to have time and locations for rehearsals, to hang posters around, advertise the gig, sell the tickets and gather an audience capable of listening, understanding and somehow reacting to music.[79]

Music as a collective process is based on several skills and a network of relationships useful for production, diffusion, and consumption of the artistic works. Pierre Bourdieu agrees that a piece of art is the result of a process when all the

---

[78] Bourdieu, 1980.
[79] Becker, 1982, p. 13–18.

elements linked to the personality of the artist are connected to the network of social relationships and economic constraints. The French sociologist thinks that the work of art cannot be considered only as of the product of a single artist or as the mere result of social factors, but as a set of several factors that highlight the role of the artist as well as the audience consuming them and the cultural models defining its value. The next paragraph focuses on some of Bourdieu's theories, helping us understand all the artistic and cultural events described in this book.

1.6 Distinction: A social critique of the judgement of taste

The forthcoming process and the network of relations Becker and Bourdieu refer to are the leading factors in the creation of the work of art, and they implicitly recall the role of the "social capital" in the artistic and cultural production.

The expression "social capital" has been introduced in literature by Pierre Bourdieu, who clearly defined the difference between the social capital and the economic and cultural one. He says that it is "a set of current and potential tools linked to the possession of a steady network of relations more or less institutionalised, and to the belonging of a group of elements with common features, connected in a strong and useful relationship."[80] The French sociologist (as well as other scholars who gave a definition this concept)[81] believes the social capital is a set of relationships perpetrated over time and a feature of the social networks. He says that these relationships are crucial to reach certain goals, referring to the network of personal relationships that individuals can turn to, to pursue their aims and improve their social position.

Bourdieu's ideas (1930–2002) refer to several sectors of the sociological debate. Starting from his work *Distinction: A Social Critique of the Judgement of Taste,* he provides the tools to understand the existing relationships among social belonging, lifestyles, taste, music, and art consumption. Even when he does not directly discuss these topics, his ideas are useful to understand the social dynamics affecting the cultural processes. Here are some key ideas of his production: the key concept of Bourdieu's works are "habitus", "field", and "social space", as they are typical of the music world.

Crespi[82] believes that Bourdieu's theories are in between Structuralism and Subjectivism. In fact, he aims to avoid both the objectivistic illusion (i.e., considering social structures as autonomous realities which are imposed on the social actors) and the Subjectivist one (i.e., seeing individuals as autonomous, not affected by practical and social constraints). According to Bourdieu, the relationship between subject

---

[80] Bourdieu, 1980, p. 2.
[81] In recent years, the idea of "social capital" has become increasingly popular in the sociological and political analysis. The expressions refer to various interpretations and come from the studies of authors including Coleman (1988), Lin (1999), Putnam (1993), Fukuyama (1995), and others who focussed on it. In this book, we only refer to Bourdieu's definition (1980).
[82] Crespi, 2006.

and structure is about a mutual interdependence, as an action is neither a mechanical reaction to preestablished norms, roles, and cultural models nor the result of aware and deliberate actions of the social actors.[83] The meeting point between action and culture is *habitus*, which is a set of "dispositions" coming from the practical experience of social life. Crespi reminds us that these dispositions are both "structured determinations, as they are a result of historical action and inter-relationships among individuals, and structured dimensions as they generate and arrange practices and individual and collective representations. In real social contexts, these limit the *field* of the actual possibilities of thought and action."[84] Someone's "dispositions" are their embedded history and make an agent choose a strategy instead of another within a certain "field." In other words, they are the reason why a person would be likely to behave in a certain way and to develop a specific taste. *Habitus* affects the traditional idea of "class." Social existence means to have a space and time in society, hold a position in a social structure, and show the signs of these structures as verbal automatisms or mental mechanisms and of the whole *habitus* generated by a specific condition. This means we depend on groups and are stuck in networks of social relationships showing objectivity, opacity, and permanence of things, and that manifest themselves in the shape of dues, debts, determinations, and constraints.[85]

According to Bourdieu, strategies, dispositions, tastes, behaviours, verbal automatisms, and mental mechanisms are not entirely caused by *habitus*, as there is always room for uncertainty. However, "the strategies' freedom would depend on the structure of the field, which has a higher or lower concentration of capital."[86]

To understand the tight relationship between improvised dimension (i.e., the degree of freedom) and the structured dimension, Bourdieu talks about when describing the *habitus*, we can refer to an example by Davide Sparti about the relationship between tradition and innovation, structure and improvisation in jazz.[87] This example might be useful to clarify how we could use Bourdieu's interpretative categories within an argument about the processes and the dynamics of music and creative phenomena. Improvisation in jazz does not mean freedom but, on the contrary, if musicians can improvise, they can do it as they know the rules and the material of their field. They know them so well that they can modify them and creatively transgress them. Sparti believes that to understand musical improvisation, we must "recall a theory of tradition and a theory of practical knowledge, that clarifies both the constraints of generative action and the special skills needed to create something new when composing music."[88] As in everyday life, you cannot start from scratch when you improvise and interpret a piece of music, but you always have the background to start from. There is a horizon of possibilities, represented by tradition,

---

[83] Bourdieu, 1972.
[84] Crespi, 2006, p. 81.
[85] Bourdieu, 1979.
[86] *Ibidem*.
[87] Sparti, 2005.
[88] *Ibidem*.

that is, a set of sources and rules that remains virtual until the musician gets ownership of it while composing. It is a toolbox to choose from when you compose music. This active negotiation begins already with musical socialisation, which is not a simple reproduction of tradition. This is because any neophyte, whilst starting to practice jazz, necessarily brings something from their own culture and experiences, from what they learned in other contexts, redefining it to inject it into the new context. The jazz player then begins to act through the contexts over time, establishing connections between contexts that appear divergent or even contrasting at first. In this way, the interfaces between contexts, music pieces, old and new, get re-designed and extended, and new bonds get tied.[89]

For example, in a solo of the 12th February 1964 on the song "My Funny Valentine", the trumpet player Miles Davis improvises, but at the same time "alludes and comments, has a conversation with, deconstructs the story of the other versions that he knows of the jazz standard, including all the previous versions played by himself." [90] If we consider tradition as a horizon where the music player acts, then the horizon moves along with the musician. The jazz player continues and modifies tradition while using it. There is no need to wonder how much "structure" we need in improvisation, but we need to note this circularity: "Tradition is both the *medium* and the product that music contributes to creating. Those who improvise have a lead role, not so much as a musician isolated from tradition, but as a music generator who reproduces, but actualises and produces tradition."[91]

Hence, we can talk about two events: the former is structured and concerns tradition and the original contexts; the latter is structuring and concerns people who improvise within these contexts. Improvised music is, therefore, an expression of a context of origin that will eventually be extended and unfolded.

Bourdieu's idea of "field" allows considering structural, cultural, and subjective elements that interact within a given social context and generate "procedures" through which a new social reality comes to life.[92] By refusing the interpretation of "linear thinking" that points out to only one factor (i.e., the relationship of production) as the "cause" of social practices, Bourdieu believes that we need to "re-design the patterns" of the relationships interconnected by several variables, referring to the "structural causation of a network of factors." There is a multiplicity of material, cultural, and social determinations, connected to each other. It is precisely the peculiar shapes assumed by these multiple relationships that configure a practical "social space."

Bourdieu conceives the "social space" as an area of relations constituted mainly on the basis of three fundamental dimensions: "capital", as a set of resources and powers that can actually be used (economic capital, cultural capital, social capital); the particular structure assumed by the capital; the evolution over time of the two

---

[89] *Ibidem*, p. 134.
[90] *Ibidem*.
[91] *Ibidem*, p. 135.
[92] Bordieu, Passeron, 1970.

previous dimensions.[93] The "social space" is an "abstract representation", a spot where you can watch the various components of the social world from. All individuals are simultaneously immersed in various fields. Each field, characterised by specific social relationships, gains partial autonomy from other social relationships, and it ends up structuring in other fields that can be then divided into subfields. Each area characterised by certain social relations (which acquires a relative autonomy in relation to other relations) ends up being structured in a field which, in turn, can be subdivided into several subfields. For example, a "field of power" will be able to divide itself into a "field of political power", that is interdependent but distinct from the "field of economic power." The "intellectual field" is also divided into various subfields, from the artistic to the scientific. In each field, the position of an agent depends on the quantity and structure of the capital (economic, cultural, and social), which they have at their disposal as they have been inherited or accumulated.

According to Bourdieu and Jean-Claude Passeron (1970), the cultural field is the so-called "market for symbolic goods or cultural messages." The traditional Marxist analysis has relegated it to the world of "superstructure", often limiting to mechanically and directly identifying conditioning structural determinations. Others have analysed it as a separate body, as a "pure symbolic market", a realm of bare forms of content and with no meaning. Bourdieu and Passeron are particularly critical of these positions, introducing and linking some important explanatory concepts, such as the relative autonomy of the cultural field, the reproductive function of class representatives, and the role of the school as the "main legitimate instance of entitlement of the cultural agent, that contributes to the reproduction of the structure of the distribution of cultural capital across classes, and its reproduction of the established class relationships." [94]

The reproduction of the relationships of each social class is the result of a pedagogical action, which does not start from a clean slate, but is applied on individuals who have received both a given cultural capital (from their family or from previous pedagogical actions) and, at the same time, a set of attitudes towards culture. Each pedagogical action has a differentiated effectiveness according to the pre-existing cultural characteristics of the subjects, and they are "social" by nature. By penalising these differences as if they were merely theoretical, schools contribute to reproduce the social stratification, and legitimise it. By doing this, the social stratification gets to be interiorised and made believe to be natural rather than social.[95]

Music (in all its forms) and art, contribute to the processes of the definition of the cultural and symbolic capital of the actors sharing the social context where they belong. However, the music events too are part of the interaction dynamics of various fields, through the combination of several social, cultural, and economic factors.

---

[93] Bourdieu, 1979.
[94] Bechelloni, 1974, pp. 10–11.
[95] *Ibidem.*

We will now focus on Bourdieu's *Distinction: A Social Critique of the Judgement of Taste*, where the French sociologist presents the results of an investigation conducted in France about the relationship between the aesthetic "taste" and social background. On the basis of an empirical research carried out on a sample arranged by gender, age, education, and profession, Bourdieu analyses how the distinction of the aesthetic "taste" appears both as an effect and as the cause of "class" distinction. In particular, the study was executed through two polls between 1963 and 1968 in France (Paris and Lille), where 1200 people had been interviewed. They belonged to different social groups, to investigate lifestyles, tastes, and cultural consumption.

By defining "taste" as "the capability to judge aesthetic values", Bourdieu demonstrates that this capability and the preferences connected to it change according to the social group where someone belongs. Taste (i.e., the judgement taste is expressed through) is a meaningful tool of social classification (i.e., perception and evaluation), that allows individuals to "label" and get labelled. Tastes preferences do not indicate a precise social status, but they do contribute to articulate and sometimes determine them. The affirmation of their own taste, through a process of cultural differentiation, is caused by a need of "distinction" and social construction of identities.

According to Bourdieu, members of the ruling class, born in a privileged social position, "distinguish themselves" as their *habitus* responds to the basic needs of involvement in the main social and cultural regulations. They can "affirm their difference, their uniqueness their distinction, without consciously looking for them. As Marco Santoro says, they stand out simply by being themselves, whilst the members of lower middle class indicate their distance from the ruling class by making too much of an effort in order to appear what they are not."[96] In fact, the lower middle class does not have embodied social structures, allowing their culture to function according to patterns of perception, evaluation, classification, and consequently according to the ruling class' *habitus*.

Bourdieu's book intends to challenge Kant's philosophy of aesthetic judgement, rather than presenting a sophisticated and rigorous sociologic investigation. As Bourdieu maintains in the preface of the English edition of his book, his purpose is to "offer a scientific argument to the outdated matters dealt by Kant in his Critique of Judgement and he indicates the structure of the social classes as the base of classification systems that structure the perception of the social world and designate the objects of the aesthetic pleasure."[97] Basically, this is the "pure" pleasure Kant talks about. By contrast to the utter doctrines about art (including Kant's critique of judgement), Bourdieu's "social critic of the taste" shows that needs and cultural practices (so as the artistic preferences) are strictly connected to education, social origins, schooling, and family background."[98] "Taste" is apparently "subjective", but it is actually "socially determined."

---

[96] Santoro, 2001, pp. XVIII–XIX.
[97] Bourdieu, 1984, pp. XIII–XIV.
[98] Santoro, 2001, pp. X–XII.

Bourdieu shows how "the universes of taste" correspond to "three different social levels and three social classes":

- the "legitimate taste", that is, the appreciation of those works of art considered "superior" which increases with the level of school education and is typical of the ruling class;
- the "average taste" referring to the preference for minor works of major arts, and is typical of the middle class;
- the "popular taste" referring to "pop music" or cultured music that has been depreciated by the its spread and other music forms with no "art", typical of the lower class.

While analysing a data chart from the research, Bourdieu says that:

> in the universe of particular tastes that can regenerate through further breakdowns, when observing the main oppositions, we can identify three clusters of taste that roughly correspond to three education levels and three social classes: the *legitimate taste*, that is, the taste for legitimate pieces of art that in this case are represented by *a Well-Tempered Clavier* [...] by the *Art of Escaping*, by *The Piano Concerto for the Left Hand* (or in painting by Bruegel or by Goya). It increases along with the schooling level, and reaches its highest frequency within the ruling class, which has a better educational value. The *average taste*, assembled the minor works of the major arts (as *Rhapsody in Blue* [...] the *Hungarian Rhapsody* or in painting, Utrillo, Buffet, and even Renoir) and the major works of art of the minor arts, such as songs by Jacques Brel and Gilbert Bécaud. It is more frequent in the middle class than in the lower class, and in the more "intellectual" parts of the ruling class. Finally, we have the *popular taste* (represented by pop music or by serious music depreciated by its dissemination such as *On the Beautiful Blue Danube* [...], *Traviata*, the *Arlesiana*, and above all songs with no artistic ambitions [...]. It reaches the highest frequency in the lower class and as opposed to schooling (this explains why we can find it in businessmen and entrepreneurs, managers but not as much in primary school teachers or cultural intermediaries).[99]

According to Bourdieu, the importance of the conditions of reception of a work of art and, above all, the changes in taste, indicate that the artistic expression is never a final product; its meaning constantly changes according to the period in time and the social context.[100] The way a book gets read or the value given to a painting is linked to the hierarchical relationships among the several social statuses, and they depend on the prestige's logic of differentiation that oversees these relationships, based on education, wealth, lifestyle, trends, institutions managing the spread of artistic culture (i.e., academies, museum, music-halls, publishing houses, etc.) and by the law of the market. In fact, Bourdieu believes that the preferences brought by the artistic taste have the symbolic function of

---

[99] Bourdieu, 1979, pp. 8-10.
[100] *Ibidem.*

retaining social or class inequalities, and it should be analysed within the processes of social reproduction.

In conclusion, Bourdieu's analysis of the way consumption and culture contribute to the reproduction of the class system within the modern societies is an overcoming of the philosophy of the School of Frankfurt. According to Santoro, "Bourdieu's effort is more relevant than Adorno's and Horkheimer's, for at least two reasons: because his analysis is both theoretical and empirical (not just philosophical) and because Bourdieu overcomes the idea sustained by the two philosophers about a cultural conspiracy."[101] In the end, Crespi highlights how Bourdieu sees the symbolic order as the leading element in the construction of the social reality, and also how he subordinates this condition to the objective structures brought by class divisions: "by doing this, he seems to have forgotten his initial purpose, to give the same value both to the subjective and objective dimensions."[102]

In this respect, Bourdieu's work seems a more sophisticated version of the Marxist structuralist Determinism, as he believes that "action" is in a subordinate position "as it's limited to bring up to date objectified cultural patterns that ultimately come from the class structures."[103]

Talking about the sensitive intertwine between taste and social classes, the researches of DiMaggio, Lamont and Zolberg,[104] highlight how the relationships between social class and hegemony are not simple at all. The relationship between taste and social classes is one of the main topics in modern sociology. The theory of the cultural capital (expressed by Pierre Bourdieu's in France and Paul DiMaggio's in the USA)[105] highlights the role of the "taste" in the process of reproduction of social inequalities: "They focus on the familiarity with art being a criterion of access to high classes [...] and about how this familiarity (as shared characteristic of the members of that class) would strengthen the social solidarity within the group, thus becoming an intersubjective criterion of belonging and recognition."[106]

However, with the advent of mass culture, the relationship between taste and social belonging became less smooth, and consequently more complex. In fact, nowadays the difference between elite art and mass art flourishes through new dimensions. There are interesting arguments about this topic, such as Néstor Garcia Canclini[107] introducing the idea of *culturas hìbridas*. This is crucial to understand the new intersections between fragments of elite and mass culture, which are part of modernity. The hybridisation between cultures and new intersection form deliver new ways of match-mismatch between ruling classes and middle classes,

---

[101] Santoro, 2001, p. XIX.
[102] Crespi, 2006, p. 84.
[103] *Ibidem*.
[104] DiMaggio, 1982; Lamont, 1992; Zolberg, 1992.
[105] Bourdieu, 1979; DiMaggio, 1982.
[106] Tota, 2002, p. 83.
[107] Canclini, 1989.

enhancing unexpected processes of identification. Tota argues that this hybridisation, on one hand, represents an actual breakdown of the barriers and the constant redefinition of symbolic and cultural borders;[108] on the other hand, it builds up new forms, both poetic and aesthetic, through which the ideologic contents of the ruling classes are defined. According to this view, hybrid art is where intertextual relations converge to produce and reproduce social inequalities.

> In modern and democratic societies, where there is neither superiority by blood nor titles of nobility, consumption becomes vital to set and communicate differences [...]. Separation of art is needed by the middle class to pretend their privileges are justified by something more than mere economic accumulation [...]. Modern societies need both divulgation (to expand the market and the consumption of goods to increase profits) and distinction (recreating signals that differentiate hegemonic sectors to tackle massifying effects of dissemination). The question now is how we can rearrange the dialectic between dissemination and distinction, in a context where museums receive millions of visitors, and classic or avant-garde literary works get sold in supermarkets or get converted into VHS, Video Home System.[109]

Cultures and the institutions representing them become instruments of comprehension and interpretation of reality, but also ways to arrange social differences. Symbolic markets deeply change, but exclusion processes do not, even though they might shift to new forms. Tota says[110] that in museums, theatres, and big concerts collective rituals of post-modernity are celebrated, and at the same time, new forms of social exclusion arise. In fact, rituals build up belongings and identities. The process from inclusion or exclusion from the ritual allows setting boundaries on the inside and outside of that context and social practice. In post-modernity, art is expressed by several forms of hybridisation, in many ways: from the various medial levels it interacts with to the multiple materials it is explained by. Only by analysing the intertwine among the several levels can we note new forms through which the practices of artistic consumption keep reproducing social inequalities.[111] Bearing in mind these ideas, the theories and analysis of the dynamics of pop music and mass cultures have been analysed in the next chapter.

---

[108] Lamont, Fournier, 1992.
[109] Canclini, 1989, pp. 31–32.
[110] Tota, 2002.
[111] Savonardo, 2010.

2 Popular Music, Urban Rhythms, and Mass Cultures[1]

2.1 Pop Music

This chapter is about the main theories of pop music, with a focus on pop and mass culture, highlighting the relevant connections to media, communication technologies, urban realities, and the youth universe.

According to James Lull, pop music is a specific, very influential form of communication that deserves serious analysis, not only in the street and tabloid press, but also in scientific writings and at universities.[2] This investigation refers to music with a strong connection to mass media, cultural consumption, and youth universe: it is the pop music, music that entertains and is consumed, considered and enjoyed as "leisure" and that has usually little to do with the classic, "serious", "cultured" or "responsible" music. Pop includes rock as well as many other music genres such as soul, reggae, country, punk, and rap. However, there is a variety of definitions for "light", "rock", "popular", and "pop" music. In fact, there is no one consistent genre referring to these words, but many overlapping music styles, expressing forms of hybridisation among styles, codes, and music genres. These have a common origin but different evolutions. Hence, it is not easy to come up with an unambiguous definition of popular or "pop" music.

In Italian, we use the word "leggera" (light) as opposed to the genres of "serious" or "highbrow" music. However, the contrast between light and cultured is paradoxical, as it automatically diminishes both genres it refers to. As we already mentioned, Adorno[3] thinks that pop music is an "inferior" product, expression of the commodification of the mass culture, and it promotes the ever-growing homologation processes. According to contemporary theories, music is "light" when it is "structurally simple, aimed to a casual and light-hearted consumption, dominated by commercial rather than artistic intentions."[4] The economic side is highlighted by the expression "commercial music", referring to music for mass consumption and created (or even "packaged") with mainly profitable intentions.[5]

---

[1] The author of the paragraph 2.4 is Dario De Notaris.
[2] Lull, 1987.
[3] Adorno, 1841.
[4] Sibilla, 2003, p. 21.
[5] Leydi, 1982.

Chiara Santoianni's definition "mass media music" is definitely more accurate, and it was used during the conference International Association for the Study of Popular Music (IASPM), where French scholars were referred to *"musique de mass medias."*[6] This definition emphasises the strong connection between pop music and mass media. Santoianni herself says that pop music is above all the "youth music" as it expresses youngsters' languages, movements, and cultures.

Then, the term "pop music" has been used by most English and American authors. As Franco Fabbri says: "since the 1980s, there was a consensus among music scholars to use the term *popular music*, both to acknowledge the role of English language as "lingua franca" (the expression is not translatable in many other languages), and to nod to the historical-economic importance of Anglo Saxon and Afro-American music; also, to accept a widely spread term (with all its limitations) not being ambiguous and less prone to misunderstandings. Nowadays, what kind of music is not for mass consumption? And how many types of music were born against pop music (rock 'n' roll, bossa nova, serious music, rap)"?[7] Moreover, Fabbri says that the constant and meaningful dialectic between popular culture and mass culture further explains "the ambivalence of a type of music with origin and roots in large sections of society and at the same time is industrially produced on a wide scale."[8]

The first definition of popular music comes from history: it refers to the music hall productions from the beginning of the century, then to the producers of songs for the mass market such as Tin Pan Alley, that is, the New York press industry and its British equivalent.[9] However, scholars went further from the historical perspective and came up with other ways to define pop music, that in many cases are not coherent or in contrast to each other. Roy Shuker mentions three main branches of definitions.[10] In the first one, popular music's definition is based on its popular nature, meaning that it reaches a large number of people and is widely appreciated. The second is about music as a commodity, as it is sold and spread through mass media. The third refers to "the existence of an actual aesthetic theory about the partial anonymity of the composers, the wide-scale distribution and the archiving on phonographic tools."[11] These approaches show how popular music is still a field open to analysis and dissertations (sometimes contrasting) that are typical of the current scientific debate and start from various historical, musical, or socioeconomic theories.

Richard Middleton is strongly opposed to the most common definitions of popular music, as he believes most of them are insufficient or inadequate. He believes that the main theoretical approaches are aimed to divide the musical field between elite or mass music, high or low, aristocratic or common, and so on. In increasingly

---

[6] Santoianni, 1993, p. 8.
[7] Fabbri, 2008, p. 4. See note 50, Chapter 1.
[8] *Ibidem*.
[9] Middleton, 1990.
[10] Shuker, 1998.
[11] Sibilla, 2003, p. 28.

complex and differentiated societies, demarcations are crucial to understand and interpret important conflicts, and social and cultural tensions. However, there is a recurring risk to engage way too rigid definitions that tend to rely on the failure of recognising the several factors and presumptions behind each definition. Middleton believes that whatever word, expression or term we use, it cannot be considered the ultimate one. Moreover "popular music" can be properly figured out only as a changing phenomenon within the whole music field. This field (as well as its internal relationships) is never fixed, but always moving.[12] Hence, "popular" culture is not "pure", but "a turf where transformations happen."[13] Middleton claims that, to examine historically framed forms of popular music, we must place them within "the whole historical–musical framework", paying attention to its constant and continuous changes.

Starting from the main theories, Gianni Sibilla[14] distinguishes between pop and popular music, saying that the former should be more generic and universal than the latter. According to the scholar, the word *popular* is intertwined with *folk*, that refers to farmers', national and traditional songs, while "pop" was born in the 1950s with youth music such as rock 'n' roll. On this matter, the Enciclopedia Garzanti reminds us that "pop" is a contracted form of *popular music* that in the Anglo Saxon countries refers to "light" music. The word "popular" highlights the mass diffusion and, differently from the word *folk*, does not refer to ethnic and authentically popular culture. [...] The main field of pop is *rock* and its subgenres (*country-rock*, *folk-rock*, *hard rock*, *soft rock*, etc.), and that is why sometimes the two terms coincide. However, of late, the term rock has been used in opposition to pop as it is "consumeristic"[15] music.

Although there are some common traits (productive, social, and historical), the word "pop" refers to a narrower and better-defined field compared to the one of popular music. The birth and intermediatic development of music genres after rock 'n' roll led to the explosion of various peculiarities of popular music, such as industrial production, the relationship with the media, public role or musicians or performers. Hence, some linguistic and communicative forms of contemporary music are typical expressions of pop, but not always present in popular, *folk*, or traditional music. They always represent increasingly expressive languages, typical of the youth universe. As Sibilla says: "In other words, pop is *popular music*, but *popular music* is not necessarily pop music."[16]

The main features of pop music are the historical period of production, textual, and linguistic forms, the social actor involved, the way they build their own identity and, above all, the relationship with the communication media. In a nutshell, Sibilla believes that pop represents a "contemporary music macro-genre, including all the

---

[12] Middleton, 1990.
[13] Hall, 1981, p. 28.
[14] Sibilla, 2003.
[15] Various, 1983, p. 556.
[16] Sibilla, 2003, p. 31.

subgenres typical of the popular music, that evolved from the advent of rock 'n' roll, and that was highlighted by the intermediatic diffusion on phonographic and communication tools."[17]

Although each form of contemporary music (including the classical one) is produced and divulged according to industrial patterns and through mass communication media, pop music is the only one to be produced and reviewed for an intermediatic diffusion: "only pop musicians are (or get made up by the industry) characters of a tale happening across several communications media."[18] Pop music product and the activities of the pop stars are indeed divulged and promoted through several media, and use at the same time various mediatic languages, through radio or web, or TV and video clips.

According to Iain Chambers,[19] the terminological change from "popular" to "pop", that happens in the middle of the 1950s, is not just a mere historical division between the generic field of consumerism music and a tighter area linked to a teenage audience. There is something more behind the abbreviation of the word than a generation gap in taste: in fact, it also suggests specific music and cultural change. The voices of Little Richard and Elvis Presley emerged from a tradition quite different from the one of Frank Sinatra, Rosemary Clooney and other icons of American pop music in the afterwar.[20]

Furthermore, the adjective "pop" is not exclusive of the music field, as it is widely used in several cultural fields. Initially, in the 1950s, they used it as a generic adjective to indicate cultural products designed for a teenage audience, but it soon acquired a wider semantic ground. David Buxton reminds the "pop spirit" of the 1950s and says that "the idea of pop" as a consistent concept started in Great Britain as a rebellion against the elitist and traditionalist nature of "serious culture." "From here, we went towards popular and commercial culture, integrated into daily life."[21] In this context, pop enhances popular culture as commercial and mass culture. *Pop art* legitimises makes "exciting and *glamorous*" the usage and aging of merchandise and consumption objects, which are a symbol of social transformations and mass culture typical of the late modernity. The artist Andy Warhol was one of the main proponents of this style, and according to Buxton, he was the link between *pop art* and music. In fact, towards the end of the 1960s, he became the mentor of the famous Lou Reed's Velvet Underground, and in one of his famous quotes, he highlights the role of pop as being able to impose a trend or a celebrity on masses. This quote stresses the ideological distances that, at that time, seem to differentiate rock from pop, that is, where rock is the voice of a romantically integralist vision of the artist, pop is a massified communication.[22]

---

[17] *Ibidem*, p. 29.
[18] *Ibidem*, p. 31.
[19] Chambers, 1985.
[20] *Ibidem*, p. 19.
[21] Buxton, 1965.
[22] Sibilla, 2003, p. 25.

In this respect, it is interesting to take a further look at the word "rock" that has been used for a long time about young, "generational" music, aimed at a specific social group. At the beginning of the 1950s, the fusion of "Black" music with White folk, meaning the fusion of the sound of blues, jazz, rhythm 'n' blues and country brought to the emergence of rockabilly, and consequently of rock 'n' roll. Music historiography and the most important academic studies suggest that the emergence of rock happened with the advent of Little Richard and, above all, Elvis Presley on the music market. From the 1960s onwards rock (shortened version of rock 'n' roll) both determined and was influenced by cultural, social, and habitual buzz typical of our time. Rock music has been the soundtrack of social commitment, the desire to communicate, the constant search for identity, the need to belong, and the longing for recognition and limelight of young people. Moreover, the so-called "cultural revolution" of the 1960s and the 1970s was generated by a strong need to react to conservatism, the hypocrisy of the conformists, to the consolidated power, and the social unrest. This necessity expressed through generational conflicts and rebellions of the kids that start rebelling against their fathers, stuck in a frozen system. Rock was the engine and propulsive thrust of protest and its dynamics, but at the same time, it was fed by them.

According to Simon Frith,[23] rock is not just a music genre but a period of music production when music romantically prioritised the value of "authenticity", trying hard not to compromise with the industry and the mass communication. Rock as generational, romantic, rebellious, and revolutionary music was moved by a sort of "ideology of authenticity", by a "specific music connotation" and by meaningful opposition to pop music. The so-called "rock 'n' roll era" ends in 1976–1977 with the emergence of punk that through its slogan "No future", proposes a philosophy of authenticity of music that (in the most romantic vision of the artist) must be pure, devoid of compromises with the market and the corruption of the modern world. This philosophy returns in the 1990s with *grunge*, even though the commercial scenario and mass media were completely different. Anyway, rock's purpose is to contrast pop and to be a "true" and "pure" music against a "light", uncommitted, entertaining, and commercial music. This contraposition is way too often merely ideologic, and ended up disappearing due to a new system of discographic production, changes of the cultural industry, and contamination across the various music genres.

2.2 Songwriting and its evolution

The topic of authenticity is related to the conflictual relationship between the Italian pop music and songwriting. In the Italian music landscape of the 1960s, the new generation and the "beat revolution" irrupted on the political social and cultural scene. It soon became a lifestyle. With the new songwriters in the 1970s, words became

---

[23] Frith, 1978.

music's weapon for social involvement and criticism. The artist becomes a focal point, the bearer of the truth, a model of identification, a real "prophet." Meeting up at gigs and marches, in the squares, and at universities, was a new way to socialise, thanks to the belonging to a specific group and the sharing of the same language and ideologic motivation. Rock concerts become a new social ritual, the "place" of collective aggregation and commonality. However, the crisis of values and ideas animating the cultural revolution in the 1960s and the 1970s, and an ever-growing awareness of the impossibility to change the reality, seemed to feed the 1980s reflux.

Individualism, Reaganian hedonism, yuppies' movement, and rampant ideology seem to have become more prominent, and the will to express themselves in a group, to react to issues, wars, massacres became weaker as nothing could have helped the situation. These arguments will be further explored later in this book, and complex cultural, social, and economic factors examined. The main point is that all the above elements somehow affect the songwriting.

The neologism "songwriter" was used for the first time in 1960, in the advertising list or the record label RCA, an American multinational company that had recently opened in Italy. The term and definition of this artistic music genre emerge from the need to commercially classify them, but would soon acquire a different function. In Italy, the "initiator" of songwriters is Domenico Modugno, who in 1958 at Sanremo had a great success with the song "Nel blu dipinto di blu" (he also wrote the music for it): the song was new, different from anything present on the Italian music scene, and with surreal and freeing lyrics. It had no precedents and was associated with an original way of singing, innovative for the Sanremo audience and music professionals. On this matter, Fabrizio De André said: "I was 18, it was 1958, the year when Modugno broke through at Sanremo with "Volare", revolutionising all our patterns and shattering all our ideas about songs, even the most progressive."[24]

The idea of a songwriter would soon evolve from a tool of commercial classification to the category of cultural classification. From an etymologic perspective, the word refers to an artist whose role is both to write and to perform the song. However, this changed over time, and it no longer identifies whoever writes the songs they sing, but the singer–writer of songs with a meaning, a piece of music and arrangement "different" from the ones of consumption songs or popular music.[25]

This music production is identifiable, thanks to the attention to subjects from daily life, its issues, and its existential, social, and political dimensions. The authors or writers are the best performers for these new themes. In the songs written and performed by songwriters, words gain a meaning giving them a literary dignity absent in other songs. The idea that whoever speaks or writes about topics and daily life experiences should also actually "live them" and communicate with the audience with no third parties is key to the symbolic creation of the authenticity of some songs. They are "different" as virtually opposed to the mere commerciality of other songs.

---

[24] De André, 1999, p. 4.
[25] Santoro, 2000 and 2010.

Since the beginning, the songwriter has been representing a cultural creation, a product born to supply a demand for authenticity that traditional Italian music (produced by an industrial machine according to fixed and unreliable patterns) can no longer satisfy.[26] According to Sarah Thornton, music is perceived as "authentic" when it sounds real or perceived as such, then it has credibility and it's genuine. In a time of never-ending representation and global communication, music authenticity is a cure both against alienation (as it offers a sense of community) and against fiction (as it amplifies a sense of what's "real").[27] Songwriting sounds real and is perceived as such against alienation and fiction.

The innovation brought by authors and performers is not confined to words, but affects culture and interpretation. By breaking the pattern of the tradition of the "Italian-style song", songwriters substitute classic romance or paradigms of the traditional Neapolitan song with modes and structures that they borrow from the French *chansonnier* and from Anglo-American rock or rhythm 'n' blues, also recuperating Italian folk. With the use of these paradigms (above all rhythm ones), which are different from the Italian melodic tradition, the songwriters bring linguistic, metric, and content innovation, typical of the cultural "revolution" they enact. American referents, such as, for example, Bob Dylan, made similar style choices, contaminating traditional folk with the languages of rock, and offering politically and socially relevant lyrics.

During the 1970s the songwriter acquires a new economic and political value. The language and music break-up with Italian tradition overlaps with the political and cultural structure brought by the students' movements of 1968 and 1977. In the 1980s, there is the ultimate consecration (but also the beginning of an identity crisis) of the songwriters, brought by the ever-growing control of the logics of market on the contents of the song, and by those social, cultural, artistic, and technologic changes that in the 1990s generated new expressions and new forms of music communication. The overall disorientation, the research of music and art identity typical of the new generation of songwriters, and the unavoidable trend towards mixing, contamination across different styles and languages (visible in all the contemporary artists), affects the songwriting, both nationally and internationally.

The image of the 1970s songwriters, who used to express themselves in an efficient and emotional way even just with a guitar and a flow of words, seems to waver against a sort of "popfunkrapjazzrock-singer-author" who collects, breaths, and expresses the several stimuli (music-related and not related) through the hybridisation across genres and styles overwhelming them. This also happened, thanks to a very fast development of technologies of communication.[28] A "pop...singer–author" like the American artist Beck (just as an example), whose albums are always diverse, produces different types of songs, each of them taking a different direction from the

---

[26] *Ibidem.*
[27] Thornton, 1995.
[28] Savonardo, 2002.

global project, to explore new expressive forms, contaminating languages of rock or folk tradition with electronic music. Through the hybridisation across rock, funk, rap, and jazz, the new songwriters convey a fragmented identity, generation, more and more "confusa e felice" (confused and happy), as the songwriter Carmen Consoli (1997) would say. "Happy" not to have limits or boundaries, happy to get out of the cage of pre-packaged styles and aesthetic labels to go looking for new emotions. They explore new contradicting realities that live together or "get confused", melt in a new hybrid music reality. This creative dimension reaches its highest expression through the "transformism" of the London pop star David Bowie (1947–2016), an eclectic artist who since the early days of his career and throughout it was able to stage all his multiple identities and all the social, artistic, and cultural changes of his time through his music and art productions in general. The "White Duke" represented a meaningful expression of the fast changes, of late modernity, and its relevant metamorphosis, through his language expressions, his diverse looks, and the sound of his albums. These experimented with various music genres, from punk to jungle, rock to dance, funk to electronic music.

These hybridisation processes are not new or exceptional. The transformations of music and social languages are always brought by the crisis of preexisting paradigms, towards innovations generated by mixing, contamination, the meeting or clash that generated rock in the 1950s, thanks to the fusion of other genres and styles. Even the songwriting of the new Millenium is basically "hybrid", a combination of rhythms and sounds where diverse and apparently distant expressive paradigms melt in a contaminated, "bastard" language. The expression "bastard" recalls a concept album by Almamegretta (1998) called "Lingo", an album of the Neapolitan band (with many international collaborations) dealing with the theme of contamination and multiculturality, both regarding music languages and the content of their songs, telling about an increasingly multiethnic and mixed society.[29] This theme reminds us of an older, famous song by the poet–songwriter Fabrizio De André called "Via del campo" (1967): "dal diamante non nasce niente dal letame nascono i fior" (nothing was born from diamonds, flowers were born from manure). This is the essence of cultural change.

Music's (and art's in general) hybridisation represents a meaningful indicator of the sociocultural transformations happening in an increasingly mixed society. A society narrated by the new songwriters, who flip the preexisting categories and offer not just emotions, but also doubts and insights. Artists became the interpreters of the "malaise" of the audience (mainly young people), who feel the need to identify themselves (even just for a season) with the most popular "singer-pop... author." Young people are confused and probably have the same need for social recognition, but they are unlikely to be inspired by the same ideological (and may be naive) motivation that in the 1970s created the figure of the songwriter as a "new prophet." This type of prophet was "designed" by the ironic verses of "Cantautore"

---

[29] Savonardo, 1999.

(the Songwriter, 1976), a popular song by Edoardo Bennato. He was one of the first artists who revolutionised Italian music in a meaningful way: "you are wise/ you bear the truth/ you are not a mere mortal/ you are not allowed to cheat/ you are a songwriter."

Edoardo Bennato is a representative of the serious Italian songwriters such as Lucio Dalla, Francesco De Gregori, Fabrizio De André, just to name a few; along with Pino Daniele, he is the highest expression of the artistic movement "Napule's Power."[30] He was one of the first to mix rock and Italian language, at a time when this kind of genre was exclusively Anglo-American, that is, of someone who could use a musically flexible language, that "sounded good" and adapted to the rhythms of rock music. The verses of his "canzonette" told about the changes and the confusion of the Italian society through music and emotions, from the 1970s till today.

During the last few decades, certainties and traditional references seem to falter in any sector, in art, society, culture, politics, and economy. The increasing confusion is expressed by the music production of the young band and through the lyrics of songwriters. An example of these is given by the lyrics of "Almeno Credo" (At Least, I Think So) (2000) by Luciano Ligabue, who is one of the main Italian rock stars. These lyrics tell in a very simple and direct way about the disorientation of the contemporary society: I believe we need a God and also a bar [...] or at least I think so [...] that when you stop hoping you start dying [...] Here no one got the instructions/I believe everyone plays by ear, in their own way/here we never had just a lonely world.

The absence of "instructions", of a destination, project, future, the presence of various "worlds" and the subjective answer to wavering are typical of what Zygmunt Bauman calls the "society of uncertainty."[31]

The contamination across music languages adversely affects the dichotomy "authenticity/light-heartedness" that affected the relationship between pop and rock and the songwriting or pop music, while the advent of new technologies brings new expressive codes and new forms of "authenticity." On this matter, Thornton[32] says that a music form is "authentic" when it becomes part of a subculture or integral part of a community. Thornton says that new technologies get "naturalised" through processes of "acculturation" and at the same time the new forms of music initially seem "stranger, artificial, not authentic"; but, as long as they get "absorbed by the culture", they become "local" and natural. Frith[33] says that new music technologies are usually opposed to nature and community. He considers them "fake and forging", and they threat the authenticity of the "truth of music." However, technology developments allow new forms of authenticity.

The efficient use of media and technology tools and the awareness of their potential are used by the pop musicians, who make the most of the new technologies, both in their communicative and creative processes, and they feed the modern popular culture.

---

[30] Marengo, Pergolani, 2003.
[31] Bauman, 1999.
[32] Thornton, 1995.
[33] Frith, 1986, p. 265.

2.3 Pop Culture, mass media, and urban rhythms

Modern popular culture as we know it, originated in the years after the Second World War. These were the years when the teenage generation was born and established, with their tendency to take on the pop culture as its philosophy of life. Pop music expresses a mass culture that is increasingly "oriented by market, urban, Americanised, standardised, technological, consumerist, progressive"[34], whose birth is generally dated around 1945. However, traces of an urban popular culture, with a modern entertainment industry, were already present, at least in Great Britain, and popular music can be traced way back: Popular music is certainly not a recent invention: the concept of "popularity", in fact, given its characteristics, cannot be associated with any definite historical period: it was probably born with the mankind. However, if the "popular" cannot be linked to a specific date, the "popular culture", that is, the culture of consumerism and mass society, has instead a definite temporal origin. Therefore, the popular music that was born from it also has a definite origin. The "teenager myth" was certainly born after 1945, but the foundations for the development of the modern record industry and popular music had already been laid in America.[35]

Pop music has got some traits typical of mass communication. Unlike classical music, pop music is inseparable from the mass market and the search for a wide audience.[36] Moreover, consumers' tastes can be influenced to a wider extent: the mass audience of pop music is itself a product of the record industry. In this sense, the ultimate goal of pop music production is more than artistic, commercial: the goal of the record industry is the economic profit. However, we will soon become aware that art and music that define pop culture are not always the result of commercial projects. As Roberto Leydi claims: "Pop music is certainly managed, in a way, by the entertainment and music industry but there are creative spaces that, at least in the moment of their emergence, escape manipulation and exploitation of the consumer system."[37]

The worldwide diffusion of pop music, with its mainly heterogeneous and mostly young audience, is favoured by its privileged relationship with the mass media. However, the relationship with the media is often contradictory, ambiguous, and uncomfortable, but essential: pop is the only music whose essence consists in being communicated by mass media.[38] For a better understanding of the modern musical phenomena, it is necessary to analyse the peculiar relationships between pop and the mass media.

Pop music is an intertextual and intermediatic phenomenon, which expresses its communicative power through a language that constantly transform itself and adapts

---

[34] Santoianni, 1993, p. 19.
[35] *Ibidem*, p. 23.
[36] Frith, 1981.
[37] Leydi, 1982, p. 352.
[38] Frith, 1981, p. 6.

to the social and media contexts in which it is manifested. Pop uses every media to reach its potential audience through different forms of communication: musical film, radio selection, television video clips, biographical or photographic book about an artist or a band, recording on vinyl, cassettes or CDs, live performances and, more recently, multiple ways of promotion and dissemination on the Web.

Radio is the most consolidated channel for the diffusion of music. It was the first communication medium to spread sound products on a large scale, significantly contributing to define the forms of production and consumption and promoting the development of pop music as a mass phenomenon. For a long time, even after the advent of TV in the 1950s, radio maintained a sort of monopoly on pop music communication. With the advent of video-musical televisions in the 1980s and then Internet in the second half of the nineties, the radio has been able to renew itself, finding new ways of expression also through the web. Music Television (MTV), You-Tube, or phenomena such as music file sharing on the Net have also introduced new forms of music communication and recontextualisation of pop songs.

The relationship between pop music and the "image" in its different forms (fixed and moving) rather than a potential conflict (theorised by sound and radio purists) has favoured the integration between different languages and expressive codes. The video has, in fact, given new life to songs and artists, but also to the musical media themselves. In fact, in the fifties, pop music was consolidated thanks to the TV without affecting the role of the radio, which is still one of the instruments deprived of listening to music productions. However, the iconic integration of the sound message has significantly influenced the very nature of pop music. The combination of sounds and images "is now one of the features that define pop itself: music was born not only to be listened to, but to be seen. This is not the case in any other contemporary music genre."[39] Moreover, the different possible combinations between music and video show how the languages of pop constantly redefine themselves in relation to the contexts in which the music itself spreads. The video clip is expressed through the recomposition of heterogeneous and preexisting sounds and images in an unpublished text, a hybrid that is no longer just a musical text, but not just an iconic one. Every visual re-elaboration of music proposes a new meaning, which is still determined by the original musical product: the video clip can interpret, visualise, metaphorise, deform the song and its interpreter, but cannot ignore them.

The mass media, on one hand, tends to determine the homologation of cultural consumers and the flattening of the audiences' tastes; on the other hand, they allow pop music, even when it offers new trends and languages, to develop and consolidate, reaching an increasingly wide audience. Mass culture tends to create identical values of consumption and the cultural industry, through the media, conveys such homologating processes: "cultural frontiers - says Edgar Morin - fall into the common market of the mass media. [...] culture in industry is the only great ground for the homogenisation of customs."[40] The modes of production and reproduction of artistic

---

[39] Sibilla, 2003, p. 256.
[40] Morin, 1970, p. 107.

forms and their relationship with the public undergo significant changes with mass diffusion: the creative genius and concept of uniqueness are replaced by collaborative processes and industrial standardisation. According to Iain Chambers, where the individual presence of a writer or painter implied a single moment of production, the collective technological processes involving radio, film, television and reproduced music fragment the figure of the artist and dilute the idea of a single point of origin.[41]

The cultural industry and the mass media play a decisive role in the processes of musical production and enjoyment, as well as in the predetermination of forms of listening and consumption. Studies on the consumption of pop music have essentially two roots, one theoretical and the other contextual. The theoretical root has a Frankfurter and Marxist matrix, which refers above all to Adorno's theories, presented in the first chapter, considers "light music" as pure music, manipulated by the entertainment industry, designed for an audience that superficially and uncritically consumes it. These considerations have influenced (with the due distances and differences) most of the subsequent studies. In fact, some studies present certain distrust and, sometimes, a sort of ideological prejudice against the industrial and standardised modes of production of pop music.

Instead, the contextual root recalls the actual growth of the music industry since the 1980s and the greater awareness of the producers themselves to be able to determine and orient the tastes of the public. The music industry is increasingly taking on the role of cultural mediator, directing the public's taste through the promotion of standardised music genres.[42] However, the awareness of the industry's influence is accompanied by an increasing pressure from the audience in the processes of negotiating the content of the music product and the way it is consumed, which considers the social and cultural differences of the users. In Sociology of Rock, Simon Frith argues that rock is a music aimed at the youth market, and this includes different groups that make different use of rock: the weather-related choices that young people can make are influenced by differences in class, gender and professional level. The leisure industry has specific effects on the recreational choices, as it determines the horizon of available options. In their leisure time, young people are not only affected by their relationship with production, as workers, but also as consumers.[43]

In his book Urban Rhythms, Iain Chambers recalls how the main criticism directed against mass or popular culture that developed after 1945 refers to its "plasticised" and "not authentic" nature. A "substitute" culture made of ephemeral emotions, dominated by Hollywood stars.[44] This criticism seems to bring together writers and observers from different political, social, and cultural areas, who found themselves surprisingly aligned in judging this phenomenon. However, in the years when pop music exploded, the real target of criticism was industrial society as such,

---

[41] Chambers, 1985, p. 12.
[42] Sibilla, 2003.
[43] Frith, 1978.
[44] Chambers, 1985.

accused of destroying the "culture" and "values" of the modern world. According to Chambers, in depth, contemporary mass culture is plastic. As in Barthes's definition, it is mass-produced, it is elastic and flexible, ductile and convenient. Although it is regularly criticised for such attributes, falsehood and artificiality are the most significant qualities of mass culture, the very idea of its infinite transformation, of ubiquity made visible.[45] And, like plastic, mass culture has placed itself like a flexible film on the surfaces and actions of our everyday life, merging them into apparently prosaic models.[46]

The relations between culture and industry, commercial production and popular taste, and the consequent development of a new aesthetic also determine a different division of labour that seems to put the traditional role of the author of the artistic product into crisis. As we all know, the disappearance of earlier cultural models and new perspectives have been accompanied by significant changes in the technological reproduction of music. Transformations had already been brought to light in 1936 by Walter Benjamin's studies on cinema and photography.

The main characteristics of contemporary mass culture are, according to Chambers, its "commercial" nature in organisation and "urban" in character. The city represents the "stage" and the main "sound-box" of pop music and its new forms of modern romanticism. The urban reality is the place of contemporary imagination, and the structures of the metropolis cross every corner of our daily life, increasingly immersed in the flow of media products of mass culture. According to Chambers, there is an individualised use and an open dialogue with the languages of contemporary urban culture in pop music, in its romanticism, in its tastes, styles and pleasures.[47] Through these languages, individuals are simultaneously the subject and object of the processes of construction of the collective imaginary.

Focusing on the concept of the city and metropolis as a privileged place to frame the historical, social, and musical developments of the mother tongue, Chambers also affirms that sounds and modern history, their combination, and contamination are all recorded in the cultural economy of urban life. According to the English sociologist, the different sounds of music provide a way to listen to the sounds and rhythms of history, music and in particular pop music, which is often considered a superfluous phenomenon, reveals profound changes in the formation of modern culture.[48]

Starting from the experience of the city of London, a space composed of different stories, different memories, different identities, Chambers offers a special cultural perspective of contemporary music. By comparing two concerts of two different musical formations that – respectively, in 1969 and 1989 – "got hold of" the city of London, playing on the roofs of its houses, the English social logo proposes a reflection on the relationships between the different forms of cultural hybridisation, musical contaminations, urban realities, and historical–cultural paths that characterise

---

[45] Barthes, 1973.
[46] *Ibidem*, p. 203.
[47] *Ibidem*, p. 208.
[48] Chambers 2001.

late modernity. Through the example of the two concerts we pass, in fact, from the pop London of the Beatles (and the Rolling Stones) to the postcolonial London on whose roofs plays a band of *bhangra* music, a hybrid genre, the result of contamination between Anglo-American sounds and Indian musical traditions. In other words, we move from youth culture, dominated by an image marked in a "white" and "male" sense, to the reconfiguration of the same urban space that now provides the "home" for other stories, cultures, and identities. *Bhangra* music, for example, does not simply represent the import of a sound or culture from elsewhere that manages to contaminate local culture; *bhangra* music itself is an expression of the cultural hybridity created within English urban cultures.[49]

Therefore, Chambers says that we can think of *bhangra* or *bhangra* rap, *bhangra* hip hop music as "a stage of musical contamination" and as a historical–cultural novelty, that becomes part of the world using the pre-existing, the languages already available, those that have already been recorded on history and culture, creating a new combination, a new configuration. The English sociologist highlights, therefore, the idea of urban space as a space where different cultures and ethnic groups meet, mix, and blend. For Chambers, it is not an addition to, or a subtraction from, the culture. The existing ones, however, are combinations that create what could be called a third space, a space in which both cultures of "origin", are questioned and modified, taken elsewhere to create a new cultural configuration. It is from there, from the musical contamination, that a historical–cultural novelty emerges that inevitably also affects the urban space and the expressive languages that characterise it.

London, like New York, Paris, Naples, Bombay – cities in which the rhythms, sounds, tensions, impulses, noises of the world merge, blend together – give life to new sounds, hybrid realities without roots and without identity or with a thousand roots and a thousand identities that share the same space. Urban realities in which the centre and periphery mingle in a simultaneously diachronic and synchronic path; where the past, present, and future coexist through the "intramezzo" (*interlude*), the "third space"[50], a hybrid space where nothing is what it was, and is not yet what it will be, constantly evolving.

Chambers, finally, dwelling on the crisis of the social sciences, affirms that the complexity and the historical–cultural reality found in contemporary youth music presents itself as something that escapes from the humanistic framework. He believes that the social sciences that historically have tried to reduce historical–cultural phenomena to a framework in which the critical lines respect and reflect the desires of the observer, where everything has become transparent, rationalized and therefore explainable and accessible, now find themselves in crisis. Music, like many other social phenomena, instead shows *something* more.[51] "Something" that young people carry, through the sounds, rhythms, and languages of pop music with which

---

[49] *Ibidem*, p. 71–72.
[50] Bhabha, 1994.
[51] Chambers, 2001.

they express themselves and get fed.[52] The new generations, of yesterday and today, increasingly use and consume sound technologies and are increasingly immersed in media, both analogue and digital, from transistors to the web.

2.4 Sound technologies

Nowadays, music increasingly represents the soundtrack of our daily life through mass and digital media. It is "widespread" everywhere and adapts to different communicative contexts: from intentional listening, through a phonographic support to live performances, from the random fruition, through the radio, of a video clip, broadcast on TV or on the web. Moreover, as already pointed out, the social history of music is strongly connected to the one of the contexts and related cultures, through which it expresses itself in different eras. In contemporary society, music pervades every space of our life, every private or public place (subways, stadiums, gyms, shopping malls, and bars), whereas in the past, music reproduction was relegated to specific contexts such as theatres, ballrooms, concert halls, or squares during specific popular or institutional festivals. The advent of new technical devices allows musical reproduction in different times and spaces: from the invention of Edison's phonograph in 1877 to the appearance of mp3 players, jukeboxes, vinyl records, magnetic tapes, CDs, radio, television, and the Web. As the places of use and the means of transmission change, there is also a gradual shift from a predominantly "audio" dimension to an "audiovideo" media consumption, starting from the graphic representations associated with the 78 rpm containers to the video clips.

In the last few years, technological evolutions have allowed for unprecedented possibilities of fruition, production, and access to an infinite number of formats and media products which, thanks to the web and digital modes, are potentially available in real time, in every place. This information, through the advent of computers and new media, loses its analogical nature of text, image, and sound, becoming a series of numerical representations through digital code and bit.

The genesis of musical reproduction is due to the acceleration of the rhythms of the industrial age and mechanisation. Its cultural geography of reference includes France, England, and the United States from where, at the end of the 19th century, the recording industry began and developed. Within a few years, a real-world record market was born, which would contribute to the process of Americanisation of Western culture and society, sanctioned by the results of the Second World War.

The invention of photography and cinema, with the possibility of fixing a visual fragment of reality on a film, had contributed to the idea of being able to capture sound as well. An idea that led the American Thomas Alva Edison, in 1876, to concentrate his studies on the "graphic recording of sound", was started twenty years earlier by the French Scott de Martinville. The phonograph soon became a sort of

---

[52] Savonardo, 2001.

ante litteram jukebox. And the subsequent diffusion of the jukebox favoured a strong recovery of the music market after the crises of 1927 and 1932, constituting the main listening instrument of the 30 million records sold during those years.[53] Through the jukebox,[54] the collective fruition of the paid music contributes to define the musical taste of social classes hitherto extraneous to popular music.

The phonograph is increasingly becoming a tool of communication in the private sphere, in domestic contexts. With the birth and spread of this instrument, music was taken away from the exclusivity of the public sphere, and the living room was transformed into a concert hall, just as it would become a concert hall in the century that followed the transition from cinema to home theatre. The domestic enjoyment of music became one of the main practices of private consumption.

In the aftermath of the First World War, the phonograph regained its supremacy as a means of communication, preceded by the press and followed by television and cars. Soon, it also became a design object in home furnishings and a symbol of distinction in terms of style and social class. Moreover, its diffusion led to a growth in supply from the music industry, with increasingly rich catalogues – from opera to jazz – intended not only for the elite but also for more and more extensive public. Its definitive consecration will come with the birth of the magnetophone and the microgroove that will make it suddenly a way to access all the music and speeches of the world.[55] The distance between the intellectual and the "man of the street" is reduced: the development of the media brought the listening of musical productions that belong to social and cultural spheres. Musical genres change and new trends and styles develop which, as in jazz – also thanks to the possibility of recording longer and longer performances on every side of the record – generate, through improvisation, real "conversations" between the different musical instruments.

The photograph of the domestic home of the bourgeoisie shows, increasingly, the presence of a musical instrument, a particular symbol of social status, which in the past had been a privilege of the nobility: the piano.[56] Its presence in the house stakes on greater incisiveness with the diffusion of lyrics to be sung with the relative musical accompaniment. Moreover, sound reproduction favoured the initial examples of "distance learning", through the acoustic study of foreign languages, and the establishment of the first "music archives", with the recovery and collection of compositions from different periods or from other nations and cultures.

The technique of duplication opens up new scenarios for the reproduction and diffusion of sound materials: just as photography makes it possible to preserve, over time, and to recover the memory of a particular fragment of reality, the reproducibility of sounds makes it possible to preserve any musical performance,

---

[53] Baldini, 2000.
[54] The word "jukebox" comes from the American jook or juke, African-American" expression meaning "dance."
[55] McLuhan, 1964.
[56] Flichy, 1991.

beyond the space–time dimension. As already pointed out, Walter Benjamin focuses on photography and cinema, on the "technical reproducibility" of the work of art and hence on the possibility of reproducing the work outside the traditional and ritual context in which it was created. In his opinion, the uniqueness of the work of art is identified with its incorporation in the context of tradition[57] and it suffers when the contexts of fruition of the work are diversified, thanks to its technical reproducibility. The possibilities of fruition determined by reproducibility have caused an epochal and irreversible transformation in the world of music, allowing the diffusion and preservation of sounds and voices in different spaces and times. With the advent of sound reproduction technologies, the performance no longer needs specific places for listening: the space–time dimension of fruition but also the relationship between object and subject, between performer and consumer gets hit.

According to Benjamin, the technical reproducibility made possible by the introduction of pre-listen media and other interesting aspects. In mass society, as already pointed out, the relationship between musical production and the artist changes, and the very idea of the originality and authenticity of the work of art changes: even in the case of a highly perfected reproduction, one element is missing: the *hic et nunc* of the work of art – its existence is unique and unrepeatable in the place where it is located. The *hic et nunc* of the original constitutes the concept of its authenticity. The whole sphere of authenticity is subtracted from technical reproducibility – and naturally not only technical reproducibility. But while authenticity retains its pious authority in the face of manual reproduction, which is usually branded by it as a fake, this is not the case with technical reproducibility. It may also introduce the reproduction of the original in situations that are not accessible to the original itself. It allows it to meet the user in the form of a photograph or disc. The cathedral leaves its location to be received in the studio of an art lover; the choir that has been performed in an auditorium or in the open air can be heard in a room.[58]

The modes of individual and collective musical enjoyment change and the traditional categories of author, composer, and work of art are questioned. These considerations will also be the subject of the reflections presented in the next chapter with reference to the use of digital technologies and creative processes. Radio plays a central role in the reflection on the technological evolution of sound and music, and the next paragraph is certainly about it.

2.5 Social role of the radio and re-tribalisation processes

During the "tribal era",[59] before the invention of writing, words could not be fixed, stopped, preserved, and/or examined later. Ideas considered this ephemeral aspect of

---

[57] Benjamin, 1936.
[58] *Ibidem*, p. 22–23.
[59] McLuhan, 1964.

words: they had neither documents, nor records or sediments, but memories; and the price for this were fatigue, mental space, and techniques, not to forget.[60]

In its radio form the word is a voice, not its transcription. The traditional radio is one of the main sources through which the word is neither transcribed in written form nor accompanied by images, but simply through the sound of the voice. With the advent of radio and other electronic media, we are witnessing the processes of "re-oralisation" and "re-tribalization." Starting at least from the mid-20th century, these processes refer to the theoretical re-descriptions of many authoritative scholars, including M. McLuhan, E. Mayr, E.A. Havelock, J. Goody, I. Watt, W.J. Ong, A. Leroy-Gourhan or, more recently, D. de Kerckhove[61] who, directly or indirectly, have dealt with the relationship among orality, writing, and electronic media.

Knowledge can be transmitted through the spoken (which is primarily a sound) or written word. Cultures without writing tend (through oral transmission) to elaborate different ways of communication, memorisation, perception of one's own knowledge. Moreover, orality always constitutes a stable character of the language and, therefore, all written texts (including musical texts) must necessarily be connected, directly or indirectly, to the sound world of the voice. According to McLuhan,[62] however, the advent of writing led to the prevalence of sight over the other senses. The pre-alphabetic tribal man lived in a world where all the senses were simultaneous and in mutual balance, with an oral culture structured by a dominant auditory sense of life. Phonetic writing and, later, printing brought to a break in the balance of the perceptive senses, typical of the tribal world, determining the predominance of the eye over the ear, of sight over hearing, favouring the processes of rationalisation and individualisation. In the tribal era, the senses of touch, taste, and hearing had an important role, which were then questioned with the assimilation of the phonetic alphabet. Technologies and electronic media, through a unified and simultaneous perception, contribute to reestablish the "sensory balance" that characterises the pre-alphabetic tribal civilisations. In particular, according to McLuhan, radio and mass media in general determine a process of "re-tribalisation", overturning the "extreme individualism" originated by literacy (reading and writing are clearly solitary experiences), and arousing the ancient experience of deep tribal involvement, a ritual of growing "sensory balance."[63] The development of electronic media also contributes, according to the Canadian sociologist, to the rise of the "global village", in which physical and cultural distances tend to cancel each other out.

Regarding orality, here are some central aspects of Walter J. Ong's theories, summarised schematically by Gianfranco Pecchinenda:

"Sight isolates the elements, hearing unifies them", states W. J. Ong (1982), before moving on to highlight the following crucial points:

---

[60] Menduni, 2001, p. 71.
[61] For further readings on this subject, please refer to Cavicchia Scalamonti, Orality and writing.
[62] McLuhan, 1964.
[63] Ibidem, p. 320.

- Sight presupposes a distance between subject and object, while hearing implies an involvement, an immersion of the subject in the object;
- sight causes the subject to subdivide, "sections" his object, while the listener, instead, perceives sounds simultaneously from every direction;
- the sound (and the word as sound) is dynamic ("it is not possible to stop the sound and have it at the same time"), the sight can instead also be immobile, static;
- sound aggregates and therefore is consequently participative, it tends towards "community" (understood in a sociological sense), tribalism, while instead sight analyses, it tends to the sociological sense), then disaggregates, abstracts, individualises;
- in order to be remembered, memorised, the spoken word must be organised in a particular way, through the use of repetitions, antitheses, thematic assonances: in a nutshell, it must be organised in necessarily rhythmic (poetic, repetitive, redundant, conservative) formulas. These are types of discourses that move tradition, holding back or attributing a negative function to anything that can be innovative, original, unpredictable, not classifiable according to pre-existing schemes.[64]

With the advent of writing, the prevalence of the eye over the ear has influenced the role of sight itself which, from a visual dimension of the images of the world, has increasingly focused on the translation into meanings of a linear sequence of alphanumeric and graphic symbols. It is a process that would have ended the transition from simultaneous thought to sequential thought, at least until the electronic (and, later, digital) era, in which new forms of simultaneous communication increasingly prevail. According to Ong, the mass media have introduced a "secondary orality" or "return" that brings man back into the world of sound, emotion, extroversion, temporal simultaneity. Starting from these reflections, a series of hypotheses have been put forward from many quarters that the electronic media, by holding back the diffusion of the culture of reading, are decisively modifying the very forms of thought, transforming it from analytical, structured, sequential, and referential into generic, vague, fragmented, discontinuous, global, holistic.[65] The French sociologist Michel Maffesoli underlines how, with modernity and the advent of mass societies, we accessed the era of "tribes", networks, small groups, ephemeral, and effervescent aggregations.[66] In his book *The Time of the Tribes. The Decline of Individualism in Mass Society*, the French scholar argues that the ideals of reason are replaced by feelings and emotions, the logic of identity the one of affection. Pecchinenda also stresses that authentic reality is not articulated in verbal prepositions, but in total emotions, such as those proposed by music which, expressing deep and involving sensations, unites different cultures, beyond linguistic differences and their prepositional articulation.[67] Referring in

---

[64] Pecchinenda, 2001, p. 52–54.
[65] Simone, 2000.
[66] Maffesoli, 1988.
[67] Pecchinenda, 2001.

particular to youth cultures and noting how the process of "music-alisation" leads to the passage from the predominance of sight to that of hearing, George Steiner believes that, among the many causes of this profound change, "the emotional, or emotional aspects, especially those derived from a desire for affectively linked community", play an important role in its genesis:

> Reading is a deeply solitary act. It isolates the reader from the rest of the presentation. It imprisons his consciousness behind immobile lips. For the lonely man, books are enough companionship. They close the door to the intruder's nose. The printed character, the need for silence that it orders, demands total isolation. This is something that modern sensibility distrusts like the plague. The contemporary soul is resolutely gregarious, displaying its emotions without restraint [...]. Recorded music is perfectly in tune with these aspirations. Sitting side by side, attention fluctuating, we are dragged by sound, individually and collectively. Here is the liberating paradox.[68]

Unlike the book, music immediately reveals itself as "common property", irreparably paving the way for a kind of re-tribalisation of society. The radio, in this respect, is transformed into an extraordinary instrument, diffusing music in every home and promoting a process of re-oralisation.

Along with the advent of the radio, technological development allows the possibility of owning in one's own home space, a tool that combines the objectives of the telegraph and phonograph, to spread sounds at a distance. However, it was not until the beginning of the 20th century that the study and experiments on electrical channels allowed human voices and sounds to be transmitted through the radio by Guglielmo Marconi, whose first experiments on wireless telegraphy were conducted between 1892 and 1897. The radio soon became a "consumer good" present in every home, but it will also prove to be much more than that: among the different media it is, in fact, the one that will perhaps have the greatest impact on communication at a distance, in the air, land, and sea.

The cultural mission of the radio has changed several times over the years, while maintaining its social function and adapting to the spirit of the times. It was born as radiotelegraphy, as a "wireless telegraph", a multi-subject communication channel with the task of transmitting the content, the message to one or more chosen recipients.[69] It represents the main vehicle of information during the Second World War.[70] Media defined the processes of transmission of news for the entire period in the collective imagination of the immediate postwar period, and the radio remained associated with war communications for a long time. Between the two wars, moreover, there was a particularly important development and diffusion. Owning a radio in the living room of one's own home became the dream of every family in the civilised world. Menduni remembers:

---

[68] Steiner, 1997, p. 91.
[69] Menduni, 2001.
[70] In Italy, Mussolini declared the beginning of the war by radio, 10th June 1940.

The war experience deeply marked the radio, even in a negative way, because it associated it in the minds of many people to the emergency, to totalitarian propaganda, to the dramas of war, while the TV is the daughter of well-being, peace, new-found serenity. However, radio was above all a private and intimate, and often clandestine, experience.[71]

Radio and cinema, from the very beginning, seem to divide the areas of entertainment: silent cinema has a monopoly on visual representation, without a sound dimension which is, instead, the prerogative of radio, which, on the contrary, does not convey images. The cinema, with its theatres, spectacularises the cities, whereas the radio characterises the private sphere, the intimate and domestic listening. Even when the cinema conquers sound reproduction, the two media continuously represent different physical and social places: the radio, at home, allows to escape the social rules required in public spaces (such as the cinema), with reference, for example, to behaviour and clothing. This dimension of perceived freedom of the user allows it to triumph also on another traditional media, the newspaper which, as Menduni says, "represents the public arena par excellence and presupposes literacy and 'commitment'."[72]

With the radio, the whole world begins to be available at any time in its own domestic context: every day the "news of the moment and that precious entertainment that had until then constituted a scarce, minimal and expensive commodity" are potentially available to every individual.[73] Moreover, the advent of stereophony will foster further significant results on sound quality, as McLuhan points out: stereophonic sound is a sound "all around" or "enveloping." Earlier, sound emanated from a single point, in accordance with the preconception of visual culture in favour of a fixed point of view. Stereophony is sound in depth, as TV is vision in depth.[74]

Born with mainly military and niche communication purposes in the early 1920s, radio, through the diffusion of information, news, and music from the world, contributes to the crisis of rural cultures and the processes of social integration. It transmits through space, overcomes physical barriers and makes transient messages available to a multitude of people. In this sense, it is a medium that brings spaces together, ensuring the rational and broad distribution of changing texts without any confinement in the place of origin or within specific cultural elites.[75] The radio, moreover, becomes the heir to the phonograph and, like the record, provides dance music at home. Therefore, it broadcasts music more than information.

With the radio and diffusion of music, the market for radio broadcasts was also born, supported by advertising for commercial purposes.

---

[71] Menduni, 2001, p. 105.
[72] *Ibidem*, p. 41.
[73] *Ibidem*, p. 43–44.
[74] McLuhan, 1964, p. 299.
[75] Hendy, 2000, p. 90.

In McLuhan's "biological" vision, the radio becomes "a kind of nervous information system."[76] McLuhan himself, in his well-known theory of "hot" and "cold" media, underlines the role of radio as a privileged medium for the diffusion of music and the socialisation of young people who, from the postwar period onwards, become the main target of radio productions.

The radio, besides being an entertainment and informational tool, suggests behaviours and reflections, provokes individual emotions and encourages active participation in social life. It expresses itself in terms of "cross-knowledge", that is, sets of partial perceptions, useful indications that are kept in memory because they are interesting and bring joy.[77] Moreover, according to Negus,[78] radios represent (paraphrasing Bourdieu) "cultural intermediaries" in the two-way flow between artists and public. Finally, the constant reduction of its size and lowering of its costs make the radio the first personal electronic medium no longer aimed at the family, but at the single individuals. Unlike television, the radio is increasingly becoming a personal mobile medium, thirty years ahead of the mobile phone.

The technological evolution gradually favours the possibility of transmitting voices and images at a distance, thanks to investments, discoveries, and research in the field of "electronics" and the cultural industry sees an extraordinary opportunity to disseminate musical and artistic productions on a large scale.

In 1931, EMI[79] was born from the merger of several companies from the various communication and media sectors: the record, radio, and television industries. The control of the different areas of communication by record labels will increasingly promote and disseminate music products on the international market.

With the spread of radio and TV in the home, the public and private spheres seem to overlap, thanks to the domestic use of works, dance, and drama. Although it is the private environment for antonomasia, the home seems to increasingly acquire a public dimension, transforming itself into a new place of social interaction and enjoyment of activities that, before the advent of electronic media, were relegated outside the domestic networks. In a few years, television inherits the social function of the rational, bringing the family together in front of a new media whose consumption takes place in the domestic context. Radio, however, gradually increasingly conquers a private dimension on the move, as a portable media that accompanies the user in public space, thanks to miniaturisation and the use of batteries in place of the electrical socket. The radio comes out of living rooms and houses, dedicating itself to young people and to music, which finds in it an extraordinary channel of communication and diffusion.[80] Baldini says:

> The "new" audience of these "new" radios were the teen-agers, who were becoming an important sector of the population from the demographic, eco-nomic and consumerist

---

[76] McLuhan, 1964, p. 317.
[77] Menduni, 2001.
[78] Negus, 1996.
[79] Acronym of Electric and Musical Industries, British record label founded in 1931.
[80] Acronym of Electric and Musical Industries, a British music company founded in 1931.

point of view [...] It is at this point that the rift is created in the musical tastes between parents, left to swing and dance big bands, and children. With the transistor radio, consumption is personalised. While in the 1930s and 1940s the family gathered around the only radio, from the 1950s onwards everyone listened to "their own" radio, which transmitted "their" music, with the "first" radio.[81]

The personalised dimension of "domestic" and private listening developed, moreover, with the invention of the microgroove, the vinyl record at 33 rpm (1947) and 45 rpm (1949). Between 1952 and 1955, in America, there was a sales boom that tripled in the following years. In 1948, with the invention of magnetic tape, the doors were opened to new ways of recording sound that will lead, in the following decade, to a revolution in recording techniques. The tape allows radios to transmit even in deferred mode by recording the grams and to control the contents with more precision. The same discography adopted the magnetic tape in 1949, also introducing the possibility of mixing several audio tracks in post-production.[82] These are the years when the phenomenon of the singer-actor-voice Elvis Presley explodes, which marks the historical record of annual sales of a single performer: the "legend" is born. But they are also the years of freedom of expression, of adolescents' protests against adults, of body language that, through dance and rock rhythm, increasingly expresses the speed and acceleration that characterises modernity, as well as the profound cultural change taking place. Rock contrasts with the slow rhythm that had characterised the music of the last century, from the waltz of the French Revolution onwards.

As Flichy points out, many observers believe that [rock] is linked to the emergence of adolescence as an autonomous age group, in conflict with the adult world. This protest music is essentially written by young people, played and sung by young people, essentially born for young people. The themes of the songs are almost exclusively about adolescence.[83] In fact, rock 'n' roll (that reached popularity with the song "Rock Around the Clock" sung by Bill Halley in 1955), became young people's favourite music genre. Frith points out: "The novelty of rock 'n' roll is that its performers are "guys like you", of the same age as you, they come from the same environment and have the same interests as you."[84] And it is precisely on young people that the music industry focuses its attention.

In America, as well as in England, leisure time conquers a new space of action: the ballroom. The jukebox makes music collective in a primitive dimension of music on demand; in the domestic context, however, the record (in all its forms) favours private and social listening. According to McLuhan, the music media (starting with the radio) offer teenagers privacy, and at the same time the same tribal bond as the world of the market, of song and resonance.[85] In this context, the teenager experiences a process of

---

[81] Menduni, 2001.
[82] Cerchiani, 2001 – Baldini, 2000.
[83] Flichy, 1991.
[84] Frith, 1978.
[85] Mc Luhan, 1964.

emancipation from family values and conditionings, increasingly conquering personal spaces even inside the house: his room becomes almost "one of a kind extraterritorial space, strongly marked by the photos of the characters he admires and by the objects-symbol of the values he shares."[86] A room in which, next to the record player, there is a radio.

The music industry (in particular, the pop one) leans towards and is influenced by the changing tastes of teenagers. The youth subcultures are shaping new trends and generating new looks and sounds that the market absorbs and directs, through different modes of consumption: "different radios, different records, different star models, different promotional activities, different purchases, for different subcultures."[87] The family increasingly consumes products and services (including the telephone), and listening to the radio characterises the different forms of domestic communication. The private dimensions and rooms of the children contrast with those of the parents. It is a contraposition of sounds and genres, but also of volumes and media (radio, television, and disco).

The postwar period after World War II is characterised by a phase of growth and development and the so-called economic boom. These were the years in which the world appeared face-to-face in two blocs, the USA versus USSR, in a cold war curtain that would last until the 1990s, marked by particularly difficult historical events, among which, just to give a few examples, the Vietnamese conflict, assassination of the U.S. President J.F. Kennedy, and Thursday protest in China. This context contributes to generate youth movements which, also through rock music, develop and spread, determining significant political, cultural, and social transformations.

A relevant example of the role of music in the construction of the collective identity of young people is undoubtedly the three days of peace and music at the historic Woodstock Festival held in 1969 in Bethel (a small rural town in New York State), where the people of rock music, the "children of flowers", and hippy culture live an extraordinary moment of aggregation and media visibility.

Among the numerous participations at Woodstock (including artists Joe Cocker, Janis Joplin, The Who, Carlos Santana, just to name a few), the performance of Jimi Hendrix remains emblematic, for its extraordinary artistic value but also and above all for the political and cultural significance of its musical intervention. His version for solo guitar of the American anthem "The Star Spangled Banner", performed during the festival, expresses a harsh metaphor against the Vietnam War, evoked by explosions and hisses originated by the distorted sounds of his Fender Stratocaster guitar, and diffused by the wall of the Marshall amplifiers. Hendrix uses unconventional distortion and techniques to create powerful sonic images, generating an explicit call to bombs, when moving away from the original melodic line, with high notes to symbolise a falling bomb and distortion to call out an explosion, or recreating the sound of a rifle firing, quickly hitting the guitar strings. The significance of

---

[86] Menduni, 2001, p. 19.
[87] Baldini, 2000, p. 17.

such a performance was not immediately grasped, it was only after a few years that music critics emphasised the revolutionary mess – essay of Hendrix's performance and his criticism of the American dream. But the choice to play the anthem also seems to be dictated by another of the artist's performances: to strongly reaffirm his being an American citizen. It was difficult to feel and to be American for those who, like Hendrix, came from two races, Black and native, both marginal and discriminated against. The performance of the American anthem also takes on a sense of identity as well as expressing an explicit break with the system and representing a clear sign of protest against the war in Vietnam. A double message, therefore, in Hendrix's sound statement: I am American, I belong to my homeland, and I repeat it, but I do not share the war and this government that is generating victims and death. Hendrix's performance at Woodstock is an example of how music can express, at the same time, belonging, recalling tradition, but also innovation, creativity, and criticism of the system.

2.6 Video clip, walkman, and personalisation of listening

The economic development of the 1950s and 1960s, and the relative prosperity of the 1950s and 1960s, brought new consumer goods, including the media. A "mass consumption" is increasingly influenced using the communication media. The individual use of products on the market is constantly influenced by the marketing strategies of advertisers, who offer homogeneous behavioural and consumption strategies. The studies of Edgard Morin[88] underline the role of advertising in the advent of artificial characters, who offer models of consumption and persuasive messages (think e.g., in the Italian context of the use of famous people to support radio and television advertising). In a structural vision of consumption, Jean Baudrillard[89] identifies in the upper classes the actors who propose and manipulate the models proposed by the media, dwelling on the apparent free choice of the actors and personal in the actions of consumption on the part of individuals: the practice of consumption follows, instead, rules ascribed and preexisting to the individual himself. In this regard, according to Bourdieu[90], through the "social habitus" – in which lifestyles are also reproduced – the collective rules according to which social actors, in manifesting their choices, also express those of the group to which they belong are spread. However, consumers personalise their choices and interpret standardised objects in different ways, also taking an active part in consumption behaviour. With regard to the relationship between media and consumption, the analyses of the Frankfurt School focus on a view of the media as an instrument of mass seduction by cultural industries, while cultural studies underline how they contribute to the construction of

---

[88] Morin, 1962.
[89] Baudrillard, 1972.
[90] Bourdieu, 1970.

collective knowledge and reflect the plurality of social classification, organising and orienting what they classify and represent.[91]

In this context, young people are among the main users of media products in general and music in particular. In the sixties, the American magazine Life describes them as "hooked on sound", that is, as teenagers listening to the transistor radio: As a familiar and domestic medium, the radio repositioned itself as a portable and personal medium. The voices of the new conductors, the DJs, and the songs of the new music, rock 'n' roll, will start to echo in the sidewalks of the streets, in the places where young people can be found and in the cars through the car radio. The radio will become a symbol of autonomy for western teenagers, finally free to bring their own music, sounds, subculture and share it with their own group.[92]

Young people gradually begin to enjoy the new domestic media tool, television. In 1946, there were only six television stations and, in less than ten years, in 1954, they became three hundred and fifty-four. These were the years in which rock 'n' roll exploded and television reproduced the radio formats of the charts on the screens, thus stealing the primacy of the generalist medium from the radio.

With the diffusion of television in the domestic environment, a new way of enjoying and promoting musical products was also born. Starting in the 1950s, in fact, through programs such as *Panorama soundie* in the USA, *Scopitone* in France, *Cinebox* in Italy, television started to offer musical performances even in the absence of the artist in the studio, through video recordings of songs interpreted by singers or bands, then broadcast on a deferred basis. One of the first examples, in this sense, is given by the television performances of The Beatles who, on the occasion of the promotion of "singles", make their own video recordings to promote their diffusion in small screen programmes, even when they are not present in the studio in real time, giving life to the first *ante litteram* video clips. Technological development influences the production and enjoyment of music and art, as well as of music and television, on many levels. According to Benjamin, in cinema technology affects production, form and production. Production becomes almost a construction. The materials - the actors' acting, for example - are assembled by the camera and director and are alienated from the reality; the detached and collaborative technique replaces the integral, spontaneous expression. In the form there is an emphasis on editing or, more broadly, on a kind of analytical critique of reality, which, through "optical tests" - close-ups, different camera angles, slow motion, and so on - manipulates the material, and through "conscious optics", reveals or represents details of everyday life that one would normally not notice.[93]

Benjamin's observations on filmic form immediately suggest comparisons with recording and music mixing techniques which, through a "collaborative" and "constructed" manipulation of sound materials, ends unprecedented reports and sound

---

[91] Grandi, 1994.
[92] Bonini, 2006, p. 26.
[93] Middleton, 1990.

details. The technology offers new perspectives of diffusion, promotion, and realisation of the artistic product.

In the sixties, an analogue multitrack recorder of two or four tracks allowed The Beatles to make their first songs, using overdubs to add new sound elements to the live performance. The result, in those years, seems exceptional but involves background noise and rustling far removed from the sound results of the digital era, where what sound can be achieved with very high fidelity and overdubs have no limits and do not affect the sonic cleanliness of the final result. At the end of the sixties, therefore, rock bands abandoned the naturalistic recording model, which was limited to documenting the band's performance by multitrack recordings, superimpositions, reverse effects, reverberation, and other sound processes that cannot be obtained by simply recording the band playing in real time. In addition, new recording techniques, creative elements, and ways of musical arrangement allow introducing new creative elements and ways of arranging music, arousing new sensations and emotions in the spectator. For example, we can think of the vocal sound impact of Queen's "Bohemian Rhapsody", published in 1975, in which Freddie Mercury overdubs his own voice several times, obtaining a very suggestive and involving choral result. "Bohemian Rhapsody" is also one of the first examples of video clips, a new language that was born at the end of the seventies to promote the top songs of an album and that is fed by sounds and video images, fragments that are composed through a montage that in a few minutes must synthesise the meaning, content, and message. Video fragments that are supported by rhythm and sound and that increasingly express the speed, the incessant rhythm of modernity. The video clip suggests a new way of conceiving and thinking pop music and, above all, proposes new ways of fruition in which the different expressive languages intertwine and integrate, arousing emotions that involve all the spectator's senses, perhaps sometimes in their imaginative abilities or simply influencing the subjective experience.

In 1975, the crisis of the music business pushed record companies to search for a new way of expression, personalities who can attract the approval of the general public, even beyond their artistic abilities. With the emergence of a culture increasingly focused on style and look, a new divisive dimension is emerging that unleashes "intense but short-lived fashions and passions that can be superimposed or interchangable and in any case deniable to the explosion of the following phenomenon."[94]

In the eighties, the pop star became the undisputed star of the domestic screen, consecrating the audiovisual culture linked to video clips. In August 1981, MTV was born, the American television channel promoted by MTV Networks and entirely dedicated to music programming. In fact, the video clip became the true fulcrum of its television and commercial soul. The world stars appear one after the other in a sort of short film, with a soundtrack interpreted by the artist himself: the video clip tells stories or offers short documentaries about the pop star or rock band on duty, through sensual shots, postcard close-ups, or special effects. In addition, the video

---

[94] Baldini, 2000.

clips allow for all kinds of manipulations of the image of the new stars, who are presented as celebrities even before they become celebrities just to attract the attention of the fans and media themselves.[95]

The 1980s are characterised by an explosion of audiovisual culture closely linked to video clips, which influenced all the factors that generated it: music, TV, and youth consumption in general. With the success of MTV, the ways of enjoying music (which can be watched as well as listened to) and its protagonists who, in full "hedonism react" and "rampant yuppism", with the explosion of an explicit culture of the ephemeral, defined by fashion, look, and appearance, seem to be valued mainly for their image and less for their artistic performance. Audiovisual technologies above all open new paths and patterns, they widen the boundaries of communication, creativity, and fruition. According to Valentina Agostinis,[96] the video clip condenses and, therefore, pulverises, fragments, and explodes everything that precedes it, making exasperated syntheses. "Thinking video-music means bringing back to the surface fragments of visions, remembering minute, impossible, grammatical passages, sensational narrative ellipses, gestures, rapid, cunning quotations, but also surprising visual impulses, electronic signs within a vocabulary that technology continuously dilates. It gives shape to everything that devours, owning looks and kisses, fears and horrors."[97]

As Baldini maintains, some of the terms used by Agostinis, such as "condensation", "pulverises", "fragments", "explodes", and "devours", can be referred to the music of the nineties, in which different styles, cultures, and fragments of different languages, meet, mingle, in an increasingly accelerated time, giving rise to new musical, artistic, cultural paths that draw from the past and present to return to the future without awareness:

> In the Nineties there was the culture of the audio-visual fragment, of speed, of the management of the already mentioned communicational complexity conveyed by MTV, that made the young people (now competent and having acquired all the necessary tools for the decoding, upheaval and editing of verse expressive sources) reject a single style imposed, especially after the advent of new navigation technologies: computer, television, radio.[98]

New navigation technologies increasingly used by the so-called X Generation or MTV Generation for which accelerated change is not a semblance of multiple reality, but a preestablished datum; not a feature of the times, but a fundamental condition of life. To deal with it, they use tools such as changing technologies, fashions, and versatile styles.[99]

---

[95] *Ibidem.*
[96] Agostinis, 1983.
[97] Agostinis, 1987, p. 169–170.
[98] Baldini, 2000, p. 47.
[99] Savonardo, 2002a.

In the meantime, the industry increasingly tends to develop portable products and instruments, such as the car stereo, which (thanks to the handy cassette tape)[100] is one of the symbols of mobility, increasingly favouring the experience and private dimension of listening, compared with the collective one. The car stereo introduces a different sound environment, different from the public one in the square and the private one in the house. An environment (the car) where naturally the user's attention is on driving rather than on music, which in turn manifests itself as a real background of the experience, as a sound of the journey. Fabbri highlights: "The music listened to in the car is always combined with running images, kerbstones and signs that parade, with discontinuous strips that run on the asphalt below us. The road in a certain sense imposes a rhythm on the music, tuning with the more regular rhythmic divisions and creating a sort of perceptual dissonance with music that has a less chronometric breath."[101]

Listening to music in motion gets a new dimension with the invention of the Walkman in 1979, in Japan, by Sony. The way of consuming music changes radically. This portable instrument of sound reproduction is not only intended for the "man in motion", but also represents private listening in an absolute way, through the headphones with which it is equipped, and which isolate the listener from the family and outside world. The portability expresses in a significant way that condition of body prosthesis and sensory lengthening introduced by McLuhan's [102] theories about ten years before. Moreover, the same body movements seem to follow the rhythm of the music on headphones, maintaining a private listening condition even when immersed in the mass. Young people wander around the squares and streets, in the subway or in shops, run in parks, and study at home listening to their music, without sharing it with others. Baldini said:

> The collective enjoyment of the recorded music [...] definitively ceases to exist: everyone listens to what they want", in an intimate, private dimension, thanks to the isolation produced by headphones. The Walkman replaces and integrates the stimuli of the public sphere with that of one's own cultural–musical tribe, which expresses itself through compilations or favourite radio stations, creating not only a new sound environment, but also new connections between the body and the music, "a real sound bubble in which young people immerse themselves, isolating themselves from all possible interference.[103]

According to Menduni, this dimension is reminiscent of Baudelaire's flaneur: "It's a new sound environment, a boundless joy to dwell in the number, the swaying, the fugitive and the infinite. Being out of the house, and yet to be everywhere in your own home, to see the world, to be at its centre and to remain hidden from it."[104]

---

[100] In 1963, Philips launches "music cassettes." They managed to sell 9,000 cassettes during the first year, and then reached the million sales over the next few years (Cerchiani, 2001).
[101] Fabbri, 1996, p. 133.
[102] McLuhan, 1964.
[103] Baldini, 2000, p. 42.
[104] Menduni, 2001, p. 43–44.

At the same time, the role of TV as a new media of musical (and commercial) communication grows allows the diffusion of video clips and creation of all-music TV channels. The new media seems to put the radio and all those who had achieved success with it in the musical field into crisis right from the start. This uneasiness is explicitly expressed by the British band Buggles who, in 1979, wrote the famous song "Video Killed the Radio Star", whose lyrics talk about the loss of popularity of a radio star, following the dissemination of video-music.[105] As for music, young people are beginning to diversify the consumption of television, by choosing television programmes dedicated to them. They manage their time as well as their style, taking inspiration from the myths, the stars that the media create and promote. Well being encourages the purchase of music and the Walkman helps stimulate listening to music trends that the radio had ignored for years.[106] With music on television, the role of disk jockey (DJ) also evolves: born during the Second World War in Europe, coinciding with the opening of new dance spaces inaugurated by the French with discothèques, the "record selector" soon becomes the most professional DJ. The role of a DJ becomes central in the space of aggregation and socialisation in which different youth tribes increasingly meet and confront each other: the discotheque, that according to Domiziana Giordano[107] is "a place where the feedback - is [...] invaded by eloquent signs of belonging to certain tribes, carried out in clothing and gestures that determine a new culture." With television, the DJ evolved into "video jockey (VJ), conductor, commentator, and interviewer in music television broadcasts.[108]

In the meantime, video clips increasingly represent the musical art of the 20th century, combining song narration with video and influencing other expressive languages such as advertising and cinema. It is no coincidence that many artists and music bands borrow directors and actors from the cinema, leading to contaminations between the different languages that, since the era of black and white television, lead to the making of musical films interpreted by singers (think of Sinatra and Elvis in America, Morandi, Albano and Romina, and Little Tony in Italy, to name a few). This is a cinematic subgenre that in Italy is commonly called "musicarello." Moreover, the possibility of making videos, superimposing images of different nature, through the technique of film editing, leads to the production of real film concerts, as in the case of the memorable Live at Pompeii by Pink Floyd, in 1972.

Television technology, which allows the artist to "enter the audience's houses", is given the possibility to preserve this performance, through the help of the video recorder and VHS: the music film market develops, in this sense, a new consumer sector. It becomes a practice for artists to accompany each individual with a promotional video and then collect them all later in a single VHS, as in a real video

---

[105] In fact, MTV will launch its broadcasting in a sarcastic and provocative way, using this video as opening.
[106] Baldini, 2000.
[107] Giordano, 2004, p. 104.
[108] In reality, the "video jockey" was meant to be the one mixing images and music. But MTV contributed to a wrongful idea about this role.

album of music memory, which allows the home preservation of the image, voice, and expressions of their favourite star. The video became the artist's new tool of promotion and in many cases, advertising was used to sell products. In this sense, "the commercial became a video clip"[109], thus creating a new subgenre, as in the case of the commercials that Michael Jackson created for Pepsi, which MTV itself won the rights to air. Also, in terms of contamination between the different audiovisual languages, the expressive codes of advertising are increasingly entering the video clips and vice versa.

With the introduction of digital technologies, as we will see in the following, the expressive and creative potential of artistic productions and the ways of musical fruition will undergo particularly significant transformations. These transformations, as repeatedly underlined, thanks to the advent of electronic media and communication technologies, will invest multiple fields and dimensions. Technological innovations determine, in fact, particularly relevant and complex sound effects, producing often positive consequences. The mass media have deeply undermined the traditional dimensions of time and space, redefining the boundaries of the relationship between the public and private spheres and, at the same time, determining the processes of homologation and differentiation. Moreover, music technologies have significantly contributed to the processes of anti-individualising re-tribalisation, multiplying the moments of aggregation and collective socialisation, but also encouraging dimensions of private listening, in the domestic and individual spheres. These are social effects that will explode in the digital age through interactivity and connectivity, investing every form of language and communication.[110]

---

[109] Baldini, 2000.
[110] Savonardo, 2010.

3 Bit culture, Sound, and Digital Technologies[1]

3.1 Liquid sounds

The previous chapter focused on pop music in relation to the sound reproduction technologies and media that characterised the music scene of the 20th century. "Analogic media" such as vinyl records and cassette tapes which, thanks to the use of a Walkman or car radio, allowed the user to listen to music on the move, outside of professional or collective contexts. Moreover, the diffusion of the cassette tape (between the Sixties and Seventies) led to the possibility to personalise the user's listening. In fact, audio recorders offer users the opportunity to make original and personal montages, pouring individual songs from other cassette tapes or from the DJs into a new magnetic tape, creating real "do-it-yourself" music compilations. The user can thus build his personal sound story, choosing the songs and their order to which he or she would like to listen to.

The diffusion of a format such as the cassette tape, accompanied by integrated reproduction and recording systems (which with high definition have then taken on the name of Hi-Fi systems), transforms the average listener into an "active" audience. The user can, in fact, through a simple domestic recorder, decompose and recompose the order of the songs of one or more albums according to his or her taste. In this sense, the "personal compilations" take on an enduring role in the active fruition of the listener who, following his or her own musical tastes, is able to create a sort of sound narration of his or her own emotions and biographical experiences. Ernesto Assante remembers how, thanks to audio cassettes, the user could extrapolate a certain number of songs from records of different artists and genres, "line them up, record them and at the end have in hand an absolutely original product, a mix tape, which was something more than a compilation, a collection. It was a lifetime object, a way of seeing the world, a photograph of reality seen from a particular point of view."[2]

The creation of a mix tape indirectly recalls the production phases. The choice of the contents and order of the tracks responds not only to commercial logic, but also to the narration that the artist intends to propose. In both cases, the music remains a

---

[1] The author of paragraphs 3.2 and 3.3 is Dario De Notaris.
[2] Assante, 2008a.

"social narrative: it tells the stories of those who make it and is used by those who listen to it to decode their own story, both individual and social."[3]

The sound scenario of the eighties opens with the diffusion on the market of the compact disc (CD), the digital support that took the place of analogic technologies. The changeover to CD breaks the direct link between the medium and its support. Listening to the vinyl record, in fact, was characterised by the background rustling, the effect of dragging the turntable stylus. The physical contact between the stylus and vinyl grooves gave back that unmistakable background sound that was an integral part of listening to music. With the CD the soundtracks are transformed into "information", that is, a series of binary numbers, read through a laser. As a matter of fact, the music is numerically coded.[4] There is no longer any "physical" contact between a cartridge and a surface, no rustling.[5] The laser "reads" the bits stored on the media and decodes them, playing the music track, through high definition sound.

However, the CD appeared on the market with a high cost (although divided into three categories, top price, average price, and cheap series) and, compared with its ancestor LP long playing (LP), has a small cover. For decades, the vinyl record had, in fact, offered fans the opportunity to listen to music with photographic images, illustrations, and lyrics of the songs, imprinted on the case of the record itself and on the paper files attached to the vinyl; elements that formed the "graphical universe." The size of the CD cover initially led to the decision to reduce the graphic and textual amount of information. Subsequently, the creation of booklets inserted in the CD case mad it possible to print the lyrics of the songs and photos of the artists.

Until 2000, the decline of the audio cassette had been limited by the absence of alternative economic technologies for home recordings, then, with the advent of digital formats such as mp3 and, therefore, with the definitive affirmation of the iPod, music users quickly "put the old magnetic tapes to sleep."

We see the transition from the analog phase, characterised by vinyl and magnetic tape, to the digital phase, marked by the CD. However, with the diffusion of the new media, music (to paraphrase Zygmunt Bauman)[6] becomes increasingly "liquid", i.e. a stream of material information. Moreover, the development of computer systems that are increasingly complex in their functions but, at the same time, increasingly consumer friendly, that is, easy to use, gives music users the possibility to personalise their listening more and more. The CD "burner" which, connected to the computer, is able to create copies identical to the original as well as to record a personal list of music tracks, offers new scenarios of active participation

---

[3] Sibilla, 2008, p. 219.

[4] Manovich, 2001.

[5] However, it is nowadays possible to get this vinyl sound effect on digital technology tools. Paradoxically, the lower the quality of the sound, the more authentic it is. According to Manovich (2001, p. 254), «typical images producedby 3D graphic seem still unnaturally perfect, too clean, nitid, geometrical. (to sort this out) we needed to lower the quality of the computer-generated images, their perfection needed to be thamed to make it closer to the imperfection of the film.

[6] Bauman, 2005.

of the user, not only in the fruition but also and above all in the musical creation. The compilation on cassette tape has favoured a first level of participation to the realisation of the sound product, through instruments and is simple but requiring, however, time and attention. The sonic computer gives the user new creative opportunities. With very simple to use, the user can extract music tracks from a CD, break them down into small parts and (create new and personal artistic productions) recompose them, burn them on a new CD. Moreover, a computer, connected to the Internet, can promote the diffusion of one's own creations beyond the borders of the home.

In the nineties, the diffusion of the personal computer (PC) at home opens the way to the so-called digital era that, starting from the end of the 20th century, would seem to determine the end of that "short century of popular music" that Jason Toynbee[7] starts in 1921, when the first regular radio broadcast starts. Digital music, which by now had lost its initial technical connotation, acquires a much broader and more nuanced meaning, with a more modern and sophisticated sound, all areas of communication, from cinema to television, from music to the Net.

In particular, "digitising" information means translating it into digits. A sound can also be digitised if it is sampled, that is, measured at regular intervals. Each sample can be encoded by a number that describes the sound signal. Any sound or musical sequence can therefore be represented by a numerical series. Images and sounds can be digitised not only point by point, or sample by sample, but also from the global structures of iconic or sound messages. In general, any type of information or message can be translated into numbers and all numbers can be expressed in binary language. Lévy points out that digitally encoded information can be transmitted and copied almost indefinitely without loss of information, because the original message can almost be reconstructed in its entirety despite the degradation produced by transmission or copying. Evidently, the same cannot be said of images and sounds recorded in analogue terms, which deteriorate with every new copy or transmission.[8]

Digital technology influences, moves, and offers new perspectives of realisation and fruition of the musical product and determines new creative opportunities. Technological progress, moreover, not only changes the distribution function and meaning of already existing works but, as Middleton argues, also stimulates new artistic techniques, new productive modes and new social relations, shifting art from the ritual or disinterested contemplation to the realm of everyday life.[9]

The era of the bit has favoured the evolution of what electronics had introduced into music through the synthesizer and, later, through sampling, a computer that converts sound into numbers. In particular, the latter was the undisputed protagonist of music production in the nineties, characterising the sounds of the end of the millennium. At the beginning, it was mainly used as a "quotation machine", an instrument that could be used to copy segments of prerecorded music that were then played

---

[7] Toynbee, 2000.
[8] Levy, 1997.
[9] Middleton, 1990.

on a keyboard in the desired tonality and rhythmic scan. However, as the sound is converted into digital data through this operation, the information can be redefined. This implies the possibility of altering the source until it renders the sound in the desired keystroke, the unrecognisable, and opens up an almost boundless field of possibilities for intervention on sound. Hip hop, techno, jungle, to cite just a few examples and, in any case, the new electronic music, are "fed" by very short sound fragments that are "stolen", that is, sampled from records already recorded, decontextualised, and then "resonated", creating new musical products in which the contours and identities of the original tracks are revealed. Moreover, also with the help of special software of different nature (commercial or not, complex or simple) and a simple PC, today it is possible to manipulate the fragments of a file (audio but also video), extrapolate them from the musical text and, through a "copy and paste" procedure, reposition them inside new sound products. A creative process leading to the contamination and melting pot of different musical experiences and that, in a postmodern perspective, redefines and recomposes already existing artistic material, determining new cultural paths.

Most of these software already makes available short sounds, digital sound samples of a few seconds (a bass drum stroke, a round of guitars, a trumpet) that the user can assemble and reassemble endlessly through the use of the loop, which is the practice of reproducing a few seconds of a repeated sound, in a circular way. The rhythmic loop of drums, bass, guitar, or even simply vocals becomes the basis of a new composition and, as Lev Manovich[10] claims, the new narrative engine of music. The most significant innovation is thus realised in the possibility, for anyone, to create music, without possessing any particular theoretical–musical knowledge. In the digital era, in fact, everyone can be, at the same time, artist, producer, record producer, and distributor of himself. Nowadays, the home studio recording, that is, the bedroom and desk of the music composer/producer, represents the main "place" of every musical production, replacing, at least in part, the traditional recording studios. These possibilities create a new type of user-artist, strongly integrated and multimedia, who uses the audio–video materials of his or her own sound experience to express himself or herself, also through the Web. Digital production activities increasingly represent, in fact, the vehicle towards which individuals, in particular young people, assert their existence: "I transmit, therefore I exist." The "cut 'n' paste" is the new rock 'n' roll: with it you can move freely on the timeline (the new dance floor) "hip/do/mount" as you prefer, as long as to the rhythm of the music. Digital editing allows you to edit audio and video with ease, offering endless combinations of editing to listener-artists, remixing and redefining the aesthetic material which, in turn, contribute to the construction of individual and collective identities. As Bonini[11] says, reality is actually real only if it resembles the imaginary, producing audio and video material, starting from one's own personal experience, meaning, above all, proving your existence.

---

[10] Manovich, 2001.
[11] Bonini, 2006.

3.2 Network, file sharing, and cross-media

Understand the radical changes that (thanks to new technologies) invest musical and artistic languages means evaluating how the advent of the Internet has changed our approach to the production and enjoyment of cultural products. As we all know, the Net was born with military purposes, between the sixties and seventies, and soon became a live communication space, as Manovich[12] points out, a "real time" screen. In fact, through the screen of a PC or mobile phone, the Net determines in real time the convergence of traditional media, favours potential access to infinite knowledge, information, media and cultural productions, and allows individuals to interact at a distance from any place, at any time. Thanks to connection and broadband (ADSL, WiFi, 4G, etc.), it is possible to exchange files (information, data, and cultural objects) wherever you are: with the Internet, distances are either zeroed or reversed. Objects geographically and culturally distant approach and reenter our space, realising, at least apparently, the metaphor of the "global village" that McLuhan had theorised long before the advent of the Internet.

Web users not only share information, but actively contribute to create it, interacting with each other. They express their ideas and voice their opinions through blogs or different online forums; participate in the writing of shared information on wiki platforms; publish photos and videos within their network of knowledge, in social media; and exchange information and their own musical "tastes." Not surprisingly, music products are among the main drivers of digital sharing. The practice of file sharing is spreading significantly at the turn of the millennium, with the birth of the mp3 compression system and the production of the Napster software. Subsequently, users continued to legally or illegally download music from the Internet, as well as buy it in digital music or traditional stores. Bands such as R.E.M. and Radiohead, or artists such as Peter Gabriel, just to give a few examples, have identified new forms of market, allowing to download the songs behind free donations or with the presence of advertising before and after listening, as in radio or TV; or, again, coming live performances, videos, backstage, and other "niche" material.[13] In addition, digital technologies increasingly allow do-it-yourself audio–video reproductions. In this regard, it is interesting to note that in the course of any pop music concert, there is an increasing number of small, acutely lit performances in the audience, supported by the arms of the audience. The lighters, which the audience used to use as a sign of participation and sharing during a live performance, have been replaced by modern mobile phone screens with which video-users can reopen the performance and stream it live to their social circle of friends. Users are able to play a personal version of the artist's concert they attended and, through sharing programs, broadcast it on the Web. The same event is, in this sense, represented by multiple audio–video fragments, each contradictory from a particular point of view, which makes every single shot unique.

---

[12] Manovich, 2001.
[13] Sibilla, 2008.

Digital technologies and the related personalisation processes seem to lead to the passage from a dimension of collective musical fruition (a homogeneous one) to a connotation of heterogeneous, personal and intimate listening.

The diffusion of "liquid music" has also been enhanced by the development of high-speed data exchange networks that allow files to be transferred quickly. This acceleration in file sharing times is making it not so necessary to store data on a physical medium: it is more useful and convenient to leave it stored on the Network and access it at any time from any computer. This power (as well as easy access to information on the Net) determines what is called information overload, typical of the digital age. The possibility of transforming all the information into bits has made a large amount of data available to anyone, but it is unlikely that it will ever be fully consulted. With the spread of streaming technologies on the Internet and simple software, the possibility of creating one's own radio station is made possible (as was already the case in the 1970s) and accessible to non-experts. Web radios started, as well as the so-called free radios of the 1970s, allowing music and words to be broadcast, at least initially and/or apparently "free" from commercial or editorial logic. Unlike the radio frequencies "on air", the Web reaches a much wider and culturally varied audience. Anyone can create their own radio station and programme schedule, escaping, at least potentially, the times dictated by the advertising winds that dominate the traditional radio landscape.

As it happened with other media, radio is also undergoing an important process of convergence.[14] It is the main mobile tool, integrated in music players, mobile phones and – with the Internet – in any type of device. Moreover, online radio takes on a new connotation, abandoning the dimension of "mass communication" and approaching that of "thematic transmission."[15] Listeners follow their online radio and web transmissions in a constant and, at the same time, changing, dynamic flow. Moreover, the experience of listening to the web radio is different from the traditional one, as it is obviously more solitary and individual: "It ranges from the (white) loneliness of the desktop to the urban loneliness of post-modern flaneurs that, with headphones on their heads and iPods in their pockets, drift in metropolitan space, a space perceived through sounds as phantasmagorical, like Benjamin's Paris covered passages."[16]

The technological product that changed the musical and cultural landscape of the last ten years has undoubtedly been the iPod, released in 2001. MP3 players were already on the market at the end of the nineties, but the marketing investment made by Apple, as well as the proposal of a particular design that would make the player also aesthetically pleasing to "wear", as well as fun to listen to, has contributed to make the iPod the digital music player par excellence. Its technology has also

---

[14] Jenkins, 2006.
[15] Menduni, 2001.
[16] Bonini, 2006, p. 18.

enhanced the hybridisation between the radio and Internet, through the birth of the phenomenon called podcasting.[17]

Through the iPod you reach the apex of listening personalisation, which began with the home gramophone. The creation of the individual compilation that characterised the mix tapes, as well as the playlist, that is, the list of songs stored on an mp3 player, responds to the customisation logic typical of consumer culture in which listeners control what to listen to, in what order and at what cost. They liberated the user from record stores and radios in the same way that record stores and radios have freed previous generations from the imposition of being present at live music performances.[18]

The users of the Net find themselves, in a multitasking perspective, to be users, distributors, and creators of contents, also musical. Such contents start from the category of user-generated content (UGC), an expression that indicates the products made by the Network users, such as texts in blogs, remixed music, or videos on YouTube. For example, it is very common to "edit" images (static or dynamic) chosen by the user-author on a more or less successful song and create unpublished, serious or sarcastic video clips.[19] The logic of the narration, which is at the base of every song, is completely redefined and reworked with the help of images, as it happens in the video clips. Music and words take on a new – and different – meaning through narration through images; in this way a new product is born that is realised in the confrontation between the author and user, putting in crisis and confusing the respective roles and that, above all, cannot be re-actualised twice in the same way.

The convergence of the media, as Henry Jenkins[20] recalls, is not only the union of several instruments in one but, above all, the fusion of several media. Texts, music, and images are mutually interconnected: it's a relationship that, in different ways, is also expressed through traditional media. Let us think, for example, of the release of films, accompanied by the sale of the soundtracks, or the compilations of the music reproduced in the film itself. The cinema "lends" its stars to music, and vice versa. This is the case of Cher, who has repeatedly switched from the role of actress to that of singer, or Jennifer Lopez, or Will Smith, as in the past it was for Elvis, just to cite a few examples. The cross-genre contamination leads to the creation and promotion of music stars and their artistic products. The release of an album is often accompanied and enriched by paratextual elements, such as backstage, videos, and interviews. Record products also invest the world of video games which, thanks to specific digital games, allows the user, through participation and interaction, to play great

---

[17] Personal option digital casting. The term comes from the crisis of iPod and broadcasting and was introduced by the English journalist Ben Hammersley (Bonini, 2006).

[18] Moore, 2004.

[19] This is the case, for example, of the song "Sunday Bloody Sunday" by U2, reconstructed with the words of George W. Bush, extracted from his public speeches, or "Endless Love" by Lionel Richie and Diana Ross which proposes – in the pictures – a love duet between Bush himself and Tony Blair.

[20] Jenkins, 2006.

3   Bit culture, Sound, and Digital Technologies

musical hits of their idols through guitar-joystick (or micro-joystick) (in the images) impersonating the artist on a virtual stage and playing music.[21]

It seems obvious that, while on one hand record companies denounce a drop in receipts from physical support due to the increasing diffusion of file sharing; on the other hand, there is an – expanding – redefinition of musical and consumer boundaries. There are, in fact, paths "from above", with the proposal of new fields of musical application (cinema, video game), to paths "from below", with young artists who emerge through the publication and dissemination on the web of their musical productions made and recorded at home.

The global online record market is currently growing. In particular, official Italian data from Federazione Industria Musicale Italiana (FIMI) for the first half of 2016, certify the overtaking of digital, streaming-driven physical product. The digital segment accounts for 51% of the total market, driven by streaming services, which account for 40% of the total market and show a significant increase. Subscription streaming grew by 68%, with services such as Spotify, Apple Music, Deezer and TIMMUSIC, against +19% for ad-supported music by YouTube. In total, in 2016, the digital market in Italy had a turnover of €26.3 million and, according to the FIMI data, 20% of music consumers access paid streaming services.

Individual songs can be downloaded and assembled into a personal compilation, purchased with the entire reference album or simply inserted into the shuffle circuit of the mp3 player. Moreover, the phenomenon of comparison and research of information related to the record player is increasingly relevant: in the Web communities of the sector, you can discuss the artist, share photos, videos, and backstage (amateur and official). If in the past, paper magazines, magazines, or fanzines were used; today, these products also take new forms in the conversion to digital. The artists themselves have adapted their websites to the new "trends", offering fans the chance to buy songs and albums online directly, expressing a particular trust in the Net for the promotion of their activity.[22] The practice to improvise live performances directly (or directly through the complicity of the audience) online on social channels is becoming more popular.

The same cultural industry is appearing on the Web, with the opening of ad hoc video channels or with the birth of new independent record labels. The Net is also particularly effective for the promotion of musicians who are known to the general public, through the pages of specialised social networks. In the same way, emerging artists share their musical productions online, singles or complete albums, under creative commons license, that is, they do not ask for any compensation from those who

---

[21] Examples are the video games Guitar Hero or Rock Band (the latter supported by MTV). The Beatles' special Beatles version was quite successful, which is combined with a guitar, microphone, and drum-joystick to create a real home music complex with your friends.

[22] Madden, 2004. In addition to the usual top-down logic (established artist-listener), there is also a bottom-up process: the possibility that anyone can now create a blog on the Internet, allowing local/emergent singers/groups/bands to promote themselves at low cost, putting their songs online and indicating the dates of any live performances.

want to "share" this or that particular music track.[23] The participation from below, typical of the Net, has also manifested through the phenomenon of smart mobs already described by Rheingold.[24] As in modern Woodstock, users meet on the Net and then find themselves in the streets or squares of a city to dance. This confirms music's ritual function, as well as aggregation, socialisation, exchange, and cultural participation.[25]

According to Jenkins, convergent culture favours "trans-medial narration",[26] a new narrative form that, using different types of media and media platforms, contributes to perfecting and integrating the user experience. Each medium by conveying new and distinct information, contributes to the development of the story and the understanding of the narrated world. By using different formats and media, it helps to create "entry points" through which the user can fully immerse himself in the narrative. The user is then called upon to reconstruct the overall meaning of an integrated work of art in various media. " Jenkins highlights two prominent factors that drive the growth of transmedia communication: the first is the proliferation of new media, such as video games, the Internet, and mobile platforms with their applications. The second is the economic incentive for media creators. By sharing assets, users can lower production costs. Cross-mediatic narration often uses the principle of hyper-sociality through story creation practices even by people who do not directly deal with the main production.

This concept is combined with the concept of cross-media, which refers to the forms of communication that pass through different media. Cross-media promotes the integrated, multiple, and transversal dissemination of content and services, with mutual contributions from various production and distribution chains and the involvement of an indefinite number of creators and distributors. It is no longer just an interpretative co-operation of data, but a generative collaboration of content. The information is completed by the cross use of the media. Cross-media is a television broadcast that interacts with the public using the blog and reading live comments from home, and cross-media is the radio announcement that links to the website to deepen the information and download data. The pop music and bit culture of the third millennium are increasingly nourished by transmedia narratives and cross-media.

---

[23] An example of this is the Jamendo.com portal. There are particular types of creative licenses: usually the products offered (text, images, video, and sound) can be reused and reworked free of charge by other users, whose obligation is to indicate in their new production the source from which they have obtained that particular element; obviously, the content recreated on the basis of this license must be redistributed according to the same license. This excludes the possibility of making a financial profit on the basis of content distributed free of charge. More information about the creative commons license can be obtained from the official website www.creativecommons.it

[24] Rheingold, 2002.

[25] This is the case of the mob dedicated to Michael Jackson after his death, just to cite an example. You can view video contributions made around the world by searching YouTube for the keywords "Michael Jackson tribute."

[26] In English "Transmedia storytelling, transmedia narrative, multiplatform storytelling" (Jenkins, 2006).

3.3 Telephone and media convergence

At the end of the 1990s, thanks to the diffusion of digital technology, the telephone also underwent a significant technological evolution. From an instrument for telephoning from a fixed location, it first became a portable telephone and then a sort of "digital telegraph on the move", with the transmission of short text messages. It then rapidly became a real pocket computer with the possibility to reproduce photos, sounds, music, moving images, radio, and television transmissions, collecting the Bytes of the Net in the palm of your hand. The mobile phone thus becomes the main example of technological convergence.[27] All the other media are collected in a single "omni-medial" instrument, thus enhancing their potential and cancelling their space–time limits. In the remediation process, the new technological product replaces other media, allowing users to be always potentially connected to the world, in any place and at any time. Their purpose is being always available.

The new generation mobile phone, with its tools, is increasingly becoming the phenomenon of "mobile privatisation" (started with the radio, television, and car), which leads to typical domestic lifestyles, even when you are away from home, generating overlaps between the public and private spheres. Raymond Williams used this expression in the 1970s precisely in reference to two social phenomena that were emerging in those years: on one hand, the trend towards mobility of individuals with the growing interconnection of places; on the other, the development of increasingly self-sufficient domestic units.[28] Although they were apparently contradictory, they were closely connected and characterised the forms of life in industrialised countries throughout the 20th century.[29]

Thanks to digital technologies, we are able to cross the world with just a few clicks, without having to move, but also without being forced to stand still in one place, as in front of the computer of our home desk. We can be witnesses to an event, filming, or photographing it, transmitting it immediately on the Net, and sharing what our "third eye" (or ears) has observed or heard,[30] highlighting that we live today in the age of information and communication because the electric media instantly and constantly create a total field of interdependent events everyone can join.[31] According to Meyrowitz,[32] the presence of the electronic media has determined the social changes that led to the advent of tribal behaviour,[33] within that "global village" where all the cultures of the world are connected to each other.

---

[27] Jenkins, 2006.
[28] Williams, 1981.
[29] Jedlowski, 2003.
[30] An example of this is the TV commercial that Samsung made for the promotion of the F480 mobile phone. The video (available to view, thanks to YouTube, looking for "Samsung Spot F480") shows a DJ who, on the stage of a concert, connects other people in different places and contexts. The result is a "concert" of sounds (and videos) from different "sources."
[31] McLuhan, 1964, p. 263.
[32] Meyrowitz, 1985.
[33] Bonini, 2006.

With the diffusion of the mobile phone among the public, especially young people, the cultural industry market has offered new consumer goods connected to the use of the mobile phone. The film and TV industry converted its offer into live web productions or streaming, free or paid for. The book industry tends to promote the production of e-books. The video game market (which increasingly includes cinema and music components) has aligned itself with small telephone displays, offering games for download for a fee. Finally, in the field of music, the market has found new paths to be followed by the integration of mp3 players in mobile phones, offering online stores that allow you to buy and download mp3 songs to listen to on the go.

In addition, unlike the traditional home phone, with its indistinct trill from device to device (subject to minor variations, always standard), the mobile phone offers the possibility of setting any sound to replace the trill, a personal sound, as a distinguishing mark, to be recognised. When you receive a message or a phone call, you can hear instead of the common driin or beep, the sound of a dog, a stadium choir or Vasco Rossi's latest hit. Whatever is audible becomes a ringtone, in a catch 22 that leads to particular and original sounds. From this point of view, the recording industry seems to have found new sources of income, while humanity appears more and more "immersed" in what Derrick de Kerckhove defines as "tertiary sensoriality."[34]

The connection between man and the media is characterised by a strong social and cultural component that is also expressed in new consumer trends. Silverstone states[35] that all communities are "virtual communities", and that within each community there are different degrees of sociality linked to the level of interaction that the media offer. The expression and symbolic definition of community, with or without electro-media, have been recognised as an essential condition of our sociality; communities are imagined, and we participate in them with or without face-to-face relations, with or without contact.[36]

The possession of the new media allows the individual to express the belonging to a particular social status; from the home television with home theatre system (comparable with the piano or gramophone of the early 20th century) to the latest generation mobile phone with video camera, GPS, touch screen, and so on, the mp3 player with the characteristic white headphones, a sign of belonging to a style (the Apple one) that makes him a part of a group ("an Apple consumer", synonymous of elegance), as well as its unconscious testimonial through the performance of the same headphones.[37] Also, USB flash drives get special designs (such as the features of a jewel to hang around the neck) as well as ornaments,

---

[34] Buffardi, de Kerkchove, 2011.
[35] Silverstone, 1999.
[36] Yesterday, p. 166.
[37] Sibilla, 2008. MP3 players are born with the convenience of being kept in your pocket hidden from whoever passes by. However, the only visible elements that signal the existence of the product and, therefore, promote it, are the headphones.

distinctive objects of a certain social status or simply "fashionable." In fact, the request for customisation of mobile phone ringtones has led to the creation of dedicated online stores. Smarter mp3 players, software that allows you to produce music, car stereos with USB inputs to connect your devices, and play and listen to the music downloaded while in the car, in the city traffic or on the motorway are also produced. The car itself is a moving extension of the home environment and, like the mp3 player, it is the perfect complement to intimate and personal listening. On one hand, if the situation is prone to be criticised by the apocalyptists who see an unstoppable technological determinism (almost as if to resume Adorno's reflections on the cultural industry); on the other hand, there is the fundamentalist vision of a "liquid" future, as Bauman[38] would say, where users suggest to the industry the productive paths to take. On the Web, the communities of enthusiasts and consumers are the ones who, through the use of merchandise (music, cinema, and Internet) guarantee the success of a product, its survival or disappearance. The most widespread products, and those that survive the times, are those that manage to frame and satisfy the tastes and desires of the user or create new ones, as in the case of Apple.

As already pointed out, the Web is constituted as a place where users can express their creativity, with the help of a single tool: computing. It is necessary to remember how this term can no longer refer to the traditional home personal computer, fixed at one place. Today's computer is integrated into a variety of devices that allow anyone familiar with computer programs to create new artistic and cultural productions.

The clearest example of this creativity which, paraphrasing de Kerckhove, we could define as "connective", can be found in the analysis of YouTube, the most popular video portal on the Internet. Founded in 2005 by Chad Hurley, Steve Chen, and Jawed Karim, YouTube has positioned itself in a few years as the archive of the "visual knowledge" of the world, so much so that it was purchased in 2006 by Google, the main search engine of the Web. Its initial motto was "the archive of your digital videos", offering users of the Web a space in which to deposit their audiovisual memories. But the explicit reference to television (tube is the cathode ray tube) could not but distinguish also the type of videos uploaded by users. It is no coincidence, in fact, that many of the videos present are taken from traditional television programming, that is, scenes from films, TV series, variety shows, cartoons, and music videos. In addition to these productions, there are also amateur productions, in the perspective of the already mentioned UGC: from the video dedicated to one's partner to the personal video-blog, through which one can express one's opinions; or the creation of particular remixes and montages of other visual products.

Just as MTV has been for television, YouTube soon became a place to merge images, music and words, through which to tell a story or spread a message, in the time of a video clip. YouTube is no longer an ordinary archive, but rather a tool

---

[38] Bauman, 2005.

where you can "produce yourself", as its new motto (broadcast yourself) says. The individuals put themselves, their face (like on Facebook), their identity or, simply, their technical and artistic skills back into play.

Moreover, we all know that the Net allows to break down spatial boundaries and, therefore, it is possible, through YouTube, to create a music band with artists coming from different places and contexts: each musician video-records his own contribution, playing his own musical instrument, which is then reassembled as if it had been performed at the same time and in the same place.[39] This particular use of the Internet and YouTube as a "global" artistic community has determined, among other things, the professional creation of the first Symphony Orchestra of the Net,[40] in which professional and amateur musicians from all over the world have video-recorded their own musical intervention, comfortably playing in their own home, and then reviewing their own contribution "reassembled" together with that of others in a real concert. These examples of artistic and creative production, more or less amateurish, suggest how communication technologies, digital media in particular, allow a widespread participation of users, in what we could define – paraphrasing McLuhan (1964) – a "global music village", where the individual can express himself but also participate, connected to other individuals, in building an original and innovative, unprecedented product.

All this shows how the transition from analogue to digital media is marked by important changes in the forms of production, sharing, and enjoyment of culture. The mere presence of the computer, as a communication tool, has had a strong impact on the way individuals interact and on the processes of construction and diffusion of cultural products. The process of cultural transcoding expressed by Manovich,[41] that is, the construction of a software culture (2008), is based on (and is conveyed through) digital interfaces where the individual interacts with the world in his daily life actions. However, the new technologies are part of a process of media "evolution", rather than "revolution" (in the Mertonian sense of the term). Whatever each new technology introduces represents the improvement of a previous technology, preserving its strengths and correcting its weaknesses: in this sense, we are witnessing a process of remediation[42] but also of convergence, that is, the fusion of several media and their contents into a single instrument.[43] This process, in particular, allowed individuals to increasingly access easily the productions of their own and other cultures. Thanks to the creation of mobile devices, the individual can always carry this vast intercultural baggage (in a process of ubiquitous computing)[44] and, at any time, they can intervene on it, modifying it, widening it, participating in the co-induction of new processes.

---

[39] www.youtube.com/watch?v=tprMEs-zfQA.
[40] www.youtube.com/user/symphony?blend=2&ob=1&rclk=cti.
[41] Manovich, 2001.
[42] Bolter, Grusin, 1999.
[43] Jenkins, 2006.
[44] Greenfield, 2006.

Through digital media, the individual can thus express themselves, without any particular technical limits or previous skills, experiencing the world[45] through screens and interfaces that are increasingly powerful but accessible, which also allow them to access information but, above all, to be reached by information whenever they feel the need to.[46]

3.4 Software culture and connective thinking

In the earlier paragraphs we dwelt on the technological and social processes that have marked the modes of musical production, distribution, and enjoyment in recent decades. Technologies such as the Walkman (late 1970s), Web (late 1990s), and iPod (early 2000s), represent the point of "evolution" of previous media,[47] determining significant social effects and offering (in different ways) new sociocultural opportunities to its users. They redefined the boundaries between the public and private spheres and promoted new ways of sharing social processes.

The transformations brought about by new technologies are particularly meaningful, but also very complex. They opened significant questions that make scientific reflection highly problematic, as well as multidisciplinary. In fact, it is necessary to consider the different cultural, social, economic, and political factors that characterise the contexts where digital technologies express themselves, to better understand the social effects that they deter. The digital divide (i.e., the impossibility for some people or communities to access digital technologies, such as, for example, but not only, of the Third World countries) connected to the economic development of the territory of belonging, cultural and social origins, and levels of education of the user powers, but also to the generational differences, has a relevant weight in the diffusion and social impact of new media.

The leaders of the social and technological transformations underway are, without any doubt, the "digital natives",[48] that is, young people born between the 1980s and 1990s and who grew up in the digital flow, in the transition from analogue to digital technologies: the "Bit Generation."[49] With this transition, the "digital immigrants", that is, the older generations, who understandably have a greater difficulty in approaching the new technologies, are challenged once again.

In any case, comparing the different researches at an international level, what emerges significantly is the active role that Network users have assumed in the last decade. It is no coincidence, in fact, that in the course of the chapter we dwelt on the phenomenon of UGC, emblematically summarised by the cover of time on the occasion of the "2006 season": "You control the Information Age. Welcome to your world."

---

[45] Jedlowski, 2003; Moores, 1993.
[46] Weinberg, 2007.
[47] Bolter and Grusin, 1999.
[48] Prensky, 2001a and 2009.
[49] Savonardo, 2013.

It is "we", the users, who control the Information Age. Each user of the Network can enter his or her own content on the Web and share it with others. Discuss and participate collectively in building shared knowledge pathways. However, at a closer look, it is also obvious that the scenario is not as "democratic" as it might seem. In addition to the widespread digital divide, there is also a participation gap,[50] that is, the lack of rights of expression (due to governmental controls) or the impossibility (due to economic issues) to make one's "digital voice" heard. Such difference is not only intergenerational, but also and above all intragenerational, they involve different levels of participation in the Network. A number of people who use the new media, surf the Web, interact and create content, are joined by individuals who do not access these technologies and, therefore, do not participate at all in the process of "connective intelligence" expressed by de Kerckhove.[51] Consequently, and beyond the emphasis that characterises the main theories on the Web, the metaphor of McLuhan's (1964) "global village" seems not to be definitively fulfilled. Moreover, just as studies on cultural hegemony and the influence of the mass media have already contradicted the theoretical analyses of the last century, the current scenario poses new and necessary reflections on the forms of economic, political, and social power connected to the development of new media.

The Web (even with its free users, who express their opinions (in blogs), their consent (for example, in American presidential elections), their dissent (as in the case of the clashes between the Iranian people and the government, just to cite an example) and their solidarity (on the occasion of earthquakes and natural disasters that upset the Earth) sees at the top of the main online sites, the presence of multinationals that, in some cases, assume monopolistic positions. It is the case of Microsoft, with its predominance in operating systems and, therefore, in the access to software; or Google, with its prominent presence in online search, or in the access to information. The dominance of this has been extended, thanks to the purchase of the YouTube portal and the offer of increasingly important web applications (email and office programs as text editors), bringing the availability of content on the Web under a single owner.

Hence, the user is the only one with the power over the Information Age – to take the cover of Time. In practice, the individual creates and feeds the contents which, however, become consultable and navigable only through the societies which manage the Web. If YouTube sees itself, for its own initial mission, as "archive of our memories" and Google as "gateway" and content indexing, at any time (for different reasons: economic, political, social, ethical, and cultural) such portals could decide to sell, close, give up, disperse, or delete the immense cultural heritage they keep online.

Furthermore, the theme of control, of the traceability of all our digital actions, of the right to privacy, increasingly often violated, of a pseudo freedom of

---

[50] Jenkins, 2006.
[51] Derrick de Kerckhove (1997) uses this expression, paraphrasing the concept of "collective intelligence" by Pierre Lévy (1994), in reference to the sharing and exchange of knowledge determined by the mutual contact between the different individuals connected to the Net.

"access" knowledge, awareness, information (which is accompanied by constant "surveillance" by those who manage the digital data, be they private or governmental subjects) asks disturbing and complex questions which, for obvious reasons, we are not able to explore further in here. However, such considerations are particularly relevant also for a deeper analysis of the logic that characterise the contemporary musical universe.

To better understand some characteristics of the new communication media, also with reference to musical phenomena, it is useful to investigate some of the main theories related to digital cultures, new media, and the Web. In this regard, it is worth pointing out that the scientific literature in this field refers to the theories of sociologists, media scholars, and mass communication but, given the complex nature of the phenomenon, it also calls for significant insights into other disciplines, ranging from economics to information technology.

Lev Manovich[52] defines the new media, through the identification of five fundamental principles. The Russian scholar points out how the new media (newly created by computer or converted from analogical sources) express themselves through a digital code: they are, therefore, numerical representations (the First principle). Thanks to these representations in the numerical form, through mathematical functions, the information and media products are decomposable into fragments and recomposed an infinite number of times, a property that makes them modular, that is, elements that enjoy their own functionality even if decontextualised (the Second principle). As already mentioned, through digital technologies, sound is converted into bits and, like other information, is translated into a file that the computer processes on the basis of binary code strings. This operation allows to extrapolate fragments of a music track and to reassemble and remix these fragments into a new sound product, independent of the original one. According to Manovich, the numerical coding of the media and their modular structure allow the automation (the Third principle) of the different procedures used for the creation, manipulation, and access to the media. Such computer applications offer users the possibility to manipulate any information (not only music, but also photos, audios, videos, etc.) through simple commands to be given to the computer that delivers the final result. In this sense, digital technologies involve the loss of direct contact between the individual and the object produced: the user's actions are, in fact, mediated by a machine, an interface,[53] to which complex operations are demanded. The files are transformed into their numerical structure, properties, and bits, are modified. The moment when objects and numbers can change, the medial objects never remain identical to infinity, but are variable (the Fourth principle), they change from user to user. Finally, as already pointed out, when managing any media object, the computer does not distinguish images from videos, texts, or sound because these elements are represented by simple numbers: it is in the return to the user, instead, that these objects need to take a form that respects the

---

[52] Manovich, 2001.
[53] Johnson, 1997.

cultural patterns through which society expresses itself. If the computation does not distinguish between a photo and a text (as both are numerical representations) the individual, on the other hand, builds his or her social reality through the distinction of cultural objects. This construction also involves the process of transcoding (the Fifth Principle) between the computer and the cultural level: digital interfaces translate and process cultural products into bits (the language of the computer) and then return them in forms comprehensible to man according to shared cognitive patterns. In the jargon of the new media, "transcoding" an object means translating it into a format. The computerisation of culture gradually produces a similar transcoding of all categories of all cultural objects. This means that cultural categories and concepts are replaced,- at the level of meaning and/or language,- by new categories and new concepts derived from ontology, epistemology and computer use. Therefore, the new media act as real precursors of this more general process of cultural re-conceptualisation.[54]

The linguistic and cultural forms of the new media are, therefore, the result of a fusion between the computer logic of the computer and the cultural level of the media. In his 2008 book *Software Culture*, Manovich says how contemporary culture is increasingly expressed through digital programs that allow us to create, reproduce, and redefine the same cultural objects with which we interact, that belong to us, that we share and inherit. Software represent today, in an increasingly pervasive way, our interface with the surrounding environment, with others, with individual and collective memory, and imagination. A "universal language" allowing the world to communicate, a "universal engine" that allows the world moving. The different systems of the modern society speak different languages and pursue different goals, but they all share the syntax of the software that allowed the birth of the global information society. This means that the different disciplines of contemporary society and culture (from the humanities to science, art studies to technology) cannot ignore its role and effects. Software culture (continues the new media theorist) is an essential component of social living, because ours is unequivocally "a software society immersed in a software culture." This consideration also applies to music production and enjoyment. Sibilla[55] points out that software also contributes to build the cultural and linguistic interfaces that determine musical production and fruition, modelling the language and social forms of digital music.

As Negroponte already stated in 1995, the transition from the old to the new media and, therefore, from analogical to digital technologies, encourages pull fruition modes alongside the traditional push ones. In fact, according to the metaphor of the American scholar, through interactive processes the new media allow the user to personalise the fruition of the contents, "pulling out" the information that he considers interesting. The traditional communication tools, instead, such as the television or radio, "push" the contents towards the user, who receives them passively. The passage

---

[54] Manovich, 2001, p. 70.
[55] Sibilla, 2008.

from push to pull is related to a change in the processes of message transmission: from a mode of communication called "one-to-many", as in the case of television, to a "many-to-many" type of diffusion, in which everyone can communicate in a way that is as easy as on the Web. Therefore, the new media brought unprecedented interaction between individuals, determining the evolution from mass media to personal media.[56]

In a nutshell, the four central aspects that, through digital technologies, characterise the processes of personalisation of media fruition are: the level of simulation of reality, degree of interactivity, personalised contents; and mobility. The user interacts with digital environments according to conceptual schemes that make interaction as natural as possible, reducing the perception of an interface between the individual and cultural object. The more "natural" actions that the user performs in the use of digital media, the lower is the perception of the medium itself within the interaction practices with other individuals and culture. Digital technologies are also characterised by the use of communication systems that can be used at any time.[57]

The first two aspects mentioned above refer to the level of "transparency" of the medium as an object external to man or integrated with his daily routines. Marshall McLuhan, as repeatedly pointed out, argues that the technological innovations of communication imply radical changes in the models of perception of the individual, encouraging the use of particular senses in relation to the development of specific media. According to the scholar, "the medium is the message" and, therefore, the message of a medium, or of a technology, is in the change of proportions, of rhythm or of patterns that introduces in the human race.[58] Communication technologies also produce organic amputations and sensory extensions, offering the organism new supports, appendages that constitute a sort of extension of the central nervous system as well as prostheses of the human body. The Canadian sociologist says that the individual and social consequences of each medium derive from the new portions introduced in our personal affairs by each of these extensions,[59] as the use of different technologies affects the organisation of the human senses. These theories seem to have anticipated relevant ideas that characterise the scientific debate on digital technologies and, with the diffusion of new media, take on new meanings.

Derrick de Kerckhove was one of the leading scholars of the connections between technologies and the human mind and commonly considered McLuhan's intellectual heir. He argues that communication technologies, by investing language and the way we use it, also invest our information processing strategies.[60] According to de Kerckhove, just as writing is not only a manual capacity, but above all represents the possibility of classifying and ordering thought, in the same way the use of new communication technologies has an immediate repercussion on our ability to develop new

---

[56] Pratellesi, 2008.
[57] McLuhan, 1964.
[58] McLuhan, 1964, p. 16.
[59] Yesterday, p. 15.
[60] de Kerckhove, 1991.

mental structures and models. Furthermore, the researcher claims that with the new media we have entered the second era of electricity: the digital era after the analogue one. The first one gave light, heat, sign transport, and power to engines, the second one became mental and organic.[61]

The media typical of the electronic period determine a new revolution of the senses, overturn linear categories and create on a global scale a new circularity with virtual boundaries. The "global village" is affected by what Ong[62] defines as secondary orality, which derives from the introduction of electronic media in literate societies and the recovery of the word in electronic form. In its analysis, Ong refers to the radio and television, while the development of digital technologies introduces what de Kerckhove defines "tertiary orality" and that characterises multimedia systems, virtual reality, and the Net: "It is an electronic orality, like the 'second', but differently from that it is based on the simulation of sensoriality, rather than on its transmission. Through, for example, the 'beep' of mobile phones or computers, tertiary orality is characterised by a tactile language that gives feedback to our actions, in a sort of organic simulation."[63]

For de Kerckhove, the "history of the senses" narrates the changes brought about by new technologies, as the abstraction and desensorialisation introduced with the alphabet is replaced today by a new sensoriality that affects our relationship with the media. In the digital age and through tertiary orality, the individual can manage the cognitive process outside the mind, through the exteriorisation of his cognitive functions, in a path that reevaluates the role of all the senses and retrieves the "intermediate" ones.

For de Kerckhove rather than "orality" it is, in fact, more properly, a "tertiary sensoriality." The digital objects that the individual encounters on the computer screen can be compared with mental objects. If the television screen, offering a frontal relationship with the viewer, has inaugurated the mass culture, the computer screen (introducing two-way interactive modes) led to "total immersion", initiating a new "culture of depth."[64] An expression of this form of culture is the "virtual reality", which allows us to enter the world of video and computer games and to probe the infinite depth of human creativity in science, art, and technology.

Central, in the theories of the Canadian scholar, is, therefore, the reflection on the sensory explosion favoured by the new instruments, which represent more "technological extensions" of our body. Derrick de Kerckhove speaks of "psycho-technology" to define "a technology that emulates, extends or amplifies the sense-motor, psychological or cognitive functions of the mind."[65] In particular, the interface has become the privileged place of information processing. The computer has created a type of intermediate cognition, a bridge of uninterrupted interaction, the corpus

---

[61] de Kerckhove in Savonardo, 2004.
[62] Ong, 1982.
[63] Buffardi, 2004, p. 114.
[64] de Kerckhove, 1991.
[65] Yesterday, p. 24.

callosus of a sort of exchange between the external world and the inside of our ego.[66] Through the new instruments, memory, intelligence, organisation of thought, classification of data, and treatment of information are externalised. These "externalised cognitive functions" operate like the human mind, but they are outside of it.

The technological progress of the 20th century first leads to an exteriorisation of the motor brain, followed by the exteriorisation of cognitive functions through a series of applications that develop an increasing hybridisation between man and machines. Among the different technological prosthesis of human organs, the computer represents the amplification and extension of the mind that produces the exteriorisation, acceleration, and sharing of cognitive processes. About this point, de Kerckhove states that the exteriorisation of the individual on the screen offers the possibility of sharing the cognitive content with other people.[67]

The connection between the thoughts and cognitive forms of different cognitive forms represents one of the most significant elements that characterise the fusion of new technologies. In front of the computer screen, thought is expressed through the "connective" condition that represents the possibility of reaching a shared elaboration of thought itself through its externalised and interactive interpretation.[68] The "connective thought" is for de Kerckhove, the cognitive product that arises from the interaction between individuals, and as such, begins with conversation and already characterises oral societies. Through new means, and in particular through the Net, however, it takes on new ways. Connectivity attributes to the word a form of thought between individuals, thought becomes a "digital object." Moreover, reiterating the lines of continuity between oral society and the digital age, de Kerckhove highlights how "modes of thought" can be traced back to the different instrumental and technological endowment of different eras. The "hypertextual thought" of the Web is an "ancient thought"; it recalls our mental associations, arises from the conversation and interactions between subjects, translates and explains the necessary links among events, situations, and information. However, with electricity and modern technology, it can express a new "essence" of the individual.

For the scholar, a significant dimension is given by the "extended real time" of the Network. With this expression, de Kerckhove means the "time of mental thought" which presents itself in similar ways to the "time of connective thought." The time of thought, in fact, extends through the decoding of new information, it can be suspended, interspersed, and interrupted by other activities and thoughts, to be resumed in several stages until the information processing is closed. In the same way, thought on the Net acts in an "extended real time" in a shared working process.

According to de Kerckhove, the connective thinking and the concept of community represent the core of the reflections on the "new digital being." The electronic communities that arise through collaborative software are formed around a

---

[66] Yesterday, p. 69.
[67] Buffardi, 2004, p. 111.
[68] *Ibidem*.

shared project and represent a "just in you" community, in passing, that exists when a connection is made around the objectives and then dissolves, or changes.[69] It is a cognitive community because it reflects the cognitive character of the Net, based on a matrix of connections between elements, objects, concepts, and thoughts. In this regard, the scholar speaks of the Web as a new "art medium" that is characterised by the two forms of "connection art" and "community art":

> I think that for music, and in general for artistic creation, besides the changes determined by new technologies, it is important what I have defined "the art of intelligence", that is the art of setting the right configurations of connections [...] in the Net. This is a form of art, it is a new art medium. Connection and community represent two forms of art today that need to be developed and understood: the art of connection (the art of software intelligence) and that of community.[70]

As Annalisa Buffardi[71] summarises, the message of the new media is substantiated in the interrelation activities of people and thoughts. However, the latter recover and enhance, through electricity, forms of interaction, modes of thought, and procedures of information processing typical of primary orality. The new media solicit our senses, even the "intermediate" ones, in a hypertextual process that translates and exteriorises the traditional human thought, generating the tertiary sensoriality and to a "new way" of being of the individual.

Tertiary sensoriality is connected to the logic of immediacy and hypermediation[72] of new technologies. Immediacy allows the viewer to feel that the medium disappeared, and the objects are before his eyes; a sensation that defines the experience as "authentic." In the epistemological sense, hypermediation corresponds, instead, to "opacity", that is, the awareness that that knowledge of the world reaches us through the media. The experience of the medium becomes itself an experience of reality. The new communication technologies are, moreover, perceived as technological tools that are domesticated and perfectly injected in the everyday life of our lives. Since the advent of the industrial revolution, in fact, cities have been the main place to install mechanical, electrical (and, nowadays, electronic) media such as cinema and television. For decades, we have filled spots in our cities with complementary and competing media; these spaces have helped reshape society and have, in turn, been reshaped by different media. These same public spaces today find themselves in a different set of relationships, made up of the "remediation" introduced by the multimedia, cyberspace of the Web, and other Internet communication services.

Analysing the concept of remediation and taking up again McLuhan, Jay D. Bolter, and Richard Grusin[73] recall how the content of one medium is semi-mediation of

---

[69] de Kerckhove in Buffardi, 2004, p. 115.
[70] Yesterday, p. 118.
[71] Buffardi, 2004.
[72] Bolter, Grusin, 1999.
[73] *Ibidem*.

another medium, in particular the one that precedes it. According to this concept, therefore, new media are the evolution of the old ones: they enhance their characteristics and offer solutions to the limits expressed by previous technology. The CD, for example, can be interpreted as the evolution of vinyl: it improves the sound quality and robustness of the material, making it more portable and less degradable over time. The mobile phone improves the functionality of the home phone, also depriving it of the need to be placed in a fixed location and generating new modes of communication.

The following paragraphs focus on some aspects related to the influence that new technologies have on creative processes, music enjoyment and production, and on the social consequences of the use of personal media in our daily lives. In particular, the aim is to suggest further ideas on some concepts that are particularly relevant in the study of the sociocultural transformations that affect the contemporary sound universe, opening up new questions.

3.5 Sounds, connections, and innovations

During the last century, radio, television, computer, Walkman, mp3 player, mobile phone, and car stereo (mobile extensions of the domestic dimension) have determined sound crossings, in time and space, contributing to the "musical construction" of personal and collective experiences and memories. Individuals of any generation are immersed in sound, feed and consume it, in a continuous process of redefinition of their identities.

Music, in fact, contributes to the processes of social construction of daily experience in which the subject is constantly immersed with the body, affections, and action: this experience is mediated by a multitude of its natural and mechanically reproduced. Most of our daily actions are, in fact, accompanied by a sound background. Waking up, walking, driving, working, and sometimes falling asleep with music or other acoustic accompaniments is for most of us a family experience, a constant. As well as the noise recurs in our urban and, sometimes, domestic context. We relate to space and time through our personal use of sound, live to the rhythm of music in domestic spaces, and sit in the street listening to our favourite songs on traditional Walkman headphones or portable digital players. We experience constant sound crossings, the polyphony of sound regulates us and is regulated by us to an increasing extent as we move through everyday life.[74] This is a structuring and very interesting process that does not yet seem to be adequately studied by the humanities and social sciences.

Among the different media, radio is the most pervasive, it potentially accompanies every moment of our daily life, and is present in every place: in the kitchen, shower, car, on the beach, at the park, in the office and, through the web radio, on our computer, while we write, read, and navigate. About this, Jo Tacchi writes that the sound

---

[74] Bull, Back, 2003.

of the radio is intimately integrated into everyday life and can be understood as an important part of domestic environments or sound landscapes.[75] Sound is endowed with meanings and implications that go beyond the immediate context and physical boundaries of the house and can create a plot within which one can move and live. This sound can be interpreted as a mediator between people in the domestic context and the outside world. The experience, activity, and meaning of radio listening in different contexts creates bridges, intersections between the private and public dimensions, but also connections through time and memory, playing a connecting role between individuals and groups of people. We can get a sense of community through listening to it and, temporarily, draw on memories, nostalgia, emotions that do not need to be rationalised or verbalised. They are lived as an aspect of everyday life as it flows and are more than a single memory or a single connection.[76]

Sounds incorporate cultural and personal meanings, while memory is, in turn, stimulated by sound. Therefore, there is a language of sound imagery through which we use sound to make sense of the world around us, but at the same time we learn culturally what a specific sound is. Forrester[77] states that a sound product has two qualitative dimensions: a nourishing one and a dissonant one. However, the two dimensions do not have to be mutually exclusive: listening to the sounds we have been fed by, and which we have imbued with cultural meanings, by placing them in a disorderly context, means giving them a dissonant value.[78] Individuals feed on the sound imagery through which they give meaning and design their own cultural universe which, at the same time, contributes to the processes of social construction of collective identities.

Music connects us to each other and, as Schütz argues, allows a mutual agreement in a relationship.[79] The forms of identification in an "us", the sense of "being together" that, for Adorno, refer to the eclipse of direct experience caused by technologically mediated forms of experience, allow us to be alone and simultaneously "together" through sound reception. With the diffusion of mobile phones, Walkman, mp3 players, analogic and digital radios, and the Net and the ubiquitous car stereos, the nature and meaning of being tuned or connected require an increasingly in-depth scientific analysis and reflection, to be conducted, with a multidisciplinary approach, within the sociology of cultural and communicative processes, but also the study of late or post-modernity technologies. In addition, the sounds, rhythms, and modes of communication of the digital universe increasingly undermine the boundaries between private and public space, between the domestic sphere and the street, between the individual microcosm and the global agora. New sound technologies provide us with all the sound we want. - Michael Bull and Les Back say that domestic sound devices allow us to recreate the

---

[75] Heels, 2003.
[76] Yesterday, p. 179.
[77] Forrester, 1998.
[78] Moore P., 2003.
[79] Schütz, 1951.

cinema in our living rooms thanks to the advent of digital sound systems with enveloping sound for our television sets. Home hi-fi systems have already achieved this for our favourite sounds.[80] Customisation and individualism have increasingly divided the spaces in the home into multiple listening (and viewing) modules. However, sound does not respect space. Thanks to media, it goes through walls, geographical, and cultural boundaries.

Music, like all forms of communication and expression, is continually being updated by technological and social innovations, in an increasingly hybrid global village where it is possible, in real time, to interact through the Net with the rest of the world, whether real or virtual, opening up countless windows on multiple cultural universes and causing a profound crisis in the traditional dimensions of space and time. In fact, Carmen Leccardi argues that if modernity has dissociated space and time, creating a global present that can be travelled quickly, late modernity has destroyed the last space–time frontiers through the creation of a "global contemporaneity", the result of digital technologies. Thanks to the diffusion of the Net it is possible to "be" in different points of the planet without crossing material spaces, in a new "geography of the impalpable."[81]

The Net, in fact, contains and allows access to all the information produced, without logical limits, in time and space. The digital archives of knowledge are not located in one place and do not possess a physical configuration, but are widespread, available everywhere. We are witnessing a significant transformation of traditional systems of knowledge storage and archiving, both individual and collective. Interactive technologies, as already pointed out, allow us to radically reconceive the modes of communication, giving the user extraordinary opportunities to build effective personal paths of knowledge and cultural consumption. In fact, they allow (or even, require) the user to act, choose, and respond to every step of the communication, helping them interact with the cultural product through an unlimited variety of paths and ways. In this, new media are as different from cinema and television as they are from texts, whose user is essentially a passive receptor of something that others have structured for themselves once and for all.

The technological revolution would seem to profoundly change our relationship with media, cultural products, and knowledge, as well as our approach to the preservation of media products and the organisation of our personal home media libraries. By dematerialising the medium, digital technology allows (or, more correctly, provides the illusion of) a practically unlimited availability of material and favours the integration of sources and references physically distributed everywhere into a single "virtual archive", provided common criteria are adopted. Moreover, all this can be potentially made available to the world community through the Network and made accessible to all. Digital archiving also undermines the intrinsic complementarity of content and physical support. The extreme ease of manipulation of digital memories, but also

---

[80] Bull, Back, 2003.
[81] Leccardi, 1998, p. 62.

the fragility of memory supports and the rapid obsolescence of the technologies that allow their "reading" and elaboration, redefines the very idea of preservation to which we are semi-accustomed.

"Vinyl records, audiocassettes, CDs have given way to digital players that can contain thousands of music files, but not only those. Furthermore, the necessity to store data is decreasing on a material medium: it is more useful and convenient to leave it stored on the Net and access it in any computer. "Liquid" music, therefore, for a semi-liquid society.

The possibility of transforming all the information into bits has put at anyone's disposal an enormous amount of data, potentially infinite, which, however, will never be fully consulted. The information overload is, in fact, a phenomenon which characterises the digital age and which opens complex reflections on the theme of access to information, as well as on the preservation, organisation, and memory of data. The Net and the new electronic devices guarantee the repayment on digital support or on the Web of sound materials, allowing to preserve a specific cultural, artistic, and musical heritage in digital archives, which, increasingly, seem to be the new tools of individual and collective memory. A memory, therefore, entrusted to technologies, which show considerable advantages but which also present multiple questions, critical nodes, and unexplored fields.

According to Derrick de Kerckhove however, "digital memory seems more reliable than organic memory", as this is more complex and more "intelligent" than the numerical.[82] Digital death in the long run may not retain this reliability because "technologies, machines and programs can change, as well as being dependent on electricity, so if you pull the plug", the memory fades.

About this topic, Pierre Lévy states that recording and archiving no longer has (can no longer have) the same sense that it had before the flood of information. When archives are rare, or at least limited, to leave a trace means to enter the long memory of men. But if memory is practically infinite, flowing, overflowing, fed every moment by myriads of receptors and millions of people, entering the archives of culture is no longer enough to differentiate.[83] Moreover, Lévy points out that you don't "expose" a cd-rom or even a virtual world: you have to navigate, dive into them, interact with them. Digital technologies require the active involvement of the user, the conscious participation of his memory in the constitution of the message.

The potentialities that digital technologies express are always linked to the different cultural, social, economic, and political factors that characterise the reference contexts. The cultural and social origins, educational levels of potential users, but also the differences in generation are relevant in the diffusion and social impact of new media. However, young people, the so-called digital natives, are among the main users of new technologies.

---

[82] de Kerckhove, 2004ª.
[83] Lévy, 1997.

3.6 Creativity and interactivity

The introduction of digital technologies radically changes the relationship between the artist and creative process. The use of technological tools such as the pioneer camera, computer, and multimedia systems influence artistic production, which is increasingly expressed through the contamination between different languages and codes. We are witnessing the birth of a generation of musicians–composers who give life to new forms of expression through a musical language that goes beyond words, sounds, and images, in a process of interactive and multimedia communication. The contamination between different languages is nourished by the cultural melting pot that is also expressed through the global citizenship of some music bands, whose artistic production is, at the same time, the daughter of no place and of all places, of an indefinite space–time dimension, of the appropriation of a glocal dimension, in which the boundaries between local and global are increasingly blurred.

However, technologies have always influenced creative processes, defining or favouring, in every time and place, the creation, development, and contamination of different languages, styles, and expressive codes. Derrick de Kerckhove, analyses the passage from a mass society to a networked one, says that there are the very close connections between the technological innovations of different eras and the related artistic–musical productions. The media theorist points out how, from the industrial revolution onwards, art has been trying "to overcome the native effects of technology" and that this trend in art "could be one of the main functions of music at every level, from the more rarefied sophistication of the isolated composer to the great hits of Madonna and Radiohead"[84].

The Canadian scientist also argues that mechanisation affects the rhythms of life, leading to "a gradual loss" of the "organic interval." According to the scholar, in fact, before the advent of machines, "the interval between men, between people" was "an interval of bodily rhythms, of distance of voices [...] an interval of human rhythms."[85] Mechanisation, industrialisation, and technological innovations have a strong impact on the rhythms of life, on the perception of time and space, and, inevitably, on creativity and artistic production. Some musical genres and forms, according to this theory, reproduce the rhythms and cadences typical of machines and means of transport, such as, for example, "the rhythm of the train", of the "locomotive", which recalls not only "the beating of the heart" but also "the beating of the heart", "blues music." For de Kerckhove jazz breaks the "mechanicity" of rhythm:

> Jazz, through what is known as "the breaks" (the time needed to improvise and dialogue between musicians) represents a new way of managing the interval that overcomes the mechanicity of rhythm. By expanding or suspending the beat, jazz throws a curve into the machine. Jazz is a winning response to mechanical rhythms.[86]

---

[84] de Kerckhove, 2004a, p. 57.
[85] *Ibidem*.
[86] *Ibidem*, p. 59.

The languages of jazz, through improvisation, interrupt the typical cadence of the rhythms of the "machine", creating "the conversation in the chain of montage", that is, the creative interaction between the musicians, the possibility of reproposing "the interval of body rhythms", of "human rhythms", introducing in the repetition and routine elements of innovation. A theory that would seem to indirectly criticise the analyses on jazz and its social functions proposed by Adorno, who, as we have seen in the first chapter, believes instead that this musical language tends (as a consumer product and through its typical rhythmic cadences) to confirm the homologating processes of industrialisation and the logic of the dominant power. In the temporary society – continues de Kerckhove – through electricity, we have again lost the management of the interval that characterises human rhythms:

> Electricity greatly amplifies the signal. It immediately follows the distortion, not only of sound, but also of the body. If Charlie Chaplin's rhythm is that of the human body subject to mechanisation, Jerry Lewis is the equivalent representation of the effect of electricity on the human body. In cinema. Jerry Lewis is Chaplin on electroshock. His latest version is Jim Carrey.[87]

Electricity determines the "distortion" of rhythm, sound, and human body. Through music, young (and not so young) people breathe, feed, and seem to feel on their skin the distortion of sounds, rhythms, words, images and "body intervals" that are expressed, if not more, through new digital technologies. New generations, born and raised within the flow that characterises the so-called postmodern era, for some scholars "post-human" and soon to be "post-digital", when transition, navigating an increasingly extensive network is a widespread condition. According to Domiziana Giordano, "The transit is the message. [...] Everything flows, everything transits. The important thing is to transit and be part of the flow."[88]

As pointed out earlier, the new digital technologies have unsurprisingly affected the different sectors of the art world and have had a significant impact both on the modes of fruition and on the creative processes. With the advent of the sampler and, subsequently, of particular PC software, the cards of creativity are being remixed, the sound "theft" of fragments of a piece of the past becomes a new vital link for the artists of the present. The digital "cut and paste" allows the revisitation or distortion of sounds, melodies, and above all preexisting rhythms, which are not resonated by new performers, but simply extrapolated from the original recordings and then suitably personalised. A rhythm, a groove of bass and drums sampled from a James Brown song, put in loop, becomes the rhythmic basis for a rap, whose author completely upsets the original idea, making it his own creation, through an unpublished language that feeds on the sounds of the past. Metropolitan rappers quote Bach, rewrite him, and make him a sound background, a landscape of collective memory, drawing (sometimes unconsciously) from the pop music of the sixties

---

[87] *Ibidem*.
[88] Giordano, 2004, p. 125.

or from cinema soundtracks, cultural heritage of the individual and collective imagination: this is a free and uninhibited use of preexisting material, which feeds on a constant and continuous interweaving between tradition and innovation. A new type of musician was born, one who is often unable to play any musical instrument but, using the sampler, computer, and a few other electronic supports, in his own home studio, is able to create products of the highest sound quality. Thanks to new technologies, music is increasingly within everyone's reach, even in the creative phase, when the artist (in this case the producer–author) seems to be, as Simon Reynolds would say, "a director who, instead of directing a group of musicians playing together, expertly arranges the skillful performances of musicians of different genres and eras."[89]

To create a musical collage in pop art and postmodern style, or to distort the original sound fragments, through filters and sound modification techniques, the use of digital technologies seems to question the very concept of author, in any form of art. Paraphrasing Walter Benjamin,[90] "the work of art" should be considered in the era of its "digital" reproducibility. The "digitisation of art" would seem, in fact, to bring to extreme consequences the processes triggered by the production and mechanical reproduction of art studied by Benjamin. The use of new digital technologies and the multiple possibilities of multimediatic interaction determine an unprecedented relationship between a composer and user. Annalisa Tota says:

> In multimedia art the artist opens the text and asks its potential user to participate to their creativity: it is a kind of tailor-made work of art, in which the consumer can ask the author to step aside to personalise a little bit the product he has in front of him. A sort of DIY art, where the boundary between author and consumer blurs, not so much in roles as in the social definition of the product. The roles are clear and distinct, but the product is born at the intersection, it is created by the encounter with a specific consumer and, above all, it can never be discussed twice in the same way.[91]

Peter Gabriel is one of the first artists who, using the enormous potential of multimedia technologies, through an interactive CD-ROM game, enjoyed feeding his "de-composed" compositions to fans, to be "recomposed" according to the taste, flair, and creativity of the potential user. Already in 1993, with the CD-ROM X-plora1, Gabriel, one of the main proponents of the contamination between different forms of expression, proposes a multimedia reworking of his musical work, implemented with the help of movies, graphics, and the possibility of interaction; among the various options, the user can rework some songs of the musician. In 1996, in EVE, he created four virtual environments for four songs, each one designed by a contemporary artist; the exploration includes the possibility to create a video,

---

[89] Reynolds, 1998.
[90] Benjamin, 1936.
[91] Tota, 1999, p. 166.

reshaping both the audio and visual tracks. In the interactive game, then, the music tracks can be broken down, divided into many small sound fragments that the user can recompose as he wants, generating his own unique "composition", independent from the original song. This sound product is, therefore, the result of the interaction between the author's original idea and the user's intervention, who in turn becomes the author or co-author of the final composition.

Pierre Lévy, with reference to the creation and preservation (and not only) of the work of art in the digital age, emphasises further significant aspects that deserve attention.

> The recording, the archive, the piece likely to be preserved in a museum, but also the messages enclosed. A painting, for example, which is the object of conservation, is both the work and the archive of the work. But the work-event, the work-process, the interactive work, the metaphorical, connected, crossed, indefinitely constructed work of the cyberculture can hardly be recorded as such, even if one photographs a moment of its process or captures some partial trace of its expression. [...] Then the creative act *par excellence* consists in producing an event, here and now, for a community, or rather in building the collective for which the event will take place, i.e. in partially reorganising the virtual world, the unstable passage of meaning that hosts human beings and their works.[92]

Lévy also argues that the genres of cyberculture belong to the order of performance, such as dance and theatre. Like the collective improvisations of jazz, *commedia dell'arte*. Similarly, to like "installations", they require the active involvement of the receiver, their dislocation in a symbolic or real space, the conscious participation of their memory in the constitution of the message. Their center of gravity is a subjective process, which dissolves them from any space-time closure.[93]

Lévy's considerations seem to bring into play all the elements that characterise artistic production, conservation, the creative process and its contents, constantly "in transit", in the "flow" of digital communication, opening new problematic questions. The creative act, "the work-event, the work-process, the interactive work, the metaphorical, connected, connected, attracted, indefinitely co-constructed work of the cyberculture" cannot be regulated as such. It is possible to capture a moment of its process or capture "some partial trace of its expression" but it is hardly "reproducible", it is realised in the interaction between the author, composer, artist, and user, co-author of the work, in a creative flow in progress.

Lévy's arguments on the "work of art" (which we could consider in the era of its "digital irreproducibility") seem to particularly undermine Benjamin's theories.[94] In fact, on one hand, the German scholar's ideas on authenticity tend to be overturned, as the work of art, in cyberculture, returns to being considered a unique and unrepeatable object that draws its value from its being *hic et nunc*; and on the other hand, the concept expressed by Benjamin on the death of the author seems to be extreme.

---

[92] Lévy, 1997.
[93] *Ibidem*, p. 150.
[94] Benjamin, 1936.

With interactive technologies, in fact, the role of the author who loses the authorship of the work in the interaction with the user, who becomes co-author and contributes to the realisation of the work itself, making it unrepeatable in the same ways and forms that that specific interaction determines.

The new digital technologies and their use seem to question and sometimes overturn the aesthetic categories and traditional artistic canons, but also our daily interaction modes. Thanks to YouTube, the home computer turns into a video jukebox of memories, a shared digital space, cultural, and musical memory always accessible and usable by everyone, always on. Our personal sound archive (made up of vinyl records, audiocassettes, CDs, and music videos) is enriched by the files available on the Net, a window on the world, and an extension of our senses, increasingly connected to other eyes, ears, and memories. With digital technologies and file sharing, each of us can customise and enrich our home media library according to our own tastes and preferences. However, the process of personalisation of listening does not originally belong to the digital culture, but can be traced back to the mix tapes of the analogue era, in particular, since the time when it was first created.

The creation of mix tapes, compilations recorded on magnetic tape (as well as the storage of certain files on an mp3 player) responds to a logic of personalisation that belongs to a relevant aspect of contemporary consumer culture. A practice that emphasises, in a significant way, the role of music as a narrative, individual, and conscious. It narrates the loves, pains, enthusiasms, disappointments, passions, political commitment, the collective effervescence of significant historical, social, and cultural moments, experienced on "one's own skin", also through the sound and words of certain songs. Verses and music that have accompanied entire generations and that, in particular, have represented the soundtrack of youth cultural events of the last sixty years, from the advent of rock music to the present day sound paths, traces of life.

The mix tape, replaced today by digital playlists, stages a unique combination of cultural products and biographical experiences; a practice that emphasises how in the contemporary world one of the primary functions of the aesthetic material consists in the incessant composition and recomposition of individual and collective identities. According to Thurston Moore, a mix tape represents a particular -form of poetry. The new poet collects and recomposes- memories, lived experiences, fragments of memory by staging his own identity. No mix comes by chance.[95]

Audiocassettes and their portable recorders have brought about other significant changes, making music consumers "mobile." The Walkman, the ancestor of modern mp3 players, revolutionises traditional ways of enjoying music. According to Bull and Back, the Walkman is the emblem of urban personalisation technologies, since it allows users to build their own individual sound world wherever they go. The experience is "aestheticised" and the world becomes what the user wants it to be.[96]

---

[95] Moore T., 2004.
[96] Bull, Back, 2003.

The public space, the metropolis is transformed into an intimate, indivisible and, at the same time, a collective and shared space. The experience of urban centres changes: walking through the city to the sound of music, through the headphones of the Walkman or iPod creates new sound territories. Visual scenarios that, they nourish a mobile listening and a soundtrack that accompanies the movement, the passage. While the body moves in tune with the music, the individual transforms the public scenario, providing new sounds and colours to the urban context. The user of the iPod changes the territorial structure of the city, in a double movement of "deterritorialisation and re-territorialisation." Through its paths, it creates new thresholds, nodes, and configurations.

Moreover, according to Jean Paul Thibaud the front door can also function as a sound door. On the one hand, the door represents a transition between two places that have a distinct status; on the other, it acts as an intermediary between two types of listening experience.[97] The threshold between public and private is defined not so much in terms of physical access (getting out of the door), but in terms of a change in perceptual orientation. It is a "paradoxical territorialisation", in the sense that such an approach to the public sphere implies restricted, private sound accessibility combined with increased visual exposure.

The walkman, iPod, like the Net or stereo of the car (an extension of the car driver's technology and a metaphor for the house in motion) transfers the private, domestic dimension into an "other" context, temporarily pouring the sounds of the "world" into the private sphere. "At the same time, the mobile phone offers the sounds of intimacy wherever the user is. Sound transforms public space into private property. My home is where my sounds are!"[98]

The new generations are immersed in a chaotic set of sounds, musical lines that offer them a "home", a "place" where they can find themselves and get to know each other through lifestyles, trends, cultures, and expressive languages. These are distinctive signs that characterise the different youth "tribes", on which the next chapter focuses.[99]

---

[97] Thibaud, 2003.
[98] Bull, Back, 2003.
[99] Savonardo, 2010; 2013.

4 Youth Cultures and the Social Role of Pop Stars

4.1 Young people as a social category

In this last chapter, we examine the close connection among pop music, the new generations, and their expressive languages, with emphasis on youth cultures and on the social role of pop stars. In particular, this paragraph focuses on youth as a social category and on some of the main sociological analyses affecting the youth universe.

In the early 1950s in America, with the economic boom and a greater purchasing power on the young people's side, the myth of teenagers was born, as already pointed out, a generation inspired by a rebellious philosophy of life, fed on pop music and, above all, became the absolute leaders of the consumer society. From the years of the economic boom onwards, in fact, we can see the stereotype of a young person who can access material and cultural consumption, whose characteristics contribute to redefine the social category of young people, but also the traditional stages of life. The push towards "modernisation", consumerism, the awareness of an accelerated pace of change and the anxieties linked to its social effects determine cultural transformations that inevitably also affect the youth universe. Moreover, the new generations prove to be the bearers of a revolutionary instinct that exploded at the end of the 1960s, in the form of a movement.

In the same period, the attention of sociological studies on youth phenomena also developed. Antonio de Lillo says that since 1970, the studies and reflections on the role of the youth component in society have been growing significantly. Some sociologists, above all from the French school, mainly interested in understanding how a radical change in society was possible, said that the revolution could only come about by the working class or young people or, even better, by an alliance between the two groups.[1]

The new generations, which have always been considered a marginal component of society, thus become the main actors of change. This historical context brings the advent of a real youth culture which, with time and constant social transformation, gives rise to well-defined and diverse "subcultures."[2] These subcultures, increasingly immersed in the urban rhythms and soundscapes of postmodernism, have expressed since the 1950s, from the Beat Revolution to the

---

[1] de Lillo, 2007, p. 12.
[2] Amaturo, 2007.

emergence of the Bit Generation, the languages and trends of youth, but also the fragmentation, uncertainty, and growing crisis of reference points that characterise contemporary society. James Lull reminds us that:

> Adolescence marks a time in young people's lives when dramatic changes take place. Is a time of confusion and resistance. Popular music adapts well to the everyday life of adolescents, as the content of its lyrics and the atmosphere that can be created by sound reflects many of their concerns. Many young people use music in their struggles with rigid power holders such as parents, teachers, leaders and other influential figures. Generally, young people use music to resist authority at all levels, assert their loss, develop peer relationships and romantic ties.[3]

The new generations are psychologically predisposed to the languages of pop music and particularly sensitive to the influence of the mass media, broadcasting and disseminating their contents. In addition, adolescents (who by their very nature have a personality "in fieri", unstructured or linked to preexisting models) are significantly exposed to the influence of the mass media and open to new cultural values and forms. Young people themselves tend to be promoters of new values, trends, and lifestyles, determining processes of transformation and combining the cultural tradition to which they belong with forms of innovation that undermine preestablished patterns. Alberto Melucci argues that every generation feels like they have the need to do something with the world they live in, "it can be crushed, it can revolt, it can enter into conflict, or it can enter into a transformative relationship; it can combine in a certain way a certain amount of transformation, chemistry across elements of tradition to elements of innovation."[4] Continuity and change, conversation and rupture represent relevant characteristics in the processes of youth identity construction and are at the basis of all forms of generational conflict. These processes are clearly influenced by the social contexts of reference. The universe of youth, its expectations, relationship with the older generations, consumer behaviour itself are strongly influenced by the structural surroundings in which young people find themselves, by the ways in which society represents itself, by the proposed goals and ideals, by the collective project (if it exists) in which the individual's actions are inserted. The analysis of the condition of young people can, therefore, only start from the youth–adult relationship, with the caveat that the two terms of the relationship also change over time and vary with the changing genres, in parallel with social, economic, and cultural changes.[5]

The age of youth is commonly considered a transitional condition which progressively leads to the abandonment of adolescence and the simultaneous assumption of the functions and competences of adulthood. The times and ways in which this transition takes place are significantly influenced by historical, economic, and cultural contingencies:

---

[3] Lull, 1987, p. 152.
[4] Melucci, 1994, p. 134.
[5] de Lillo, 2007, p. 12.

The transition in contemporary societies is marked by the overcoming of thresholds, which are essential to be able to cover on a permanent basis those social conditions that distinguish the adult individual and differentiate them from the adolescent.[6]

Nowadays, this process of transition seems to extend exponentially, the category of young person seems to extend without time. The traditional distinctions by age group open up and the idea of youth expands. Each individual can perceive his or her condition as young as unfinished and even as unfinishable. In a context characterised by the fragmentation and crisis of the traditional categories of time and space, young people, who find themselves in a world where the access to the labour market is increasingly difficult and the labour market itself is increasingly precarious, "lengthen their condition as non-adolescents and non-adults." Canevacci says that this ritual of transition becomes endless: there is no longer that historical time as a certain moment when someone changes "status", but this time is pluralised and stretches without limits. The clear and fixed delimitation determined by objective social or linguistic (teen...ager) rules of being young has collapsed. One is no longer young in an objective or collective way, but transitive. People transit along a variable condition and indeterminable, some of them cross it according to modalities determined by the momentary individuality of the subject-youth, from the bargaining between its various, heterogeneous, multiple selves.[7]

From this point of view, young people increasingly live a "momentary individuality", they express themselves through multiple identities, in different and increasingly complex contexts, where their endowment of cultural and social capital becomes decisive in their interaction with the world. Using an analogy, Antonio de Lillo argues that the two cultural models prevalent among today's young people are those he defines as "the yachtsman" and "the surfer":

> Those who possess sufficient cultural and social capital to guarantee them control over the situations in which they find themselves living, are able not to let themselves be trapped by the fragmentary nature of their lives, but they always have some fixed reference point, which allows them not to lose their way, managing to manage the breadth of the boundaries of their identity. This does not happen to those who are socially or culturally deprived, to those who let themselves be carried away by the emotions or events of the moment, riding the wave, but not knowing if it will take them somewhere or overwhelm them. [...] The sailor knows how to steer his own boat, has a destination and follows a course, has the technical tools and knowledge necessary to cope with the difficulties of sailing. Being a surfer also requires skill, but you are much more dependent on the shape, height and direction of the wave you are "riding" and if you use a board that is not suitable for that type of wave it is almost inevitable that you will be swept away.[8]

---

[6] Buzzi, Cavalli, de Lillo, 2002, p. 20.
[7] Canevacci, 199, p. 31.
[8] de Lillo, 2007, p. 14.

This distinction of the youth universe, even if "simplified", explains how the study and understanding of the new generations is particularly complex. In this respect, and taking a step back, it is useful to recall the concept of "generation." According to Karl Mannheim,[9] "generation" is a sociological category that must be understood, by analogy with "class", as a social position. This collocation unites and conditions individuals born in the same period if they potentially share the same social events and if these experiences determine generational links between those exposed to the same situation. "The affinity of individuals depends on the availability of a limited historical-social space of possible experiences that involves the tendency to behave, feel and think in specific and recognisable ways or styles."[10] This process tends to occur when the exposure on crucial events occurs in the formative years, that is, those of youth.

Anyway, the meaning of generation can take on different connotations than simple belonging to a specific age group, for example, when referring to the Beat Generation or the generation of 68. In fact, as Loredana Sciolla states, it is not important to have the same age to be part of "that" generation: it is sufficient that individuals live their most formative years in the period of time considered relevant. In this case it is time, with the potential experiences and important events that characterise it, that represents the constitutive character of a generation.[11]

Mannheim[12] also points out (referring to the relationship between conservation and change) that each generation, in particular historical and social conditions, develops a distinctive identity, and that the natural alternation on the social–historical scene not only expresses a continuation of the social order; however, in the absence of specific circumstances and events, generations can also represent a factor of change and innovation.

The analysis of musical languages, lifestyles, and youth trends represents a privileged viewpoint to understand the new generations and the social changes young people are leading actors of.

4.2 Cultural studies and youth subcultures

Pop music, from the fifties onwards, brings on new fashions, customs, and habits that affect the universe of young people, with related social and economic repercussions. Even fashions, as phenomena of collective behaviour, are part of the processes of socialisation and identification of the new generations. Through them, young people tend to on one hand, take an original and distinctive stance vis-à-vis the system and, on the other hand, to gain the approval of others, recognition, and integration into the peer group. This mechanism also contributes to the formation of musical subcultures.

---

[9] Manheim, 1928.
[10] Sciolla, 2008, p. 10.
[11] *Ibidem*, p. 7
[12] Manheim, 1928.

4 Youth Cultures and the Social Role of Pop Stars

According to Gallino,[13] the "subculture" represents a subset of both material and immaterial cultural elements (values, knowledge, languages, norms of behaviour, lifestyles, and work tools) and is typically used by a given sector, segment, or layer of a society. It differs from counterculture, which is characterised by alternative structures and explicitly political and ideological forms that are in radical opposition to the dominant culture. The concept of subculture, one of the most successful in the sociological literature of popular music, suggests the idea of a close connection between music consumption and class membership. In the subcultural approach, music becomes a symbol that expresses the values of subordinate class groups that, through it, stand out from the rest of the society: mods, skinheads, teddy boys, punk, and so on. Music becomes a symbolic expression of alienation and deviance through the identification of a unique and different style. The subculture imposes itself as the style of a group, which attracts to it differs from the hegemonic culture.[14]

The main contributions to the cultural approach refer to the Centre for Contemporary Cultural Studies, founded at the University of Birmingham in 1964, England, and its Working Papers in Cultural Studies, culminating in Hall's and Jefferson Resistance through Rituals' collection of essays.

The perspective of cultural studies considers "culture" as something inextricably intertwined with the experiences and practices of social actors. Cultural forms reproduce themselves in the daily life of individuals and are constantly reformulated and innovated by them. A culture is such if it is socially shared; however, the same society can be home to different and conflicting cultural orientations: culture also represents a field of tensions, compromises, and permanent conflicts between different social groups.

In this sense, the scholars of the cultural studies explicitly manifest their interest in Gramsci's scientific work and his theoretical approach that culture is intended as a field of struggle for hegemony between classes. It is a perspective that underlines how subordinate classes are temporarily influenced by "superior" classes but also able to "resist" such influence. Culture expresses a constant multiplicity of orientations in the future, where the disappearance of certain "subcultures" is matched by the emergence of others such as, for example, the juvenile ones. Moreover, according to this approach, media and consumption seem to be the most effective instruments of the dominant classes to impose their hegemony on society. Their diffusion would tend to erode preexisting cultural differentiations and generate a homogenisation of tastes and orientations.[15]

The best-known book in this branch of studies is Dick Hebdige's *Subculture: The Meaning of Style*. According to the author, music represents a lifestyle and a response to class alienation. Between "style" and musical languages, between social choices and messages contained in pop music lyrics there is a relevant connection

---

[13] Gallino, 1978.
[14] Sibilla, 2003, p. 73.
[15] Jedlowski, 2009.

that determines a set of "meaningful practices." In reference to the mod subculture, Hebdige points out that "at some point when they came home from school or work, the mods disappeared: they were sucked into an underground of basements, discos, boutiques and record stores hidden under the layer of the normal world and in contrast to it."[16] It is an underground dimension thathelped build their "lifestyle" and identity. Hebdige's basic idea is that the peculiar values of a specific subgroup are a reflection of those expressed by a specific subgenre of pop music: consuming a certain type of music, in certain places, is a way of affirming one's identity. The users of pop music, of a specific genre, thus differentiate themselves from other listeners and the rest of society. This theoretical approach, of clearly Marxist origin, tends to underline the ideological function of music as a method of contrasting the "hegemonic culture": Drawing inspiration from the work of Roland Barthes, Hebdige considers the clothes and music of teddy boys, mods, skins, and Rastas as challenges to the symbolic order that paved the way for the even more aggressive antagonism of the punk style. This type of "semiotic guerrilla warfare" acts as a "noise" in the silent operation of the dominant ideology. Subcultures, therefore, become a "form of resistance in which the direct experience of objections to the dominant ideology is indirectly represented in the style."[17]

Hebdige is also the first to attempt to outline a study of the meanings of musical consumption, taking into account not only the sound aspects but also the visual and iconographic ones. However, the limit of the subcultural approach consists in the contradictory status attributed to music as such, without actually clarifying its position and meaning. The analysis of "Significant practices" reveals, in fact, its limits precisely in the inability to explicitly define the traits of homology between culture and musical text. Sarah Thornton also highlights how the classical studies of the Birmingham school place the media in opposition to and after the emergence of the subculture. In fact, Hebdige considers mass media, commerce, and related processes as ways to "incorporate" subcultures into a dominant culture that absorbs them, effectively demolishing them. According to Thornton, he tends to study already labelled social types (mods, rockers, skinheads, and punks), but does not pay systematic attention to the effects of various media labelling processes. Moreover, Hebdige's concept of mainstream is, according to the sociologist, abstract and nonhistorical: Hebdige and Mungham define subcultures and the mainstream as opposites of each other. Their being antithetical derives in part from the ideologies of high culture, of which the two formulations are part. Hebdige sees the mainstream as bourgeois and the youth subculture as artistic avant-garde. Mungham sees the mainstream as a stagnant "mass", and only the deviants and others are, to imply, creative and capable of change. Although the two definitions of mainstream are assigned to different class characteristics, both are devalued as a normal and conventional majority.[18]

---

[16] Hebdige, 1979.
[17] Thornton, 1995.
[18] *Ibidem*.

Rather than suggesting a comparative study, taking proper account of various social and economic factors and "comparing the ethical and political problems involved in celebrating the culture of a social group against another", according to Thornton, the theorists of the Birmingham school "invoke the chimera of a negative mainstream."[19] The sociologist believes that to study youth cultures it is appropriate to overcome the dualism between dominant ideologies and subversive subcultures, taking into account the role of the mass media in the processes of definition and labelling of subcultures. Furthermore, Thornton identifies subcultures in "cultures of taste" which, in turn, are identified in the media, through the media, and by the media. Thornton, therefore, clearly tends to overcome the binary dichotomies and oppositions proposed by Hebdige: avant-garde versus bourgeoisie, subordinate versus dominant, subculture versus mainstream, commercial versus alternative. According to the sociologist, there is, in fact, a dialectical relationship between the multiple factors in the field and the mass media contribute significantly to determine the formation and circulation of what, paraphrasing Bourdieu, Thornton defines "subcultural capital."

The following theoretical reflections offer a conceptual and terminological reformulation of the classical categories of the Birmingham school. To indicate the youth subcultures of late modernity, new expressions such as neo-tribes,[20] post-subculturalists,[21] lifestyle and scene[22] have been adopted. However, in the different sociological approaches to pop that refer to the school of Birmingham, "music is understood and studied above all as a product that reflects the culture of youth, in its rituals and myths; as a cultural factor of socialisation."[23] The most recent studies tend to go beyond the limits of the classical approach of cultural studies, preferring the idea that social actors have a relative autonomy, and that society is neither a place of a generalised consensus nor that of a permanent conflict, but rather the arena of an incessant and variously negotiated production and reproduction between the different actors, of the ways in which reality is interpreted and through which individuals act and express themselves.[24]

4.3 Youth, rap, and change

The transformation processes affecting late modernity have a strong impact on the new generations, and young people are among the main protagonists of the social and cultural transformations of our time. The progressive crisis of the traditional referents, certainties, and prospects for life, led to the disappearance of the "future" and of all forms of planning. Hopes and utopian expectations collapse, whereas the

---

[19] *Ibidem*.
[20] Bennett, 1999a.
[21] Muggleton, 2000.
[22] Bennett Peterson, 2004.
[23] Sibilla, 2003, p. 75.
[24] Jedlowski, 2009.

experience of the present time becomes central, *hic et nunc*, "living for the day." Bauman argues that "nowadays, everything seems to be conspiring against permanent certainties, projects that last a lifetime, forcing social actors to make choices and constantly re-assess their priorities."[25] The process of individualisation is increasingly characterised by the diffusion of a feeling of insecurity as a normal condition of daily life, which profoundly affects the sense of individual and collective identities, a scenario that Beck recalls in his books,[26] highlighting the deep crisis that affects contemporary society. The scholar highlights the current processes of gradual disintegration of classes, family, and traditional production units, focusing on new demands and new working conditions, which are accompanied by a constant sense of insecurity.[27]

Carmen Leccardi points out that when uncertainty increases beyond a certain threshold and almost identifies with everyday life, the traditionally understood planning capacity, that is the long-term "life project", is inevitably compromised.[28] The social acceleration and the climate of uncertainty that characterise the "second modernity", in addition to the crisis of "long-term projects", also tend to modify the temporal structure of identity, leading to processes of self-construction. However, some surveys[29] highlight how young people are open to react to the absence of certainties, elaborating responses capable of neutralising the fear of the future and clearly expressing the tendency to open up to unpredictability in a positive way. The new generations seem to consider the possibility of even sudden changes of course and of building responses in "real time", reacting to unpredictability. The speed and social rhythms of late modernity young people live with, allow them to "seize the moment" and to face the opportunities of the "here and now" as they arise.[30] For the new generations, the uncertainty of a future without a project implies the predisposition to identify possible solutions from time to time. The innovative aspect that seems to characterise the new generations is, therefore, "the ability to accept the fragmentation and uncertainty of the environment as a fact that cannot be eliminated, to be turned into assets through a constant exercise of awareness and reflexivity."[31]

The young people of the third millennium, increasingly, "stage" themselves and their inner world on social media and blogs, accessible to all users of the Network. Immersed in digital technologies, in an increasingly dissolved space–time dimension, and living in an age characterised by acceleration, they find themselves in a paradoxical condition of slowing down, of "prolonging youth", of "juvenile dilation." From a position of those who, through technological innovations, can "navigate" without limits, breaking down the barriers and constraints of time and space,

---

[25] Crespi, 2005, p. 10.
[26] Beck, 2000 and 2002.
[27] Crespi, 2005.
[28] Leccardi, 2005.
[29] Crespi, 2005.
[30] Leccardi, 2005.
[31] *Ibidem*, p. 57.

to a condition of imprisonment, in the cages of an increasingly dissolved time in a "diluted youth."[32] The difficulty of accessing labour market, of reaching economic autonomy and, therefore, of entering the world of adults, co-encourages young people not to choose, leaving them in a condition of "timeless youth."[33] In a complex society that is changing at great speed, that is experiencing significant transformations and is also characterised by profound territorial differences, the understanding of the world of youth is, for the social sciences, particularly relevant in interpreting change.

Musical languages, in addition to representing the main expressive models in which the new generations can be recognised, also seem to significantly characterise the contemporary world. Children of the "society of uncertainty,"[34] young people (who are known to being characterised by a scarce propensity for certainties or, in any case, by a vague sense of "indefiniteness" in the perception of their own identity and social position) represent, with their manifestations, language, and culture, an extraordinary indicator of late modernity.[35]

The new generations live in a reality built and inherited by others, often perceived as alien, but which is not the only one possible. Young people too often are precarious, uncertain, disoriented, and without stable points of reference. Young people who have never had "the ground beneath their feet", for whom every "instruction booklet" has always been only partial or anyway, "one of the many" feasible.[36] As Franco Ferrarotti says, they are the very same young people who have a primary need to belong to a recognisable herd and who have found the "home" in the music that they feel they no longer have elsewhere.[37] Behind the "organised noise" of the great rock concerts, according to Ferrarotti, hides a strong push towards utopia, an ancient desire for transcendence able to embrace this "people of evicted people." The status of evicted people is a condition not only physical, it upsets the soul, involves the mind, and makes one feel in a kind of no man's land, from where one leaves to look for other places, other spaces, and new references. Music is a language that aggregates and welcomes young evicts, helping them find new places. "Living" music means to look for a place other than the parish or the party headquarters. A place where the rhythm of rock, often criticised as "evanescent", "ephemeral", does not give elements for planning, but certainly inspires it, unlike party politics that do not contain the germs of utopia that young people thirst for.

Thornton states that youth subcultures (where subcultures mean "cultures of taste") are essentially musical subcultures.[38] Young people listen to more music than anyone else. Television for new generations is largely music television, just as new media are increasingly used to listen to music. Young people's leisure time and

---

[32] Savonardo, 2007a.
[33] Dal Lago, Molinari, 2001.
[34] Bauman, 1999.
[35] Pecchinenda, 2001.
[36] *Ibidem.*
[37] Ferrarotti, 1996.
[38] Thornton, 1995.

identity increasingly revolve around different sound languages. These considerations are largely supported by the results of the most recent studies on the condition of young people in Italy. The centrality of music in the daily life of new generations is a constant accompaniment and soundtracks during the day of the very young at various times. Moreover, as Maria Teresa Torti recalls, contrary to the current stereotypes that link the consumption of popular music to areas of mere escape and homologated entertainment reserved for young people with few resources, recent surveys place music as a qualifying dimension of the process of existential evaluation and of the path of growth and socialisation of young people.[39] In a nutshell, paraphrasing a famous song by the singer–songwriter Edoardo Bennato, they are not "just songs."

In the mid-eighties, a new form of expression and social denunciation exploded in the world, originating in the seventies and starting from musical sounds such as rap and hip hop, to assume, in Italy, with the movement of posse, new and surprising connotations, contaminated by the sounds, words, and rhythms of urban reality. Rap becomes the language and the most effective tool to communicate the malaise and discomfort of young people, attracting them to themes such as marginalisation, unemployment, fight against the mafia, and rocket attacks. The rappers, moreover, to make their lyrics more direct and disruptive socially and politically committed, recover the dialect by rediscovering the musical and cultural memory of our country, in a process of reconstruction of a territorial identity and a sense of belonging, which is also expressed through contamination with "other" cultures. Rap, an expression of hip hop culture, takes its origins from the sounds of Jamaican reggae and develops in the United States, and then spreads all over the world, from the Bronx to Scampia, taking on new characteristics in different contexts, and giving rise to multiple forms of musical hybridisation. As Chambers points out:In New York, towards the end of the seventies, young people of color permeated with the same culture that generated graffiti artists with spray cans and "break dancing" acrobats, used the simplest and most popular equipment in the field of sound recording (cymbals and microphones) and transformed them into real musical instruments. Rap is the sound system of New York: the culture of young black people in Harlem and the Bronx that successfully transforms technology into a new cultural form. Rap is the sound graffiti, a musical spray that blends the black rhythms and verbal gymnastics of the street jargon with the flow of words that a tightrope walker disc jockey churns out while manipulating the turntable platter.[40]

The sounds, rhythms, melodies, and noises of urban realities represent the wise sound in which rappers express themselves. They represent cultural spaces where the centre and periphery mix, in a simultaneously diachronic and synchronic path, where past, present, and future coexist. Urban scenarios where the disruptive force of the languages of that young universe emerges in a significant way (the ones that, amid discomforts and uncertainties, starting from increasingly glocal contexts, such as Naples), at the same time periphery and centre of the world seems to shout out loud

---

[39] Torti, 2002.
[40] Chambers, 1985.

"nuje vulimme 'na speranza", just like the rappers Nto' and Lucariello in the end track of the TV series inspired by Gomorrah by Roberto Saviano.

The urban reality of Naples, which has always lived the condition of territory "in transit", border, hybrid place, and crossroads of different cultures, in a dichotomous process characterised by strong localisms and openings and outward leaps, represents an interesting example of a postmodern city. A city where contaminations are dominant and musical expressions, from Arabonapoletan Arabic–Neapolitan melodies to Afro–American, and metropolitan rhythms, manifest themselves through the same moods and drives of the community. In Naples, these processes along with the characteristics of the territory, contributed to nourish that unique, unpublished musical panorama, which has given shape to expressions that are often very different, but which can be traced back to the same matrix of volcanic and magmatic nature.

Living under the volcano is a daily reminder of one's own mortality, this is perhaps the key to the schizophrenic energy of the city, its languages of exultation and despair, its extremes of physical violence and mental resignation. In Naples, one is constantly aware of not simply living an urban experience, but of living urban life as a problem, question, and provocation. By building and reassuring itself through words, the city is constantly caught between lamenting about the past and fantasies about the future, whereas the present sometimes goes unnoticed, abandoned. Naples is ineluctably transformed from a self-referential monument to an intersection, a moment of encounter, a place of transit, and centre and periphery of a wider network. Separated from its moorings, the city begins to drift, to enter into other contexts. Naples is perhaps the symbol of the city struggling, of the city as a crisis. The city does not stop to be framed by a unique, rational, static scheme, but escapes predictable schemes to become a floating signifier, moving between a hundred interpretations and a thousand stories. Gateway to the South, a virtual bridge that creates openings, ruptures, and exchanges towards other worlds, centre of a strong marginality and spearhead of a cultural universe, Naples expresses itself, however and since ever, as a proactive and productive place where, the invention starting from "other" cultures allows to mark other traces, paths, and cultural and musical projects.

The Neapolitan song, in its different forms, has always told, documented, and represented the thousand faces of Naples, its segments, systems, subsystems, stratifications, and modifications that have characterised the history of the city. Moreover, the diffusion of Neapolitan song in the world, through the musical editions of the sector, has given birth to the first forms of cultural industry on an international level. Looking carefully at the lyrics, music, and interpretations, it is evident how much the song functions as a "seismograph" of urban reality, recording transformations and changes towards continuous references to social, everyday life, the community, news events, but also to different cultural contaminations. The "facts" of the collective are "staged" according to the plots of a sociality that is based on two orders of reference: on one hand there is membership, forced or smug, that is, a restricted and contextualised location, whereas on the other there is a sort of openness, which can reach bewilderment, where (for better or worse) the cultural and then musical influences of other paradigms of humanity are accepted. This last aspect seems particularly interesting: it expresses a postmodern behaviour, in which the "song" merges different cultural and musical experiences, adopting and reworking on them liberally. Analysing the song means, therefore, to manipulate a kind of taxonomic system of cultural universes, worlds, and world views that cost a lot of money. The many facets of that particular and complex kaleidoscope, that is Naples.

The languages of creativity, urban cultures, and youth subcultures that characterise the Neapolitan city and Campania are many. The sounds, rhythms, and melodies of artists such as Almamegretta, 99 Posse, A67, Co'Sang, Lucariello, Clementino, and Rocco Hunt (just to name a few recent examples), break the harmony of oleographic melodies to give voice to an expressive alphabet where dialect is a breaking code and challenges mainstream languages. In this sense, Naples shows itself as a place of contradiction to the homologation of the rest of the country.

The city has always been the cradle of a peculiar artistic effervescence that is expressed through an interesting musical variety, ranging from traditional melodic song, recognised and appreciated all over the world, to the reality of neomelodic music, expression of a subculture of alleys, passing through the research in the tradition of Roberto De Simone and the Nuova Compagnia di Canto Popolare, classical song of Roberto Murolo, irony of Renato Carosone, strong rock of Edoardo Bennato, Mediterranean blues of the "half-black" Pino Daniele, multiethnic soul of the scugnizzo Nino D'angelo and musical production of 99 Posse and Almamegretta, expression of a subcultural metropolitan subculture that the Co'Sang, and A67 of Scampia, through the languages of rap and not only, "stage" from one of the most controversial districts of the city. According to Chambers, the hip hop culture, different characteristics and dimensions of rap, which exploded as a phenomenon in the late 1980s, were already incubating in previous decades: the global presence of rap music declined in thousands of local dialects; the complete fusion of technique and language where the means of musical reproduction (the micro-phone, the turntable, the sampler, the computer) become the tools of musical production, while the mediator (the DJ) becomes the medium; the perpetual search for different sounds under the label of 'World Music'; the full realisation of the metropolitan aesthetics of collage and DIY;[41] the languages of hip hop are the result of technological evolutions and artistic and social processes that, from reggae to funk, rock to dance, have favoured the development of new creative trends.

Rap represents one of the many expressive languages of young people with "different identities" or always in search of an identity, protagonists of a sort of "cultural nomadism" and children of the "global village." Young people who, together, go to Seattle, Prague, Genoa, or Porto Alegre, to the World Social Forum, to challenge and utopically stop globalisation, a "modern form of colonisation" and "exploitation of man on man" of which they themselves are an expression. "Leftist extremists, priests, ecologists, anarchists, boy-scouts, fans of Bob Marley and John Lennon, rave-goers,

---

[41] Chambers, 1985.

social centres, fans of St. Francis and those of Che Guevara, students of economics and training systems, computer hackers and organic food growers",[42] the so-called "Seattle pole" or "no global" seems to be, in short, made up of subjects belonging to different categories that give life to a sort of unprecedented transversal social chain. Music reaffirms its role as a unifying flag, driving force, and soundtrack of a common social path. The youth with its music groups and its fans is inscribed in collective phenomena and makes music its own flag. These phenomena produce a modification of the interaction among the subjects that are part of it, in which solidarity and a collective social consciousness are awakened. Music, therefore, as an instrument of cohesion and expression of a sort of anti-individualising retribalisation of those who oppose, for example, global homologation.[43]

Children of the so-called society of uncertainty, of all possible realities and none at all, of an increasingly insistent disorientation, young people find in the music an instrument of identification, aggregation, and, sometimes, liberation from anxiety and conflict.

Unavoidable conflicts in those who, looking for their roots which are increasingly difficult to identify, experience new paths towards new cultural coordinates and generate new expressive models which, for the social sciences, represent important signals for understanding change. Musical and artistic hybridisations represent a significant indicator of the social and cultural transformations taking place in an increasingly hybrid society, where the development of communications, media, and digital technologies has caused a violent acceleration of the processes of contamination between different forms of language.[44]

The new "urban poets", the latest generation rappers who feed on the contamination of different artistic languages and digital technologies, give life and voice to the Bit Generation, which expresses itself, communicates, socialises, and creates a new sound narration of urban and social reality through social media.

4.4 Bit Generation

The changes that affect communication technologies significantly influence the forms of socialisation, consumption, and lifestyles of the new generations, and influence the social dynamics that affect the youth universe.

There are many definitions attributed to the "young" generations, in historical, social, and cultural moments, consumption of specific technologies or in reference to particular marketing strategies: Generations X, Y, MTV, C, Net, App Generation, and digital natives, just to name a few. However, in agreement with Fausto Colombo who, in collaboration with Giovanni Boccia Artieri and other scholars, has published an in-depth study on the relationship between media and generations in Italy,

---

[42] Jovanotti, 2000, p. 17.
[43] Savonardo, 2001.
[44] *Ibidem.*

"many of the definitions or labels of the national marketing (although useful to ask the question of the role of the media in the construction of the various generations) are sometimes overlooked, and must be taken by sociology more as a stimulus than as real interpretative categories."[45]

The complexity of the multiple factors that influence and intervene in the construction of the experiences and identities of the different generations must not, in fact, be reduced by deterministic and defining approaches. We must consider the dialectic and mutual influence of the different elements that come into play, to be able to grasp the universe of youth in its different dimensions.

Aware of the limits that definitions and simplifications determine, the expression Bit Generation means (although it might be tricky to give a satisfactory definition) the youth universe, feeding and expressing through "software culture",[46] immersed in "tertiary sensoriality" and in that "connective" and hypertextual ideas,[47] typical of the digital experience.[48] In this perspective, we do not wonder (paraphrasing banally two wise men who have characterised the scientific debate) "if the Internet makes us stupid"[49] or "why the Net makes us intelligent"[50], but what are the "influences"[51] (rather than the impact) of the "digital experience" of digital technologies on different forms of communication, socialisation, consumption, and youth cultural production.[52] This expression was also chosen due to the explicit reference to the Beat Generation, the literary and musical art movement that developed between the 1950s and 1960s in the United States. This movement contributed to determining expressive, cultural, social, and political forms meaningful for the youth universe of those years, significantly influencing subsequent generations and the sociological debate on youth.

Beat was rebellion, beat, and rhythm, the beat of jazz music, of be-bop, and of the cadence of the verses in the poems. Beat was the discovery of oneself, life on the road, sexual freedom, drugs, human values, and collective consciousness. Nowadays, Beat is connection, sharing, and participation. The Bit Generation, with its expressive and creative languages, is influencing contemporary societies as well as the young protagonists of the Beat Revolution have characterised, on the cultural, social, and artistic levels, the historical period from the 1940s to the 1970s.

The expression Beat was coined by Jack Kerouac in 1948 in an interview during which, talking about past generations and not wanting to attribute any definition to his own, Kerouac said: "Ah, this is nothing but a Beat generation." The conversation was then published in 1952 in the New York Times Magazine under

---

[45] Colombo, 2012, pp. 19–20.
[46] Manovich, 2008.
[47] de Kerckhove, 1997, 2001 and 2004.
[48] Savonardo, 2013.
[49] Carr, 2010.
[50] Rheingold, 2012.
[51] Lévy, 1997.
[52] de Kerckhove, 2016.

the title "This is the Beat generation", which drew the public's attention to the literary and cultural movement that reached extraordinary popularity in the late 1950s. The cult reference book of this movement is Kerouac's *On the road*, written in 1951 and published in 1957. The novel describes the lives of the young people of the Beat Generation and their unscrupulous, wild, and free world view. An autobiographical novel that represents a new approach to writing and recounts epic car journeys across the American continent, mixing extraordinary landscapes, a deep and new sense of friendship, the poetic and romantic idea of freedom and intensity of life, through encounters with marginalised people, intellectuals and workers, amid new musical and cultural trends. The Beat Generation rebels against the traditional cultural and social formalities, starting and feeding the fight against racism, for the emancipation of women, for sexual freedom, for the rebellion of the marginalised. The movement emerged at Columbia University in 1943, when a group of students, poets, writers, including Jack Kerouac (1922–1969), Allen Ginsberg (1926–1997), and William Burroughs (1914–1997) began to hang out, artists and intellectuals who express themselves with visionary and psychedelic texts, through political instances, such as Marxism, but also anarchy and, in general, rebellion against conformism. They are the main actors and proponents of the Beat Revolution, which anticipates the other Cultural Revolution, that of 1968. The world was changing and the Beat Generation carried the flag of change high, through visionary ideals, in an America struggling with the Cold War, with the fight against communism and repression, in a society "without hopes and without a future", characterised by a thousand contradictions, constantly threatened by the risk of a nuclear conflict, driven on one hand by unbridled consumption and on the other by conformist models of life. The sense of uneasiness and anxiety runs through the consciences of the new generations who reject modern society as a block, estranging themselves from everything and closing themselves in an exclusive world, with an attitude that does not aim to demolish institutions but simply to deny the falsehood of the community and evade social schemes. Behind their provocative attitudes, there is no ideological will to change the social system, but detachment. Escape, travel, and nomadism, the intellectual attitude that inspires them, pushes them to accept life in its free flow, rejecting conformism for a spontaneous and free sociality.

The Beat Generation is expressed through the traditional media and thanks to them, they divulge their own artistic and cultural productions, vision of the world, and the political and social demands of which it has been the bearer. Today, the Bit Generation is increasingly expressed through digital media. Young people of the third millennium are among the main users of new technologies. They navigate, create, communicate, express themselves, give life to artistic productions that feed (unconsciously) from past, present, and future, attracting new interactive tools. The "children of virtual flowers", surfers of the Internet, for whom "accelerated change" represents a predetermined datum, seem to master these technological tools and the different opportunities offered by the Net, even if sometimes they ignore the risks. The sociologist Amato Lamerti defines the young as "androids" from the "electronic body", which use the technologies as an extension of the senses, but also of the "mind" and of their "thoughts."[53] That same "digital thought" de Kerckhove refers to in analysing how the human mind has transformed itself with the use of increasingly evolved communication tools, in the transition from a mass society to a networked society.

As pointed out in the previous chapter, the new technologies have deeply reconfigured the scenario where the consumption and cultural practices are expressed; a reconfiguration that has significantly affected the new generations, contributing to the definition of new forms of socialisation and communication. Young people anticipate changes, express them, determine them, and are the main protagonists.

The development of mass and digital media played a pivotal role in the diffusion of youth cultures and movements which, since the 1960s, have almost always been accompanied by a significant social and civil commitment. However, in reference to political participation in recent decades, young people seem to have lost their social and political subjectivity, increasingly recalling what Ilvo Diamanti defines as the "invisible generation",[54] a generation that is difficult to identify from a social point of view and apparently very distant from the scenarios of youth political participation in 1968. Young people appear to be self-absorbed, less idealistic, ready to identify strategies for adaptation to a society that is increasingly fragmented and characterised by a global economic and social crisis. The new generations find themselves overwhelmed by a process of transformation that involves society, behaviour models, and the sphere of values and ideologies (and therefore of politics), a transformation that plunges young people into a condition of isolation, disorientation, and uncertainty, and that pushes them to distance themselves from the traditional politics that cannot adequately represent their needs.

These considerations should be placed in a broader analysis that takes into account the complexity of the factors that characterise the youth universe, also in relation to the development of communication technologies and the crisis of traditional forms of participation. The most recent social, logical, and political studies, but also the new forms of youth protest and dissent, show that disaffection towards politics does not necessarily correspond to a lack of interest in civil commitment. Political socialisation (bringing not only processes of individual construction of a civic identity but also allows democratic political culture to reproduce itself) passes through new forms of collective action which contain, as a whole, a certain amount of "political" commitment and which scholars now define as "unconventional participation" in its moderate and/or radical forms.

According to Ulrich Beck, there is an opening of the boundaries of politics, a sort of migration of politics from institutional spheres to other sectors not directly connected to it, a shift in the attention of young people from ideological content to everyday practices.[55] It would be appropriate to ask ourselves whether we can really speak

---

[53] Lamberti, 2004.
[54] Diamanti, 1999.
[55] Beck, 1986.

of an "invisible generation", bent on its own subjectivity, or rather of a generation that has moved its interests elsewhere, through new paths, forming and structuring social identity in new ways.[56] Moreover, the languages, expression, and communication skills of the new generations change rapidly, triggering transformations that traditional politics seems unable to grasp.

The generations of the third millennium and the different movements that represent them, increasingly, find in the Net a relevant instrument of civil, social, and political participation of amplification of dissent and of response to the economic and existential crisis.

The Net is turning into a real digital marketplace: it is a juncture, and not a replacement for the real one, a telematic agora in which politics and citizenship are discussed and which makes the young users of the Web visible also on the social scene. The political movements that also developed through digital media, such as the Meetup and the Five Star Movement of Beppe Grillo (www.beppegrillo.it), have populated the Italian squares with hundreds of people, generating a particularly significant youth participation, online and offline, and playing a central role in the political debate, also with important electoral consequences. This participation, which received considerable media exposure, has been, due to its protest tone and the way it is not exactly in line with the traditional language of politics, welcomed as an expression of antipolitics or "qualunquismo." However, these phenomena represent, more likely, a tangible sign of an epochal change in the forms of social and civil participation of young people who no longer seem to recognise themselves in a political and institutional system in crisis and are unable to cope with the changes and innovations that are sweeping the world.

Traditional politics is far removed from young people who keep declaring they do not trust governments, political parties, and institutions, as well as downgrade political activity among the last places on the scale of values. Yet, as the most recent studies on the world of youth show, the rejection of politics by the younger generation is not simply a response to the "crisis of values" or the diffusion of individualism. On the contrary, it goes hand in hand with a sense of solidarity and commitment to the increasingly widespread remoteness, which shows a strong interest in social participation and civil commitment, in nontraditional forms. The new generations seem to move on small local objectives, from the fight against the TAV to the waste emergency, showing how the Net is not only a communication tool, but a totally new political model: a form of direct democracy, from the bottom up, that manages to skip the mediation of the professional politicians. From the V-day, promoted by Grillo, to the electoral success of the Five Star Movement, young people show that they discovered new forms of active social participation through the Net.

The intolerance and lack of interest in political life arise from the difficulty of understanding its meaning through obsolete and complex rituals and languages,

---

[56] Caputo, 2007.

which the new communication methods tend to simplify. Moreover, the discomfort and de-orientation of young people are probably due to the more general crisis of the social and political systems which, inevitably, strongly affects and conditions the dynamics that regulate the universe of youth. In a world that changes so fast, where innovations and accelerations invest and influence the languages of the Bit Generation, which seem to interpret and anticipate change, politics, in addition to giving concrete answers, we should rethink the ways of communication, adopting new forms of expression, closer to the youth universe.

The openness of young people to new forms of communication, the widespread technical ability to use them, their predisposition to sociality seems to be in contrast with fears of solipsistic withdrawal often overshadowed by those who tend to emphasise the risk of isolation induced by a continuous use of computing or smartphones, but brings with it new potential pathologies. Anyway, young people appear open-minded, curious about the new, and above all interested in communication with their peers. The Internet, in fact, is an extraordinary tool to build relationships, in a web galaxy increasingly populated by a generation of very young people who, right on the Net, build their networks and, therefore, that social capital on which they feed even in real life. Bourdieu says that if the social capital is "the set of actual or potential resources linked to the possession of a stable network of more or less institutionalised relationships"[57] of mutual knowledge and recognition, and if it is incorporated in the relationships among people, web communities are potentially a particularly effective tool to generate and feed the social capital of Web users, even if, in this case, it is more difficult to speak of "stable relationships", considering the "liquidity" of the Net. The diffusion of the Web and the possibilities of interaction offered by ICT seem to contribute, therefore, to the creation of social capital but also to strengthen democratic possibilities and civic engagement, so the connection Internet–citizenship–democracy could be a virtuous circle. Young people are the promoters of this change even if they use the Internet mainly to create friendly relationships and/or as a medium of communication and are not always aware of the potential risks that the Web hides. Risks, in part already underlined in the previous chapter, which refer, for example, to the different forms of dependence on digital technologies or to the protection of one's privacy, in the delicate relationship between the public sphere and private dimension, are increasingly unstable.

The new digital technologies and their use seem to put into question the classic categories with which we interpret the world. Our routines and modes of interaction in everyday life change, where the private sphere is increasingly confused with the public sphere and the traditional dimensions of space and time seem to be in crisis. Through the use of social media, young people live the daily experience overlapping the public and private dimensions, and vice versa, in a continuous game of constant cross-references and intersections.

---

[57] Bourdieu, 1980, p. 2.

Giovanni Boccia Artieri points out that the Net represents a cultural device that incorporates a dual perspective: a tension between public and private and at the same time a new "public" dream that produces, distributes and consumes with the awareness of being public in public. Meaning, with the awareness of being in an environment where links, relationships and the possibility to address an indistinct public intertwine in a new mixture that produces relevant ways of representing one's own sphere (of interest, motivations, impulses, etc.).[58] This cultural phenomenon particularly affects the processes of social construction of individual identities which, in the case of the new generations, are clearly being defined. The youth age is commonly considered a transitory condition, of transition, from adolescence to adulthood. This condition in constant becoming favours the predisposition to change and places young people, who are clearly in training and with an as yet unstructured personality, in a continuous dialectic between routine and innovation.

In a society where everything changes quickly, innovation seems to be routine. As Gabriella Paolucci points out, "the familiar, the habit, the known", no longer seem to consist of the "always the same", how much from "always new." In a nutshell, the new is becoming "ordinary"[59] and young people have to deal with this form of "routinized innovation." The same personality on training, in transit, not yet structured, allows the new generations to manage change, reacting to the unpredictability of events and innovation processes. A response to uncertainty and crisis is represented by creativity, a resource young people are significantly endowed with, and which is expressed not only in art, but in all social and cultural spheres.

Popular music turns out to be an instrument of social connection for young people and the pop stars in which they recognise themselves represent, if anything, significant points of reference for their growth. The next paragraph focuses on the social role of rock stars.

4.5 Symbolic power of the rock star

The purpose of this chapter is to open new perspectives on the social role that artists play in pop music. In particular, starting from the conceptual categories expressed by Pierre Bourdieu and in relation to the wider debate on the subject, the paragraph focuses on the symbolic and cultural power of pop stars in contemporary society.

According to Bourdieu,[60] within "social fields", individuals occupy different positions, depending on the type and amount of resources available to them, in terms of social, cultural, and economic capital. These positions are closely linked to the "power" that the individual holds. Power is less pervasive and affects different types

---

[58] Boccia Artieri, 2012, p. 13.
[59] Paolucci, 2007, p. 136.
[60] Bourdieu, 1979.

of actions and encounters. In fact, even though there is a general tendency to associate power with the political sphere, individuals also commonly cite other forms of power that have little or nothing to do with politics and the state. They express or help establish relatively strong relationships or networks of power and domination, between individuals or groups of individuals, who occupy different positions in the fields of interaction.

Symbolic power comes from the activity of producing, transmitting and recreating symbolic forms with meaning. Symbolic activity is a fundamental aspect of social life and affects all forms of interactions between individuals. According to Bourdieu, symbolic systems not only exercise functions of communication and social integration, but also represent powerful tools of domination as true constituent agents of reality. [61] The very tight connection between social and cognitive structures is thus configured as "one of the most solid guarantees of social domination", because it can "come into the world, acting on the representation of the world."[62] As Gabriella Paolucci still reminds us, according to Bourdieu, symbolic power exerts the most effective form of violence we can conceive: it forces the "dominated" to actively collaborate in their domination. Through the concept of symbolic violence, Bourdieu emphasises the active collaboration of the dominated to the mechanisms of domination, which is exercised through incorporated forms of existing power relations, which appear as "natural" relationships.

John B. Thompson emphasises that, in symbolic practices, individuals use different types of resources to fix and transmit information, recognition, and respect. In producing symbolic forms, actors perform actions that can intervene in the course of events: "Symbolic actions can provoke reactions, induce others to act or respond in certain ways, [...] to assert their support for a state of affairs or to raise a collective revolt."[63]

For Thompson, as for Bourdieu, the "symbolic power" refers to the ability to influence the actions of other individuals and to create events, producing and transmitting symbolic forms. Although symbolic activity is a pervasive aspect of social life, there are several institutions that, throughout history, have taken on a particularly important role in the accumulation of tools for knowledge, information, and communication: religious institutions, educational institutions, and institutions of communication, whose function is the large-scale production and overall dissemination in space and time of symbolic forms.

Among the main languages of communication, music (cultured or popular, traditional or innovative) has always contributed significantly to the processes of construction and consolidation of symbolic content. The role of pop stars in the field of music, as testimonials and through their songs, is becoming more and more important in the promotion of consumer products and in relation to specific social, institutional, and political communication campaigns: this shows how the symbolic power they

---

[61] Paolucci, 2009.
[62] Bourdieu, Wacquant, 1992b, p. 123.
[63] Thompson, 1995.

express and the consensus they produce is increasingly pervasive, in relation to the social, institutional, and political world, in reference to audiences and the sociocultural contexts they address. Think, for example, of the artists who, in the United States, take part in presidential campaigns in support of one or other candidate, directing consensus; the use of pop stars and their songs in advertising, and directing consumption; the social and civil commitment to environmental protection of artists such as Sting; or the initiatives for the cancellation of the public debt of Third World countries promoted by Bono Vox of U2, just to mention a few particularly significant international cases. These activities spring multiple reactions among the various audiences (consensus and dissent, approval and criticism, and support and boycott) in relation to the various stakeholders they directly or indirectly address and with reference to the various interests in the field.

These specific activities of pop stars, which strictly speaking go beyond musical activities, can be read from the Bourdieusian perspective, according to which the relationship between the "field of power" and the "intellectual field" has always been particularly meaningful. To better understand this relationship, it is necessary to take into account, first of all, the fundamental dichotomous expression in the analysis of the French sociologist: "dominant/dominated." Bourdieu uses the terms "domains", "dominant", "dominated" and the expressions "dominated fractions of the dominant classes" or "dominant fractions of the dominated classes" also with regard to the relations between "intellectual field" and "power field." More precisely, he focuses on the socially constituted habitus of artists and writers, on their positions within the intellectual field, in a given epoch and in a given society and, therefore, on the relative "aesthetic or ideological positions objectively connected to the positions occupied."[64] For Bourdieu, as the intellectual and artistic field acquires autonomy and, at the same time, the social status of producers of symbolic goods increases, the intellectuals progressively enter into the game of conflicts between fractions of the dominant class on their own account, and no longer only by proxy or delegation. With the growing autonomy of the artistic field and the development of the market for symbolic goods, the purely intellectual characteristics of the producers of these goods acquire greater explanatory force. In reference to France at the end of the 19th century, the sociologist divided the intellectual and artistic field into three strands: "social art", "art for art" and "bourgeois art":

> The "bourgeois" (dominant-dominated) artists and writers enjoy the recognition of the bourgeois public (sometimes obtaining almost bourgeois living conditions) and therefore, they feel entitled to consider themselves as spokespersons of their own class, to which their work is directly addressed. Instead, the proponents of "social" (dominant-dominated) art find in their economic condition and in their social exclusion the foundation of solidarity with the dominated classes, solidarity whose first principle is always hostility towards the dominant fractions of the dominant classes and their

---

[64] Bourdieu, 1971.

representatives in the intellectual field. Supporters of art for art occupy a structurally ambiguous position in the intellectual field [...] The position where they find themselves forces them to think of their aesthetic or political identity in opposition to both "bourgeois" artists [...] and "socialist" artists or bohemian artists [...]. Depending on the political conjuncture, these contrasts can be simultaneous or consecutive.[65]

If this distinction emerges from the observation of France at the end of the 19th century, the contemporary art field would no longer seem to reflect the tripartite nature of bourgeois, social and art for art. According to Marco d'Eramo, the collapse of the Eastern regimes led to the disappearance of that figure, central in the twentieth century, of the "dissident intellectual" who proposed himself symmetrically to the East and West. Instead, a bland form of bourgeois art thrived, especially with regard to the anxiety of social recognition and economic integration: "Art for art aimed at deferred recognition (fame after death). Today the criterion of glory seems to have disappeared, replaced by that of success. But the success does not admit a true autonomy of the aesthetic, so the modern artist mimics the disinterest of the artist who creates inspired."[66]

More generally (also with reference to the social role of artists and the relationship between the field of power and the intellectual field), it should be stressed that it is no longer possible to trace the reflection on the dynamics of power back to a monolithic vision of the dominant class, meant as a homogeneous and shared group that produces and reproduces, in a constant process of sound construction, the ideology necessary to legitimise the status quo. This traditional definition does not, in fact, take into account the complexity of the stratification processes in contemporary society.

The dominant class cannot be univocally conceptualised, for at least two reasons: the complexity of the criteria on which the processes of social exclusion and inclusion are based; and the fact that there is no dominant class identifiable as such, but rather several social groups that compete with each other in a constant process of negotiation of mutual power. In this sense, the material bases of ideologies are no longer reducible exclusively to the social class. In this direction, the strand of studies on subcultures is expressed, with particular reference to youth and musical cultures. According to the approach of the cultural studies of the Birmingham School, in fact, the very concept of subculture subverts any class membership.

In any case, the present analysis has as background the theoretical framework of Richard Middleton, who considers popular music as a cultural phenomenon and pop culture as the ground on which the main social transformations take place. Starting from the School of Birmingham, all sociological approaches to pop music are oriented to the study of musical phenomena as products of youth culture and popular music as a cultural factor of socialisation, recognition, and construction of individual

---

[65] *Ibidem*.
[66] d'Eramo 2002, pp. 24–25.

and collective identities. In this perspective, according to Middleton, the rock star represents the centre of what we can call the sphere of identification.[67] Young people from different eras and contexts recognise and identify themselves in the popstar to which they refer, following a specific musical genre or subgenre, whether it is an expression of the dominant or "alternative" culture.

Moreover, some genres or musical productions represent a clear expression of the rejection of traditional politics by new generations and tend to awaken collective social consciousness, staging forms of solidarity and civil commitment. Think, for example, of the language of rap, used by young people to communicate malaise and discomfort, against a social system that generates marginalisation, unemployment, malfeasance, and racism. In this sense, pop music is a significant tool for reaction and cohesion.

In this context, the symbolic actions that can be traced back to the protagonists of the star system could contribute, recalling Thompson, to solicit reactions, induce others to act or respond in certain ways,[68] for example, by encouraging the consumption of a particular product of the market. Directly or indirectly, artists of recognised reputation (thanks to their social role, reputation, prestige, and credibility) have the potential to induce their fans to assert their knowledge for a state of affairs or to rise up in a collective revolt.[69]

The processes of "mass seduction", operated also through pop stars and with particular reference to different youth audiences, can encourage significant reactions, depending on the social, economic, and cultural contexts of belonging.

In contemporary societies, this form of power is closely connected to the role of the media, which, to a greater or lesser extent, contribute to amplify and spread artistic and cultural productions, enhancing the capability for persuasion and seduction of the artists themselves. The capability is linked to the social reputation deriving from the artistic activity and its related (and possibly future) prestige, to the recognition and media visibility, but also to the authenticity and credibility expressed by the musical production, and not only, of pop or rock stars.

As already pointed out, according to Simon Frith,[70] "rock" can be traced back to a period of musical production when music itself has romantically placed the value of "authenticity" in the foreground, attempting (at least in theory) not to get involved with industry and the media. In this sense, rock has been characterised by a sort of "ideology of authenticity" and a significant "opposition" to pop music, understood as "light", disengaged, entertainment, and commercial. A contrast that is very often only ideal (considering that rock is a product of the market, as is pop music), and that with the change in record production systems, the transformations of the cultural industry and the contamination between different musical genres has gradually faded.

---

[67] Middleton, 1990.
[68] Thompson, 1995.
[69] *Ibidem.*
[70] Frith, 1978.

That said, the rock concert represents a new social ritual, a "place" of collective aggregation and sharing and the artist is increasingly a point of reference, repository of truth, model to recognise yourself, model to be a part of the world, "new prophet" to whom you entrust your emotions. A "prophet" that Pink Floyd, in their concept album The Wall in 1979 and in the 1982 film of the same name, provocatively denounce as a potential "dictator", underlining the increasingly "omnipotent" role of the rock star, capable of guiding and orienting the masses, in a context in which the consumer and communication society and the star system follow the logic of the market, pushing the artist to do the same. It is a vision that recalls the processes of homologation and standardisation and Adornian theories on popular music and the cultural industry.

Since the second half of the last century, pop music concerts have increasingly represented real collective rituals with an international character (from the first performances of Elvis or The Beatles to the more recent phenomena of "stardom" expressed by Madonna, Michael Jackson, or Lady Gaga) and different musical expressions have often taken on political and social values inspired by a new solidarity. For example, we can think of concerts for developing countries, such as the Live Aid of 1985, promoted by artist Bob Geldof, or those for the protection of the environment, such as the Live Heart of 2007, conceived by Al Gore, former vice president of the United States, or the different forms of solidarity of the music world in favour of populations affected by natural disasters, just to cite a few examples.[71] In this sense, it is useful to mention the activism of many Italian arts such as the singer–songwriter Luciano Ligabue who, for the Ministry of the Environment, in 2007, promoted, with his interpretation of the song "And yet it blows" by Pierangelo Bertoli, the awareness campaign for the protection of protected areas or that, as testimonial of Amnesty International, with the song "My name is never again" (1999), supports an anti-war charity campaign, together with colleagues Piero Pelù and Lorenzo Jovanotti.

A civil commitment against all forms of violence that also follows the rapper–guru–singer–songwriter Jovanotti who, with the song "Salvami" (2002), described by the artist himself as "a desperate cry of hope against the war", expresses his dissent against the military intervention resulting from the violent act of terrorism against the two towers of New York. Jovanotti has also taken a stand for the cancellation of the debt of Third World countries by industrialised countries, a commitment that has seen him leading an effective and innovative media initiative. In fact, using the television space and the extraordinary audience of the Festival of Sanremo 2000 where he was a guest, Jovanotti addressed the then Prime Minister Massimo D'Alema with a disruptive and never-before-commercialised rap in his finger, asking the Italian government to commit itself to debt cancellation:

> I now turn to Mr D'Alema / I take advantage of the microphone to talk about this problem / who knows how many people have already raised the issue / but I would

---

[71] Savonardo, 2010.

like to use the microphone and television / to ask you from here to give a profound sign / to the issue of the foreign debt of many countries in the South of the world / which are suffocated by the accumulated gap / towards the rich governments of the so-called industrialised world / countries that for centuries have been colonised / and then drowned in the sea of a progress difficult to sustain / for lack of infrastructure and zero power decisional / at the not at all round table of the world bank / and the international money fund / cancels the debt...

Beyond the social and civil content of Jovanotti's rap songs, it is interesting to focus in particular on the effective use of the "microphone" and "television", that is, media and technological instruments, and on the awareness of the potential of these tools typical of the entire artistic activity of rap for and of the new generation of singer–songwriters who, having grown up in the digital age, use new technologies in a significant way both in communication and creative processes. These initiatives highlight the social and "political" role of pop stars and their symbolic power.

There is no doubt that each of the events mentioned has triggered debates and conflicts between supporters and detractors, for ideological, political, social, cultural, or economic reasons linked to groups of power, pressure, and opposing interests. However, these events and the stars who took part in them were celebrated by the international media, generating a production of symbols and meanings which, through the language of emotions, provoked reactions on a large scale and on different audiences which, in different ways and with different tendencies within them, underwent the charm, charisma, and power of seduction of the artists involved. From this point of view, to conclude, recalling and integrating Bourdieu's theories,[72] with the growing autonomy of the intellectual and artistic field, and the rise of the social status of producers of symbolic goods, pop stars (also thanks to the increasingly pervasive use of communication tools) would seem to gain a significant explanatory force, even if within the logic of the star system which, in any case, tend to condition the expressive and creative freedom of the individual artist. The development of the market of symbolic goods, which is increasingly characterising the recording and media industry, allows the producers of these goods to acquire an ever-growing importance and incidence in social dynamics. Pop stars and "stars" of the national and international music scene, through the dissemination of cultural values and models conveyed by artistic activities and productions, seem to assume an increasingly significant role in helping to orient and direct their audience.

As has been pointed out, the relationship between social structures and similar systems seems to play an increasingly significant role in helping to guide and direct their target audience because it can intervene on the world, acting on the representation of the world.[73] Artists act on the different forms of "representation" of reality, knowing and legitimising the values, interests, and visions they carry, within the dynamics characterising the relationship between the intellectual field and the field

---

[72] Bourdieu, 1971.
[73] Bourdieu, Wacquant, 1992b.

of power. Moreover, music, like art, is a cooperative process in which, in addition to the personality of the artist, "personal support" and public itself play a decisive role. The set of interactions between different social actors contributes to define the artistic field, differentiating it from other forms of production. Music implies competences of different nature and a network of relationships useful for the production, promotion, diffusion, and consumption of artistic products. The work of art is the result of a collective process, where the individual personality of the artist is connected to the network of social relations and to a set of economic and cultural conditioning. These factors also have a strong impact on the definition of the public role of the pop or rock star and its related social influence, which is mainly expressed and nurtured through the emotional sphere.

"The time of emotion" is the title of Luciano Ligabue's contribution, offering a reflection on creative processes, concluding our journey through sounds, rhythms, and musical languages.

Afterword. The Time of Emotion[1]

by *Luciano Ligabue*

I have always thought that any form of communication, to be effective, must respect or, even better, reflect the need that produces it. A need that, in terms of urgency, cannot but be catalogued among the primaries. This is basically because it has to dealwith another vital need that is as vital as it is precious: emotion, for the sender as for the receiver. And any mode of expression, whether artistic or not, if it truly comes from such an essential need, is necessarily linked to emotion. I would like to ask you now to forgive me for the abuse I will make of the word "emotion", but then (as this is what I am talking about), it remains the most accurate term that I can use and no synonym could effectively replace it.

Pier Vittorio Tondelli, who besides, being a great author, was also my fellow citizen, he said that the only possible writing was the so-called "emotional writing." It is an example of a type of expression that cannot allow the shyness of your own emotion. On the contrary, it must allow the urgency that causes it to overcome the technical quality of the sentence, the chosen lexicon, and the relative punctuation. Kerouac himself was a clear example of that search for emotional purity in his own writing. I think it is no coincidence that his style has been accused by many of being reduced to mere typing on a typewriter. Such a strong accusation is the proof of a very strong emotion felt, even if it is a negative one. So, this is the evidence that Kerouac's intention was fulfilled anyway, and that his writing was successful.

Thomas De Quincey argued that emotional literature is a powerful literature. And then he divided literature into two large groups: knowledge and power, concluding that as the former ages and disappears without leaving any trace, the second one exists, as long as the language lasts. Louis-Ferdinand Céline said "my emotional meter takes over everything. My books take over everything." He then added that his goal was to return all the emotion of spoken language through written language.

Back to Tondelli, to finally conclude with the quotations, he ended a short text about writing with these words: "the emotional text fucks the inconsolable loneliness of being in the world." A conclusion that is perhaps excessively romantic and that may be could even appear paradoxical, given that reading and writing are

---

[1] The text takes its cue from Luciano Ligabue's doctoral lecture, held on 28 May 2004, at the University of Teramo, where he was awarded an honorary degree in Publishing, multimedia communication, and journalism.

notoriously solitary activities. But, in reality, it is a conclusion that brings us back to the starting point, that is, to the need for a strong circulation of emotions, as authors and as readers too: as human beings. My personal experience has led me to develop a thesis, obviously equally personal: the song has the ambition to pursue the same model of emotional purity.

You can imagine how much I owe to this instrument of popular communication, but I would like to point out that the considerations I will make will perhaps see me more as the user than as the author. First of all, let me focus a list of faults, or alleged faults, that music in so many years of life has never been able to correct itself.

In the meantime, a problem of space: the song, for its brevity and the constraints imposed by the music that composes it, forces the author to a limited use of one, two, or three hundred words. So, it forces them to a synthesis operation. Moreover, the author is often obliged not to use the words they want to use so much as those that perform a rhythmic or respectful or even rhyming function. In a nutshell, especially words that "sound."

Another limitation is that of a structure that has always been faithful to itself: verse-refrain -verse-chorus. Many a times it becomes verse-bridge-refrain and in a smaller number of possibilities there is a digression, otherwise called "c" or special, which is usually used after the second chorus. Regardless, we are always in front of the same type of "cage." A consolidated structure that, over time, has proved to be the only one, almost as if it were an unmodifiable code, able to keep the song's characteristics that are so vital to its natural predisposition to be a popular instrument. Another problem is the famous old query of the notes that are only seven in number (actually twelve), and therefore the resulting combinations would always and only be what they are. Furthermore, we should not forget to consider that, in the meantime, the songs already written (and therefore the combinations already used) are millions.

But are we really sure that the ones I have just mentioned are flaws? Personally, I do not think so. Let us review them one by one.

The small space and the consequent need for synthesis if on one hand are a limitation, on the other, they force the author to work until he comes across the necessary emotion: Necessary and "collected", because in the song there can be no dispersion. Above all, when they will have to do without specific words or literary images they like, but none of them fit the sound of the song (by the way, I frequently renounce subjunctive forms when I feel that they oppose a sensation of speech that in some cases seems to me necessary), the author, in forcing themselves to words that "sound" by force, will have to make sure that the emotion remains alive word by word, sound by sound.

With all the relief they will feel in front of a refrain that finally communicates what they wanted, with the necessary lightness, with the feeling of precision that will testify to the emotion they experienced writing it even with the musicality of the words as fluid as necessary. Obviously, as long as the refrain comes to life. And speaking of refrain, the obligation to the consolidated, and almost inevitable structure – verse-bridge-refrain will naturally take the author to different levels of emotional intensity depending on the "part" he is writing. Knowing well that the temperature of the chorus will have to be the hottest, the temperature of the verse will have more possibilities in terms of nuances and that of the bridge will have the function implicit in the name itself, that is, it will act as a bridge. Based on this, it seems that one can use a sort of "technique of emotion", while, in reality, the author gets only a sort of awareness that alerts them to the fact that, if I add that emotional thermometer, certain parts will not work until they are spawned by the appropriate emotion.

As far as the musical part is concerned, it is true that there are twelve notes and that there are many songs written, but even these data force the writer of a new song to break new ground that should be as personal as possible, as the emotion that will flow into an airy or, in some way, into a significant melody that must be personal as well. In this regard, we can give the example of the blues, which always uses only three chords (which in the end are always the same), and even fewer notes than other musical genres (the blues scale is pentatonic and therefore composed of only five basic notes). The result is that the emotion transmitted by anyone who puts so much emotion in a few notes, played so slowly, is much greater than the one shot by any guitarist who is mainly concerned to show his technical skill and speed of execution. All in all, the "constraints" of the song are the ones to actually guarantee the presence of emotion, the proper one, the one that should justify its writing and circulation.

Over time, I verified that my most successful songs are the ones I have written in less than an hour. Obviously, I happened to verify that, with a more careful and precise work, somehow more rigorous, refined images, and ambitious passages, qualitatively better on paper, but their combination with the music gave a result that had, somehow, little strength compared with the (let us call it) "unconsciousness" of impulse writing. I do not want to bother with the romantic and a bit too elitist concept of "inspiration", but rather with the "time of emotion", a time that matures in a different way according to the personal stages of the author's life, a time that it is never possible to provoke or in duration. But curiosity, indignation, one's own vulnerability or fragility, the enthusiasm of a phase of life can certainly foster it.

Many authors claim that writing every day leads to the arrival of "that" time. Personally, I happened to use that method. But, to separate it from the fact that it can work and the quality it manages to produce, it still seems like a way to besiege emotion, to conquer it, instead of leaving it to its natural time. Waiting for those, the times of the need to reckon, there are just a few management and design tricks. Compared with the three forms of expression, I have used today, in each one of them the balance between management and emotional need can change a little bit, but the latter is still dominant. Writing a story where the structure can be rather "elastic" and free from schemes, is for me very similar, in emotional terms, to that of the song: it is somehow "feverish" because it is closely linked to the intensity of the generating emotion.

The writing of a novel involves more of a design phase as far as the structure itself is concerned. And, certainly, there is the need for a degree of coldness in the composition, analysis, and evaluation of the setlist. However, even in that case, for the realisation of the outline you can only act on the wave of an emotion capable of producing the various parts. From then on, once we have moved on to the chapters, it is worth talking about stories and songs. When writing screenplays, the management phase becomes even more present. It is necessary to design its structure in the various phases that make it up usually: pre-release, crisis, resolution, and finale. But above all, it is necessary to reckon with the actual economic, and also visual, feasibility of each scene. However, coming back to myself, this kind of verification was done only after I had written the scenes (once again) on an emotional impulse. The direction, eventually, is based on what an oxymoron can be: the design of emotion. It is a constant discussion with all the collaborators for the realisation of many small pieces of films of a few seconds that, by the way, are never shot sequentially. So, with the further complication of not proceeding following an emotional flow, but realising parts that will be thought at the head of some already shot or at the tail of others yet to be filmed. But even in that case, once the setup time is over, every minimal sequence will work only if in those few seconds there will be all the emotion brought by the director of photography with his lights, filters, and lenses, the set designer who made the set, the cowriter who helps the characterisation of the characters with styles and colours, the operators and cameramen who shoot and make the dollies spin and, of course, by the actors.

Going back to the song, speaking of managing and designing, here too there are some techniques. Let us call them little mischief or shop tricks, which usually a somewhat experienced author or composer uses in the illusion to dominate it. Concision, meanwhile. A song should be within five meters, better if four or even three. However, it cannot be said that, for example, "La locomotiva" by Francesco Guccini, which lasts nine minutes, is not a popular song.

Usually, writing in a minor key helps communicate maliciousness, or sadness or introspection better, whereas writing in a major key predisposes to communicate clearer, more open, lighter feelings. And yet, Lucio Battisti's "Ancoratu", written in a minor key, recounts the joy of a mental reunion. On the contrary, "La donna cannone" by Francesco De Gregori and "Com'èprofondoil mare" by Lucio Dalla have been written in a major key. Beautiful, but with all the characteristics usually found in songs in minor tonality.

It is generally advised to avoid describing current events with the motivation that the song would soon grow old. But the history of the music is full of songs that are the photograph of a precise moment and that, somehow, are updated over the years. Because this is another of the song's great powers, that of being "different" in time, thanks to new (coincidentally) emotional interpretations of a listener who is gradually changed by life.

Then, you know that using a tempo in three-fourths or six-eighths you will generally get an undulating, fluid result, with melodic possibilities of considerable openness. It is still known that the use of low frequencies puts the listener more quickly in communication with the more primitive and physical, also sexual, part of the listener. And that using harmonic rounds familiar to the listener's ear makes contact more immediate. Even today, I still find it almost miraculous that such different songs with such different intentions, contents, and atmospheres are so different, as different as

"Stand by me", "The sky in a room", and "God is dead", all of which share the same chord sequence.

But no matter how many tricks a songwriter may know, it is easy enough to say that, on their own, they will produce little and that, above all, they will never be enough to "tame" a song. Because, otherwise, each one would be a success. And here we come to one of the greatest qualities of the song: its elusiveness. François Truffaut claimed that the songs he loved the most were the stupidest. I am convinced that the most integer intellectual who declares only passions for jazz or classical music or the certain so-called "high" music, in the darkness of the booth (not electoral but) of his shower, he can sing many pop melodies that he will never confess, but that remain in his head all day long.

Unpredictable, unpredictable and powerful, the song. So powerful that it does not care about any kind of social, ethnic, age, religious, or sex distinction. For it, all ears work. How many times have you heard that certain genres, one for all rock, are dead? How many times have you read or heard about new waves of fashions or trends in which to place some of them? How many times have you come across an adjective that clumsily tried to specify its identity? Love song, social, psychoanalytical, political, or existentialist? How many times, have you noted that the song does not care about all those jumbles and makes its way or not depending on mysterious elements that surely go beyond certain "belonging"? They tried to make a geometric analysis of it by establishing that melody is the horizontal part and harmony the vertical one. They tried to reduce it to a simple algebraic sum. In other words, the song would be "only" the emotion of the author of the words plus those of the composer of the music, arranger, producer, player, and more naturally that of the singer. If the combinations of notes are many, imagine how many can be those of the emotions of those who contribute to its writing and realisation.

Without considering that the song is emotion in motion, and therefore doubly elusive, because the live performance renews and changes it every time who sings or plays or listens to it. Because, then, the sum of the former is still missing a determining factor: the emotion of those who listen to it. A song is always the result of the encounter between the pen (or the piano or whoever writes it), the voice of the person who sings it, and the ear of the person who listens to it. This is not to continue to stir in the obvious, nor to let go of a small anatomical–vibrational observation, but to remember the power of the feeling of identification that a precise combination of melody, harmony, rhythm, words, and voice can produce in those who are emotionally "tuned" to a particular moment in their life.

And if I speak of "precise union", it is not by chance. Because another fundamental characteristic of this communication tool is its unrepeatability. Francesco De Gregori claims that the song is like a pair of shoes made by a shoemaker. A handcrafted work made with the instruments you own at that moment: it is unique. Perhaps this minimal definition has produced a somewhat ungenerous image with respect to the quality he was able to produce, but it clarifies his thought on the theme of unrepeatability. Fabrizio De André said: "I don't have any absolute truth to believe in, I don't have any certainty in my pocket and, therefore, I can't give it to anyone and it's already very good if I can give some emotion." And here we go back to the starting point. I ask you to forgive me if I have made several generalisations about the song that, actually, as you well know and as I have pointed out till now, it is composed of many small independent units and therefore not able to be classified.

All the differences between intentions, type of involvement, and quality of the authors; all the differences in form, sound waves, arrangements, all those of the song; in short, all the many differences between each song I do not allow an overall analysis if not, in my humble opinion, for the presence of the emotion that must originate it. I like to think that one cannot objectively decide whether a song is good or bad. I like to think that evaluations are always strongly subjective on the basis of the different emotional effects, very difficult to analyse, that song has had on the person who judges it. And, finally, I like to think that the songs that more than others ended up in the life of a large number of people are all the result of the emotion that originated them: written just because someone needed to say those things.

Maybe all this is nothing more than a kind of self-conviction as emotion is an integral and maybe cumbersome, if not overwhelming, part of my nature and in this way, I tried to pass off as a theory what was a point of view. And what I presented to you was a point of view in full. One thing I am certain of, though, is the expressive need resulting from that emotion manages to defeat a form of presumption that I find very annoying: the almost intolerable presumption for which you write a song thinking that there will surely be someone who will listen to it.

References

AA.VV., 1983, *La nuova enciclopedia della musica*, Garzanti, Milan.
Abruzzese A., 2012, *La bellezza per te e per me. Saggi contro l'estetica*, Liguori, Naples.
Abruzzese A., Borrelli D., 2000, *L'industria culturale*, Carocci, Rome.
Abruzzese A., Morcellini M. (edited by), 1995, *La comunicazione*, Stampa alternativa, Viterbo.
Adorno Th.W., 1941, «On Popular Music», in *Studies in Philosophy and Social Science*, vol. 9, (translated by M. Santoro, *Sulla popular music*, Armando Editore, Rome, 2006).
Adorno Th.W., 1949, *Philosophie der neuen Musik*, J.C.B. Mohr, Tübingen (translated in *Filosofia della musica moderna*, Einaudi, Turin, 1959).
Adorno Th.W., 1955, *Prismen. Kulturkritik und Gesellschaft*, Suhrkamp Verlag, Frankfurt am Main (translated in *Prismi. Saggi sulla critica della cultura*, Einaudi, Turin, 1972).
Adorno Th.W., 1956, *Dissonanzen. Musik in der verwalteten Welt*, Vandenhoeck und Ruprecht, Göttingen (translated in *Dissonanze*, Feltrinelli, Milan, 1981).
Adorno Th.W., 1960, *Mahler. Eine musikalische Physiognomik*, Suhrkamp Verlag, Frankfurt am Main (translated by *Mahler. Una fisiognomica musicale*, Einaudi, Turin, 2005).
Adorno Th.W., 1962, *Einleitung in die Musiksoziologie. Zwölf theoretische Vorlesungen*, Suhrkamp Verlag, Frankfurt am Main (translated in *Introduzione alla sociologia della musica*, Einaudi, Turin, 2002).
Adorno Th.W., 1968, *Alban Berg. Der Meister des kleinsten Übergangs*, Verlag, Vienna (translated in *Alban Berg. Il maestro del minimo passaggio*, Feltrinelli, Milan, 1983).
Adorno Th.W., 1969, *Stichworte. Kritische Modelle*, Suhrkamp Verlag, Frankfurt am Main (translated in *Parole chiave. Modelli critici*, SugarCo., Milan, 1974).
Agostinis V., 1983, «Editoriale», *Segnso* special number *Suonoimmaginerock*, n. 8, may, p. 12.
Agostinis V., 1987, «Pensare videomusica», in the catalogue of *Music in Film Fest*, Vicenza, pp. 169-170.
Alberoni F., 1963, *L'élite senza potere*, Bompiani, Milan.
Amaturo E., 1993, *Messaggio simbolo comunicazione. Introduzione all'analisi del contenuto*, Carocci, Rome.
Amaturo E., 2001, «I suoni, le parole, gli interpreti», in Savonardo L. (edited by), *I suoni e le parole. Le scienze sociali e i nuovi linguaggi giovanili*, Oxiana, Naples.
Amaturo E., 2007, «I giovani: problemi di definizione», in Savonardo L. (edited by) *Figli dell'incertezza. I giovani a Napoli e provincia*, Carocci, Rome.
Amaturo E., Savonardo L., 2006, *I giovani. La creatività come risorsa*, Guida, Naples.
Assante E., 2005a, «I ragazzi della musica da computer», *la Repubblica*, 13th february.
Assante E., 2005b, «La rete ha cambiato musica», *la Repubblica*, 17th october.
Assante E., 2008a, «La prima compilation della nostra vita», *la Repubblica*, 8th june.

Assante E., 2008b, «Il fascino del lato B», *la Repubblica*, 12th august.
Baldini D., 2000, *MTV. Il nuovo mondo della televisione*, Castelvecchi, Rome.
Baltzell E.D., 1979, *Puritan Boston and Quaker Philadelphia: Two Protestant Ethics and the Spirit of the class Authority and Leadership*, The Free Press, New York.
Barthes R., 1973, *Mytologies*, Seuil, Paris.
Baudrillard J., 1972, *Pour une critique de l'économie politique du signe*, Gallimard, Paris (translated in *Per un'economia politica del segno*, Mazzotta, Milan, 1974).
Bauman Z., 1994, *Alone Again. Ethics After Certainty*, Demos, London (translated in *Le sfide dell'etica*, Feltrinelli, Milan, 1996).
Bauman Z., 1998, *Globalization. The Human Consequences*, Polity Press, Cambridge (translated in *Dentro la globalizzazione. Le conseguenze sulle persone*, Laterza, Rome-Bari, 1999).
Bauman Z., 1999, *La società dell'incertezza*, il Mulino, Bologna.
Bauman Z., 2005, *Liquid life*, Polity Press, Cambridge (translated in *Vita liquida*, Laterza, Rome, 2006).
Bauman Z., 2008, *The Art of Life*, Polity Press, Cambridge (translated in *L'arte della vita*, Laterza, Rome, 2009)
Bechelloni G., 1974, «Introduzione a due voci», in Bourdieu P., Passeron J.C., *La riproduzione*, Guaraldi, Rimini.
Beck U., 1986, *Risikogesellschaft. Auf dem Weg in eine andere Moderne* (translated in *La società del rischio. Verso una seconda modernità*, Carocci, Rome, 2000).
Beck U., 2000, *La società del rischio. Verso una seconda modernità*, Rome, Carocci.
Beck U., 2002, *Individualization*, Sage, London.
Becker H.S., 1963, *Outsiders. Studies in the Sociology of Deviance*, The Free Press of Glencoe (translated in *Outsiders. Saggi di sociologia della devianza*, Abele, Turin, 1991).
Becker H.S., 1982, *Art Worlds*, University of California Press, Berkeley (translated in *I mondi dell'arte*, il Mulino, Bologna, 2004).
Benjamin W., 1936, *Das Kunstwerk im Zeitalter seiner technischen Reproduzierbarkeit*, Suhrkamp Verlag, Frankfurt 1955 (translated in *L'opera d'arte nell'epoca della sua riproducibilità tecnica*, Einaudi, Turin, 2000).
Bennett A., 1999a, «Subcultures or Neo-Tribes? Rethinking the Relationship between Youth, Style and Musical Taste», *Sociology*, vol. 33(3), pp. 599-617.
Bennett A., 1999b, «Rappin' on the Tyne: White hip hop culture in Northeast England - an ethnographic study», *The Sociological Review, February*.
Bennett A., 1999c, «Hip hop am Main: The localisation of rap music and hip hop culture», *Media, Culture and Society, January*.
Bennett A., Peterson R.A., 2004, *Music Scenes: Local, Trans-Local and Virtual*, Vanderbilt University Press, Nashville.
Berger P.L., Luckmann T., 1966, *The Social Construction of Reality*, Doubleday and Co., Garden City, New York (translated in *La realtà come costruzione sociale*, il Mulino, Bologna, 1969).
Bettetini G. et al., 2005, *I nuovi strumenti del comunicare*, Bompiani, Milan.
Bettetini G., Colombo F., 1993, *Le nuove tecnologie della comunicazione*, Bompiani, Milan.
Bhabha H.K., 1994, *The Location of Culture*, Routledge, London-New York.
Boccia Artieri G., 2012, *Stati di connessione. Pubblici, cittadini e consumatori nella (Social) Network Society*, Franco Angeli, Milan.
Bolter J.D., Grusin R., 1999, *Remediation*, The MIT Press, Cambridge (translated in *Remediation*, Guerini, Milan, 2002).
Bonini T., 2006, *La radio nella rete. Storia, estetica, usi sociali*, Costa & Nolan, Milan.

Bourdieu P., 1971, *Champ du pouvoir, champ intellectuel et habitus de classe* (translated by Pierre Bourdieu. *Campo del potere e campo intellettuale*, Manifestolibri, Rome, 2002).
Bourdieu P., 1972, *Esquisse d'une théorie de la pratique*, Droz, Paris-Genève.
Bourdieu P., 1979, *La distinction*, Éditions de Minuit, Paris (translated in *La distinzione. Critica sociale del gusto*, il Mulino, Bologna, 2001).
Bourdieu P., 1980, «Le capital social», in *Actes de la Recerche en Sciences Sociales*, 3, pp. 1-6.
Bourdieu P., 1984, «Preface», in Bourdieu P., *Distinction. A Social Critique of Taste*, Harvard University Press, Cambridge 1984.
Bourdieu P., Passeron J.C., 1964, *Les Heritiers*, Éditions de Minuit, Paris.
Bourdieu P., Passeron J.C., 1970, *La reproduction. Eléments pour une théorie du système d'enseignement*, Éditions de Minuit, Paris (translated in *La riproduzione*, Guaraldi, Rimini, 1974).
Bourdieu P., Wacquant L., 1992a, *An Invitation to Reflexive Sociology*, The University of Chicago Press, Chicago.
Bourdieu P., Wacquant L., 1992b, Rèponses. Pour une Antrhopologie reflèxive, Ed du Seuil, Paris (translated in *Risposte per un'antropologia riflessiva*, Bollati Boringhieri, Turin, 1992).
Brancato S., 2000, *Sociologie dell'immaginario. Forme del fantastico e industria culturale*, Carocci, Rome.
Breton P., 2000, *Le cult de l'Internet*, La Découverte, Paris.
Buckingham D., Willet R., 2006, *Digital Generation. Children, Young People and New Media*, Erlbaum, Mahwah.
Buffardi A., 2004, «Il pensiero digitale e l'arte della connessione. Conversazione con Derrick de Kerckhove», in Savonardo L. (edited by) *Musicman_machine. Arte e nuove tecnologie nell'era digitale*, Graus Editore, Naples.
Buffardi A., 2006, *Web sociology. Il sapere nella Rete*, Carocci, Rome.
Buffardi A., de Kerckhove D., 2011, *Il sapere digitale. Pensiero ipertestuale e conoscenza connettiva*, Liguori, Naples.
Bull M., Back L. (edited by), 2003, *The Auditory Culture Reader*, Berg, Oxford (translated in *Paesaggi sonori. Musica, voci, rumori: l'universo dell'ascolto*, il Saggiatore, Milan, 2008).
Burgess J., Green J., 2009, *YouTube. Online Video and Participatory Culture*, Polity Press, Cambridge.
Buxton D., 1975, *Le rock: star system et société de consommation*, La pensée sauvage, Grenoble (translated in *Il rock. Star system e società dei consumi*, Lakota, Rome, 1987).
Buzzi C., 2010, «I giovani e la transizione all'età adulta», in Associazione Italiana di Sociologia (edited by), *Mosaico Italia. Lo stato del Paese agli inizi del XXI secolo*, Franco Angeli, Milan.
Buzzi C., Cavalli A., de Lillo A. (edited by), 2002, *Giovani del nuovo secolo. Quinto rapporto IARD sulla condizione giovanile in Italia*, il Mulino, Bologna.
Buzzi C., Cavalli A., de Lillo A. (edited by), 2007, *Rapporto giovani. Sesta indagine dell'Istituto IARD sulla condizione giovanile in Italia*, il Mulino, Bologna.
Canclini N.G., 1989, *Culturas híbridas. Estrategías para entrar y salir de la modernidad*, Grijalbo, México (translated in *Culture ibride. Strategie per entrare e uscire dalla modernità*, Guerini, Milan, 2000).
Canevacci M., 1999, *Culture extreme. Mutazioni giovanili nei corpi delle metropoli*, Meltemi, Rome.
Cantelmi T., 2009, *L'era digitale e la sua valenza antropologica: i nativi digitali*, www.medicinalive.com/psicologia-e-medicina-della-mente.

Caputo A., 2007, «La partecipazione giovanile», in Savonardo L. (edited by), *Figli dell' incertezza. I giovani a Naples e provincia*, Carocci, Rome.
Carr N., 2010, *The Shallows. What the Internet Is Doing to Our Brains*, Norton, New York (translated in *Internet ci rende stupidi? Come la Rete sta cambiando il nostro cervello*, Raffaello Cortina, Milan, 2011).
Castells M., 2000, *The Rise of the Network Society*, Blackwell, Cambridge (translated in *La nascita della società in Rete*, Università Bocconi Editori, Milan, 2002).
Cavalli A., 1980, «La gioventù: condizione o processo?», *Rassegna Italiana di Sociologia*, XXI, 4, pp. 519-542.
Cavalli A. (edited by), 1985, *Il tempo dei giovani*, il Mulino, Bologna.
Cavicchia Scalamonti A., Pecchinenda G., 2001, *Sociologia della comunicazione. Media e processi culturali*, Ipermedium, Naples.
Cerchiari L., 2001, *Il disco. Musica, tecnologia, mercato*, Sansoni, Florence.
Chambers I., 1985, *Urban Rhythms. Pop Music and Popular Culture*, Mac Millan, London (translated in *Ritmi urbani. Pop music e cultura di massa*, Arcana, Rome, 2003).
Chambers I., 2001, «Ritmi urbani, ritmi di identità. Suoni e scenari sulla strada oltre l'umanesimo», in Savonardo L. (edited by), *I suoni e le parole. Le scienze sociali e i nuovi linguaggi giovanili*, Oxiana, Naples, 2001.
Coleman J., 1988, «Social Capital in the Creation of Human Capital», *American Journal of Sociology*, 94, Supplement, pp. 95-120.
Colombo F. (edited by), 2005, *Atlante della comunicazione: cinema, design, editoria, internet, moda, musica, pubblicità, radio, teatro, telefonia, televisione*, Hoepli, Milan.
Colombo F., 2012, «Come eravamo. Il ruolo dei media nell'identità generazionale», in Colombo F., Boccia Artieri G., Del Grosso Destreri L., Pasquali F., Sorice M. (edited by), *Media e generazioni nella società italiana*, Franco Angeli, Milan.
Crane D., 1992, *The Production of Culture: Media and Urban Arts*, Sage, London (translated in *La produzione culturale*, il Mulino, Bologna, 1997).
Crane D. (edited by), 1994, *The Sociology of Culture*, Blackwell, Oxford.
Crespi F., 1998, *Manuale di sociologia della cultura*, Laterza, Rome-Bari.
Crespi F. (edited by), 2002, *Le rappresentazioni sociali dei giovani in Italia*, Carocci, Rome.
Crespi F. (edited by), 2005, *Tempo vola*, il Mulino, Bologna.
Crespi F., 2006, *Manuale di sociologia della cultura*, Laterza, Rome-Bari.
Crespi F., 2013, *Esistenza-come-realtà. Contro il predominio dell'economia*, Orthotes Editrice, Nocera Inf.
d'Eramo M., 2001, «L'inafferrabile giovinezza. A proposito di una categoria», in Dal Lago A., Molinari A. (edited by), *Giovani senza tempo. Il mito della giovinezza nella società globale*, Ombre Corte, Verona.
d'Eramo M. (edited by), 2002, *Pierre Bourdieu. Campo del potere e campo intellettuale*, Manifestolibri, Rome.
Dal Lago A., Molinari A. (edited by), 2001, *Giovani senza tempo. Il mito della giovinezza nella società globale*, Ombre Corte, Verona.
De André F., 1999, *Come un'anomalia. Tutte le canzoni*, edited byR. Cotroneo, Einaudi, Turin.
de Kerckhove D., 1991, *Brainframes. Technology, Mind and Business*, Bosch & Keuning, Utrecht (translated in *Brainframes. Mente tecnologia e mercato*, Baskerville, Bologna, 1993).
de Kerckhove D., 1994, «Remapping sensoriale nella realtà virtuale e nelle altre tecnologie ciberattive», in Capucci P.L. (edited by), *Il corpo tecnologico*, Baskerville, Bologna.

de Kerckhove D., 1995, *The Skin of Culture. Investigating the New Electronic Reality*, Sommerville, Toronto (translated in *La pelle della cultura. Un'indagine sulla nuova realtà elettronica*, Costa & Nolan, Genoa, 1996).
de Kerckhove D., 1997, *Connected Intelligence. The Arrival of the Web Society*, Sommerville, Toronto (translated in *L'intelligenza connettiva. L'avvento della web society*, Aurelio De Laurentiis Multimedia, Rome, 1999).
de Kerckhove D., 2001, *The Architecture of Intelligence. The Information Technology Revolution in Architecture*, Birkhäuser, Boston (translated in *L'architettura dell'intelligenza. La rivoluzione informatica*, Testo & Immagine, Turin, 2001).
de Kerckhove D. (edited by), 2003, *La conquista del tempo. Società e democrazia nell'era della rete*, Editori Riuniti, Rome.
de Kerckhove D., 2004a, «Gestire l'intervallo», in Savonardo L. (edited by), *Musicman_machine. Arte e nuove tecnologie nell'era digitale*, Graus Editore, Naples.
de Kerckhove D., 2004b, *The Body Electict Inside Out*, www.vodafone.com/flas/receiver/10/articles/pdf/10_01.pdf.
de Kerckhove D., 2016, *La rete ci renderà stupidi?*, Lit Edizioni, Rome.
de Lillo A., 2007, «Prefazione», in Savonardo L. (edited by), *Figli dell'incertezza. I giovani a Napoli e provincia*, Carocci, Rome.
de Notaris D., 2010, *Vite condivise. Dal newsgroup al social network*, Ipermedium libri, S. Maria Capua Vetere.
Del Grosso Destreri L., 1968, «La sociologia della musica: situazioni e prospettive», *Studi di sociologia*, year VI, fasc. II, pp. 155-179.
Del Grosso Destreri L., 1989, *La sociologia, la musica, le musiche*, Unicopli, Milan.
Del Grosso Destreri L., 2002, *Sociologia delle musiche. Teorie e modelli di ricerca*, Franco Angeli, Milan.
Denora T., 1986, «How is extra-musical meaning possible? Music as a place and space for "work"», *Sociological Theory*, 6(2), pp. 84-94.
Denora T., 2000, *Music and Everyday Life*, Cambridge University Press, Cambridge.
Denora T., 2003, *After Adorno. Rethinking Music Sociology*, Cambridge University Press, Cambridge.
Diamanti I. (edited by), 1999, *La generazione invisibile. Inchiesta sui giovani del nostro tempo*, Il Sole 24 Ore, Milan.
DiMaggio P., 1982, «Cultural entrepreneurship in nineteenth century Boston: The creation of an organizational base for high culture in America», *Media, Culture and Society*, 4, pp. 33-50.
Drotner K., 1999, «Dangerous media? Panic discourses and dilemmas of modernity», *Paedagogica Historica*, 35(3), pp. 593-619.
Engel H., 1960, *Musik und Gesellschaft. Bausteine zu einer Musiksoziologie*, Berlin, p. 9.
Fabbri F., 1996, *Il suono in cui viviamo. Saggi sulla popular music*, Feltrinelli, Milan.
Fabbri F., 2008, *Around the clock. Una breve storia della popular music*, Utet, Turin.
Ferrarotti F., 1966, *Idee per la nuova società*, Vallecchi, Florence.
Ferrarotti F., 1996, *Rock, rap e l'immortalità dell'anima*, Liguori, Naples.
Ferri P., 2011, *Nativi digitali*, Mondadori, Milan.
Flichy P., 1991, *Une histoire de la communication moderne. Espace public et vie privée*, La Découverte, Paris (translated in *Storia della comunicazione moderna. Sfera pubblica e dimensione privata*, Baskerville, Bologna, 1994).
Forrester M., 1998, *Auditory Perception and Sound as Event: Theorizing sound imagery in Psychology* in «Sound Journal», 1, <http://www.kent.ac.uk/sdfva/sound-journal/forrester001.html>.

Frith S., 1978, *The Sociology of Rock*, Constable, London (translated in *Sociologia del rock*, Feltrinelli, Milan, 1982).
Frith S., 1981, *Sounds Effects. Youth, Leisure and the Politics of Rock'n'roll*, Pantheon, New York.
Frith S., 1986, «Art versus Technology: The strange case of popular music», in *Media, Culture and Society*, VIII, 3rd, july 1986.
Frith S., 1988, *Music for Pleasure*, Polity Press, London (translated in *Il rock è finito*, EDT, Turin, 1990).
Fukuyama F., 1995, *Trust: The Social Virtues and the Creation of Prosperity*, Free Press, New York (translated in *Fiducia. Come le virtù sociali contribuiscono alla creazione della prosperità*, Rizzoli, Milan, 1996).
Gallino L., 1978, *Dizionario di sociologia*, Utet, Turin.
Gilmore S., 1987, «Coordination and convention: The organization of the concert world», *Symbolic Interaction*, 10, pp. 209-227.
Giordano D., 2004, «The transit is message», in Savonardo L. (edited by), *Musicman_machine. Arte e nuove tecnologie nell'era digitale*, Graus Editore, Naples.
Grandi R., 1994, *I mass media fra testo e contesto*, Lupetti, Milan.
Greenfield A., 2006, *Everyware: The Dawning Age of Ubiquitous Computing*, New Riders Publishing, Berkeley.
Hall S., 1981, «Notes on deconstructing the popular», in Samuel R. (edited by), *People's History and Socialist Theory*, Routledge, London.
Hall S., Jefferson T., 1976, *Resistance Through Rituals: Youth Subculture in Post-War Britain*, Hutchinson, London.
Hebdige D., 1979, *Subculture. The Meaning of Style*, Methuen, London (translated in *Sottocultura. Il fascino di uno stile innaturale*, Costa & Nolan, Geova, 1983).
Hendy D., 2000, *Radio in the Global Age*, Polity Press, Cambridge (translated in *La radio nell'era globale*, Editori Riuniti, Milan, 2002).
Horkheimer M., Adorno Th.W., 1947, *Dialektik der Aufklärung*, Querido Verlag, Amsterdam (translated in *Dialettica dell'illuminismo*, Einaudi, Turin, 1997).
Horkheimer M., Adorno Th.W., 1956, «Soziologische Exkurse», in *Frankfurter Beiträge zur Soziologie*, vol. IV, Frankfurt am Main (translated in *Lezioni di sociologia*, Einaudi, Turin, 1966).
Horrigan J.B., 2007, *A Typology of Information and Communication Technology Users*, Pew/Internet www.pewinternet.org/Reports/2007/A-Typology-of-Information-and-Communication-Technology-Users.aspx.
Jedlowski P., 2003, *Fogli nella valigia. Sociologia, cultura, vita quotidiana*, il Mulino, Bologna.
Jedlowski P., 2009, *Il mondo in questione. Introduzione alla storia del pensiero sociologico*, Carocci, Rome.
Jedlowski P., Leccardi C., 2003, *Sociologia della vita quotidiana*, il Mulino, Bologna.
Jenkins H., 2006, *Convergence Culture: Where Old and New Media Collide*, New York University Press (translated in *Cultura Convergente*, Apogeo, Milan, 2007).
Johnson S., 1997, *Interface Culture. How New Technology Transforms the Way we Create and Communicate*, HarperEdge, New York/San Francisco.
Jovanotti, 2000, «Le ragioni del popolo di Seattle», *la Repubblica*, 5th october.
KNEIF T., 1966, *Der Gegenstand musiksoziologischer Erkenntnis*, in «Archiv für Musikwissenschaft», 23/3, p. 216.
Lamberti A., 2004, «Ma i giovani sognano pecore elettriche?», in Savonardo L. (edited by), *Musicman_machine. Arte e nuove tecnologie nell'era digitale*, Graus Editore, Naples.

Lamont M., 1992, *Money, Morals and Manners: The Culture of the French and the American Upper-Middle Class*, Chicago University Press, Chicago.

Lamont M., Fournier M. (edited by), 1992, *Cultivating Differences. Symbolic Boundaries and the Making of Inequality*, Chicago University Press, Chicago.

Leccardi C., 1998, «Tempo, mutamento sociale e figure della soggettività», in Melucci A. (edited by), *Fine della modernità*, Guerini, Milan, 1998.

Leccardi C., 2005, «I tempi di vita tra accelerazione e lentezza», in Crespi F. (edited by), *Tempo vola*, il Mulino, Bologna.

Leccardi C., 2010, «Cittadinanza culturale e cosmopolitismo. I giovani come "buoni cittadini"», in Mandich G. (edited by), *Culture quotidiane. Addomesticare lo spazio e il tempo*, Carocci, Rome.

Lévy P., 1994, *L'intelligence collective. Pour une antropologie du cyberspace*, La Découverte, Paris (translated in *L'intelligenza collettiva. Per un'antropologia del cyberspazio*, Feltrinelli, Milan, 2002).

Lévy P., 1997, *Cyberculture*, Éditions Odile Jacob/ Éditions du Conseil de l'Europe (translated in *Cybercultura. Gli usi sociali delle nuove tecnologie*, Feltrinelli, Milan, 1999).

Leydi R., 1982, «La musica di consumo», in Calendoli G., Pierce R. (edited by), *Storia universale della musica*, Mondadori, Milan.

Lin N., 1999, «Social networks and status attainment», *Annual Review of Sociology*, 25, pp. 467-487.

Lull J., 1987, *Popular Music and Communication*, Sage, London.

MacBride P.K., 2006, *Brillant. Internet per gli over 50*, Milan, Pearson.

Madden M., 2004, *Artists, Musicians and the Internet*, Pew/Internet, www.pewinternet.org/Reports/2004/Artists-Musicians-and-the-Internet.aspx.

Maffesoli M., 1988 Le temps des tribus, le déclin de l'individualisme dans les sociètès de masse, Universitè Renè Descartes, Parigi (translated in *Il tempo delle tribù*, Armando, Rome, 1996).

Maffesoli M., 1996, *Éloge de la raison sensible*, Grasset, Parigi (translated in *Elogio della ragione sensibile*, Seam, Rome, 2000).

Magrini T., 2002, *Universi sonori. Introduzione all'etnomusicologia*, Einaudi, Turin.

Mannheim K., 1928, Das Problem der Generationen, in "Kölner Vierteljahreshefte für Soziologie", n. 7 (translated in *Le Generazioni*, il Mulino, Bologna, 2008)

Manovich L., 2001, *The Language of New Media*, The MIT Press, Cambridge (translated in *Il linguaggio dei nuovi media*, Olivares, Milan, 2002).

Manovich L., 2008 (draft), *Software Takes Command*, http://lab.softwarestudies.com/2008/11/softbook.html (translated in *Software culture: Società, informazione e conoscenza nell'era del software diffuso*, Olivares, Milan, 2010).

McLuhan M., 1964, *Understanding Media*, The MIT Press, Cambridge (translated in *Gli strumenti del comunicare*, Net, Milan, 2002).

Melucci A., 1994, *Creatività: miti, discorsi, processi*, Feltrinelli, Milan.

Menduni E., 2001, *Il mondo della radio, dal transistor ad Internet*, il Mulino, Bologna.

Merriam A.P., 1964a, *The arts and antropology*, in «Horizons of Antropology», Aldine Publ. Co., Chicago.

Merriam A.P., 1964b, *The Anthropology of Music*, Northwestern University Press, Evanstone (translated in *Antropologia della musica*, Sellerio, Palermo, 1983).

Meyrowitz J., 1985, *No Sense of P7 lace*, Oxford University Press, New York (translated in *Oltre il senso del luogo. Come i media elettronici influenzano il comportamento sociale*, Baskerville, Bologna, 1993).

Middleton R., 1990, *Studying Popular Music*, Open University Press, Buckingham (translated in *Studiare la popular music*, Feltrinelli, Milan, 2001).
Moore P., 2003, «Susono ettario e identità culturale nell'Irlanda del Nord», in Bull M., Back L. (edited by), *The Auditory Culture Reader*, Berg, Oxford 2003 (translated in *Paesaggi sonori. Musica, voci, rumori: l'universo dell'ascolto*, il Saggiatore, Milan, 2008).
Moore T., 2004, *Mix Tape. The Art of Cassette Culture*, Universe Publishing, New York (translated in *Mix tape. L'arte della cultura delle audiocassette*, Isbn Edizioni, Milan, 2008).
Moores S., 1993, *Interpreting Audiences. The Ethnography of Media Consumption*, Sage, London (translated in *Il consumo dei media*, il Mulino, Bologna, 1998).
Morcellini M., 2007, «Giovani e nuovi media», *Quaderni di Sociologia*, n. 2, pp. 3-10.
Morcellini M., 2013, *Comunicazione e media*, Egea, Milan.
Morcellini M., De Nardis P. (edited by), 1998, *Società e industria culturale*, Meltemi, Rome.
Morin E., 1962, *L'industrie culturelle*, Le Seuil, Paris (translated in *L'industria culturale*, il Mulino, Bologna, 1974).
Morin E., 1970, «Il grande pubblico», in Rivolsi M., *Comunicazioni e cultura di massa*, Hoepli, Milan.
Muggleton D., 2000, *Inside Subculture: The Postmodern Meaning of Style*, Berg Publishers, Oxford.
Negroponte N., 1995, *Being Digital*, Knopf, New York (translated in *Essere digitali*, Sperling & Kupfer, Milan, 2004).
Negus K., 1996, *Popular Music in Theory. An Introduction*, Polity Press, Cambridge.
Ong W.J., 1982, *Orality and Literacy. The Technologizing of the World*, Metheun & Co., New York (translated in *Oralità e scrittura*, il Mulino, Bologna, 1986).
Paolucci G., 2007, «La routine dell'innovazione», *Quaderni di Teoria Sociale*, n. 7, pp. 131-140.
Paolucci G., 2009, «Pierre Bourdieu: strutturalismo costruttivista e sociologia relazionale», in Ghisleni M., Privitera W. (edited by), *Sociologie contemporanee. Bauman, Beck, Bourdieu, Giddens, Tourine*, Utet, Turin.
Pecchinenda G., 1999, «Ri-tribalizzazioni. Riflessioni su musica e sociologia», reface to Savonardo L., *Nuovi linguaggi musicali a Naples. Il Rock, il Rap e le Posse*, Oxiana, Naples.
Pecchinenda G., 2001, «Almeno credo! L'identità incerta: tra musica e sociologia», in Savonardo L. (edited by), *I suoni e le parole. Le scienze sociali e i nuovi linguaggi giovanili*, Oxiana, Naples.
Pecchinenda G., 2002, «Musica e tecnologie della memoria», in Savonardo L. (edited by), *I suoni e le parole. Le scienze sociali e la musica d'autore*, Oxiana, Naples.
Pergolani M. e R. Marengo (edited by), Enciclopedia del PopRock Napoletano. Da Roberto Murolo alle Posse, Edizione RAI ERI, Rome.
Petrucciani S., 2007, *Introduzione a Adorno*, Laterza, Rome-Bari.
Pomian K., 1999, *Sur l'histoire*, Gallimard, Paris (translated in *Che cos'è la storia?*, Bruno Mondadori, Milan, 2001).
Pratellesi M., 2008, *New Journalism. Teorie e tecniche del giornalismo multimediale*, Mondadori, Milan.
Prensky M., 2001a, *Digital natives, digital immigrants: A new way to look at ourselves and our kids*, www.marcprensky.com/writing.
Prensky M., 2001b, «Digital natives, digital immigrants, part 2: Do they really think differently?», *On the Horizon*, NBC University Press, vol. 9, n. 5, October.

Prensky M., 2001c, *Digital natives, digital immigrants: A new way to look at ourselves and our kids*, http://tinyurl.com/ypgvf.

Prensky M., 2009, «Sapiens digital: From digital immigrants and digital natives to digital wisdom», *Innovate – Journal of Online Education*, February-march, www.innovateonline.info/index.php?view=person&id=98.

Putnam R.D., 1993, *Making Democracy Work*, Princeton University Press, Princeton (translated in *La tradizione civica nelle regioni italiane*, Mondadori, Milan, 1993).

Reynolds S., 1998, *Generation Ecstasy. Into the World of Techno and Rave Culture*, Routledge, New York (translated in *Generazione ballo/sballo. L'avvento della dance music e il delinearsi della club culture*, Arcanamusica, Rome, 2000).

Rheingold H., 2002, *Smart Mobs: The Next Social Revolution*, Perseus Publishing, Cambridge (translated in *Smart Mobs: Tecnologie senza fili, la rivoluzione sociale prossima ventura*, Cortina, Milan, 2003).

Rheingold H., 2012, *Net Smart. How to Thrive Online*, MIT Press, Chicago (translated in *Perché la Rete ci rende intelligenti*, Raffaello Cortina, Milan, 2013).

Rognoni L., 1959, «La musicologia filosofica di Adorno», in Adorno Th.W., *Filosofia della musica moderna*, Einaudi, Turin.

Sachs C., 1962, *The Wellsprings of Music*, Martinus Nijhoff, Den Haag (translated in *Le sorgenti della musica. Introduzione all'etnomusicologia*, Bollati Boringhieri, Turin, 2007).

Santoianni C., 1993, *Popular music e comunicazione di massa*, Edizioni Scientifiche Italiane, Naples.

Santoro M., 2/2000, «La leggerezza insostenibile. Genesi del campo della canzone d'autore», in AA.VV., *La nuova sociologia della musica, Rassegna Italiana di Sociologia*.

Santoro M., 2001, «Presentazione», in Bourdieu P., *La distinzione. Critica sociale del gusto*, il Mulino, Bologna.

Santoro M., 2006, «Adorno e la sociologia critica della musica (popular)», Presentazione in Adorno Th.W., *Sulla popular music* (edited by), Armando Editore, Rome.

Santoro M., 2010, *Effetto Tenco. Genealogia della canzone d'autore*, il Mulino, Bologna.

Sapadin L.A., 1988, «Friendship and gender: Perspectives of professional men and women», *Journal of Social and Personal Relationships*, 5, pp. 387-403.

Savonardo L., 1999, *Nuovi linguaggi musicali a Napoli. Il Rock, il Rap e le Posse*, Oxiana, Naples.

Savonardo L. (edited by), 2001, *I suoni e le parole. Le scienze sociali e i nuovi linguaggi giovanili*, Oxiana, Naples.

Savonardo L. (edited by), 2002a, *I suoni e le parole. Le scienze sociali e la musica d'autore*, Oxiana, Naples.

Savonardo L., 2002b, «Musica e nuove tecnologie», *Next. Strumenti per l'innovazione*, n. 15, S3, pp. 50-56.

Savonardo L., 2003a, *Cultura senza élite. Il potere simbolico a Napoli nell'era Bassolino*, ESI, Naples.

Savonardo L., 2003b, «Musica, cultura e memoria digitale: l'Archivio sonoro della canzone napoletana», *Matrix*, anno I, n. 4, pp. 107-122.

Savonardo L., 2003c, «99Posse. L'hipfolkrap e la parola come arma impropria», in Pergolani M., Marengo R. (edited by), *Enciclopedia del PopRock Napoletano. Da Roberto Murolo alle Posse*, Edizione RAI ERI, Rome.

Savonardo L., 2003d, «Almamegretta. L'utopia delle anime migranti», in Pergolani M., Marengo R. (edited by), *Enciclopedia del PopRock Napoletano. Da Roberto Murolo alle Posse*, Edizione RAI ERI, Rome.

Savonardo L., 2003e, «Musica e società. I suoni della città porosa», in Pergolani M., Marengo R. (edited by), *Enciclopedia del PopRock Napoletano. Da Roberto Murolo alle Posse*, Edizione RAI ERI, Rome.

Savonardo L. (edited by), 2004a, *MusicMan_Machine. Arte e nuove tecnologie*, Graus Editore, Naples.

Savonardo L., 2004b, «Figli dei fiori virtuali. Riflessioni su giovani e musica», *Sociologia della comunicazione, Comunicazione, Conoscenza, Tecnologia*, XVIII, 34, pp. 123-136.

Savonardo L. (edited by), 2007a, *Figli dell'incertezza. I giovani a Napoli e provincia*, Carocci, Rome.

Savonardo L., 2007b, «Innovazione e creatività», *Quaderni di Teoria Sociale*, n. 7, pp. 193-216.

Savonardo L., 2007c, «Linguaggi musicali, giovani e new media», in Bertirotti A., Strollo M.R., (edited by) *Traghettare il pensiero. La musica come "variabile Caronte": contributi pedagogici e sociologici*, Franco Angeli, Milan.

Savonardo L., 2010, *Sociologia della Musica. La costruzione sociale del suono dalle tribù al digitale*, Utet, Turin.

Savonardo L., 2013, *Bit Generation. Culture giovanili, creatività e social media*, Franco Angeli, Milan.

Savonardo L., 2015, *Sociologie de la musique. Construction sociale du son des tribus au numérique*, Editions Academia - L'Harmattan, Louvain-la-Neuve.

Savonardo L., 2017, *Pop music, media e culture giovanili. Dalla Beat Revolution alla Bit Generation*, Egea, Milan.

Savonardo L. and others, 2010, «Mediateche domestiche: una storia sociale», in Mandich G. (edited by), *Culture quotidiane. Addomesticare lo spazio e il tempo*, Carocci, Rome.

Savonardo L., Caputo A., De Notaris D., Bruno E., 2007, «Consumi culturali e new media», in Savonardo L. (edited by), *Figli dell'incertezza. I giovani a Napoli e Provincia*, Carocci, Rome.

Savonardo L., De Notaris D., 2010, «Musica, new media e culture digitali», in Savonardo L. *Sociologia della Musica. La costruzione sociale del suono dalle tribù al digitale*, Utet, Turin.

Schönberg A., 1950, *Style and Idea*, Philosophical Library, New York (translated in *Stile e idea*, Feltrinelli, Milan, 1980).

Schütz A., 1951, «Making music together. A study in relationship», in *Collected Papers vol. II: Studies in Social Theory*, The Hague, Netherlands, pp. 159-178 (translated it «Fare musica insieme. Studio sulla relazione sociale», in Schütz A., *Frammenti di fenomenologia della musica*, Guerini e Associati, Milan, 1996).

Sciolla L., 2008, «Presentazione», in Mannheim K., *Le Generazioni*, il Mulino, Bologna.

Serravezza A., 1980, *La sociologia della musica*, EDT/Musica, Turin.

Shuker R., 1998, *Key Concepts in Popular Music*, Routledge, London/New York.

Sibilla G., 2003, *I linguaggi della musica pop*, Bompiani, Milan.

Sibilla G., 2008, *Musica e media digitali. Tecnologie, linguaggi e forme sociali dei suoni, dal walkman all'iPod*, Bompiani, Milan.

Silverstone R., 1999, *Why Study the Media?*, Sage, London.

Simmel G., 1881, «Psychologische und ethnologische Studien über Musik», in *Zeitschrift für Völkerpsychologie und Sprachwissenschaft*, Dümmlers Verlagbuchhandlung, Berlino (translated in «Studi psicologici ed etnologici sulla musica», edited by De Martino G., Fanini S., in appendix Federici M.C., D'Andrea F. (edited by), *Lo sguardo obliquo. Dettagli e totalità nel pensiero di Georg Simmel*, Morlacchi, Perugia, 2004).

Simmel G., 1900, *Philosophie des Geldes*, Duncker & Humblot, Lipsia (translated in *Filosofia del denaro*, Utet, Turin, 1984).
Simone R., 2000, *La terza fase. Forme di sapere che stiamo perdendo*, Laterza, Rome-Bari.
Sparti D., 2005, *Suoni inauditi. L'improvvisazione nel jazz e nella vita quotidiana*, il Mulino, Bologna.
Sparti D., 2007, *Musica in nero. Il campo discorsivo del jazz*, Bollati Boringhieri, Turin.
Steiner G., 1997, *Errata: An Examined Life*, Weidenfeld and Nicolson (translated in *Errata. Una vita sotto esame*, Garzanti, Milan, 1998).
Tacchi J., 2003, «Nostalgie e radio accese», in Bull M., Back L. (edited by), *The Auditory Culture Reader*, Berg, Oxford 2003 (translated in *Paesaggi sonori. Musica, voci, rumori: l'universo dell'ascolto*, il Saggiatore, Milan, 2008).
Tessarolo M., 2001, «I suoni e le parole dei giovani: una rivolta contro il disincanto», in Savonardo L. (edited by), *I suoni e le parole. Le scienze sociali e i nuovi linguaggi giovanili*, Oxiana, Naples.
Thibaud J.P., 2003, «La composizione sonora della città», in Bull M., Back L. (edited by), *The Auditory Culture Reader*, Berg, Oxford (translated in *Paesaggi sonori. Musica, voci, rumori: l'universo dell'ascolto*, il Saggiatore, Milan, 2008).
Thompson J.B., 1995, *The Media and Modernity. A Social Theory of the Media*, Polity Press, Cambridge (translated in *Mezzi di comunicazione e modernità. Una teoria sociale dei media*, il Mulino, Bologna, 1998).
Thornton S., 1995, *Club Cultures: Music, Media and Subcultural Capital*, University Press of New England (translated in *Dai club ai rave. Musica, media e capitale sottoculturale*, Feltrinelli, Milan, 1998).
Torti M.T., 2002, «Musica e notte», in Buzzi C., Cavalli A., de Lillo A. (edited by), *Giovani del nuovo secolo. Quinto rapporto IARD sulla condizione giovanile in Italia*, il Mulino, Bologna 2002.
Tota A.L., 1999, *Sociologie dell'arte. Dal museo tradizionale all'arte multimediale*, Carocci, Rome.
Tota A.L., 2001, «Musica e vita quotidiana: la composizione musicale dell'esperienza», in Savonardo L. (edited by), *I suoni e le parole. Le scienze sociali e i nuovi linguaggi giovanili*, Oxiana, Naples.
Tota A.L., 2002, «Stili in rivolta? Musica e mass media», in Savonardo L. (edited by), *I suoni e le parole. Le scienze sociali e la musica d'autore*, Oxiana, Naples.
Toynbee J., 2000, *Making Popular Music, Musicians, Creativity and Institutions*, Arnold, London.
Weber M., 1921, *Die rationalen und soziologischen Grundlagen der Musik*, Drei Masken, München (translated in «I fondamenti razionali e sociologici della musica» in Weber M., *Economia e società*, V, Edizioni di Comunità, Milan, 1961).
Weinberger D., 2007, *Everything is Miscellaneous*, Times Books, New York.
Williams R., 1981, *The Sociology of Culture*, University of Chicago Press, Chicago.
Willis P.E., 1977, *Learning to Labour: How Working Class Kids get Working Class Jobs*, Saxon House, Farnborough, Hants.
Zolberg V.L., 1992, «Barrier or leveler? The case of art museum», in Lamont M., Fournier M. (edited by), *Cultivating Differences. Symbolic Boundaries and the Making of Inequality*.
Zurletti S. (edited by), 2006, *Th.W. Adorno 1903-2003. Una ragione per la musica*, Cuen, Naples.